Worth the Try

VALERIE PEPPER

Cover Design & Illustration: Sam Palencia, Ink and Laurel

Edited by Katie Awdas at Spice Me Up Editing

Published by Stafford Lane Publishing, LLC

ISBN 979-8-9888570-8-2

This book was powered by rugby thighs, so it's only fitting that I dedicate the book to them. So here's to those magnificent legs, and to the very real people who play the game.

Before heading onto the pitch, please be aware of the following content warnings: infertility of FMC; FMC followed by private investigator; cyberbullying. While all of these have been treated with the utmost care, your mental health is most important. Be careful with yourself.

Chapter 1
Elodie

"YOU'RE BEING LET go."

Air whooshes from my lungs as my stomach clenches. The world tilts and dims, and my palms sting with how hard my nails are digging into them. Fired. I'm being fired. From the only job I've had my entire career.

"But—" I can't finish. I can't *breathe*. A wave of dizziness overtakes me, and I unclench my fists only to grip the sides of the chair.

Slowly, as if it's paining him just as much to say this as it is for me to hear it, Dan from HR slides a stapled set of papers across the desk, the movement serving only to draw attention to the golden name plate glinting mere inches from his wrist. A golf club is engraved on either side of his name. A distant thought hits, and I wonder if our company gave that to him, or if someone else did—his mom, maybe, or a partner.

Wait. Not *our* company. Not anymore. Because Dan just fired me. He can wrap the message up in whatever words make him feel better, but the result is the same.

My knuckles blanch. I think I might be sick.

The chair squeaks as Dan leans forward and speaks again. "We've, ah, we've put together a severance package. I think you'll find it's incredibly generous."

I stare at him. *Generous* would be not firing me. But he looks so upset, so uncomfortable about delivering this news, that I feel bad for him.

He must see something in my expression, because his own falters. "Elodie, I'm so—"

I snatch the papers from the desk, startling Dan with my movement. It startles me, too, if I'm being honest, because I'm *nice*. Disney princess level nice. It's literally my most defining trait. Unless you count my hair, which has its own zip code most days.

Trying not to let the pages shake in my hand, I scan the words. The terms really *are* good. Six months' severance with the promise of glowing reviews to potential employers, three months of them paying for insurance, and a meeting with a staffing agency to help me with next steps.

The start of a migraine begins to form around the back of my head. Or maybe that's just the nausea. My mouth is dry.

Dan produces a pen and moves it close. "You've been an incredible person to work with. So nice."

See? *Nice.*

Which is, apparently, not enough. Even though it should be. What happened to being rewarded for loyalty? For dedicating years of my life and more creative ideas than I could count to the most boring marketing team to ever walk the face of the planet? Not that they deserved them. Clearly.

"But Fore Gone is going in a different direction, and your role is being absorbed into a regional position."

My eyes snap up. "Is Carolyn Ackerman getting it?" She's been my boss on the events team for the last five years, and not once has she liked any of the event ideas I pitched. *Too risky, too gaudy, too pricey*, and on and on.

He winces. "Yes."

Of course she is. And is Carolyn nice? No. No, she is not. *"You get more bees with honey, Elodie."* Despite the years of silence, I can still hear my mother's sugary drawl as she scanned me from head to toe, her lips pinched, before sending me out to walk in yet another beauty pageant.

I grab the pen and click the top, managing to suppress my mother's voice and my own defeated sigh as I sign and date the agreement. It's a great pen, with smooth black ink and a comfortable grip. Dan produces a second copy for my signature, then countersigns both and returns one to me.

Sliding the pages into my hands and folding them in half, I tell him, "I'm keeping the pen." My voice is flat. A calm sort of numbness fills my chest, and I'm grateful. Better to be numb than shrieking.

"Of course," he says. As if it's every day that he fires people and they declare they're keeping the pen. Maybe it is. Maybe they do.

Dan stands, and I follow. I know what's next. At least, I can guess at it.

Sure enough, an empty box awaits me when I get back to my cubicle. A strangled laugh escapes. Eight years I've been here, still in a cubicle, and all I have to show for it is a severance package and a cardboard box. Eight. Years.

How is this happening?

I clear my throat. "You don't have to stay here."

Dan shifts on his feet and wrings his hands. "I, um." He looks around and lowers his voice. "I have to."

Now a laugh really *does* come out. "What do they think I'm going to do? Throw my laptop? Flip a table?"

Erica's head pops over the top of the cubicle, her big brown eyes growing increasingly round as she takes in the scene unfolding right before her. "Oh, hell no!" she says, her eyebrows furrowing as she glares at Dan. "You can't be serious."

"It's okay, Erica." Lies. All lies. It's not okay. It's not remotely okay. But what is Erica going to do about it? What am *I* going to do about it?

I know exactly what I'm going to do: Pack up eight years of dedication to an events team where I wasn't appreciated, was regularly treated as an entry-level employee, and where I went absolutely nowhere. *That's* what I'm going to do about it.

"Uh, no, it's *not* okay," she shoots back, echoing my thoughts as she rounds the corner. "What in the fresh hell is this, Dan?"

He looks at her helplessly. "It's not my fault."

Erica sucks her teeth. "Damn, Dan. I knew you were spineless, but I thought you'd at least have our backs when it came down to it."

Dan straightens. "I *do*."

"Then what's this?" Erica gestures at me.

I ignore them, dropping my bags of Blow Pops and sour gummy worms into the box.

Next are the framed pictures: me and my parents at my college graduation. Me and my best friend Kari on our girls' trip to the Bahamas, both of us grinning like fools while we pose with the pigs on Big Major Cay. A picture of Fenian, my old German Shepherd, tongue lolling as he looked out from the top of a mountain we'd hiked up in East Tennessee when I was in undergrad.

Then the other detritus of office life: a congratulatory handwritten note on hitting my five-year anniversary. A pair of Fore Gone logo'd sunglasses from last year's senior marketing retreat. The little microphone statuette commemorating the time I won my team's "Communicating in the Moment" award. An Atlanta Granite bobblehead from when Kari got us front row seats to one of the professional rugby team's game last year.

It doesn't even take five minutes. Eight years, packed up in five minutes. Something warm and spiky bubbles in my chest as I grab my purse, pick up the box, and look at Erica and Dan. "I'm ready."

Erica stops mid-rant. "Oh. *Oh.*"

I smile, the gesture automatic and fake, trained into me until I could hold it for an hour straight. "I'll be fine. Erica, you have my number. Let's grab those margaritas we talked about next week. Dan? I suppose you have to walk me out?"

He nods stiffly, turning and leading the way.

Erica pulls me into a side hug, the smell of her vanilla perfume wafting over me. "I'll miss you, Elodie."

I smile back and blink away the tears that threaten. "I'll miss you too, Erica."

"E-squared forever!" she calls out as I turn to go. "And fuck that bitch Carolyn," she mutters.

I snort out a laugh, and my voice is watery when I respond, "E-squared forever."

Dan waits downstairs in the lobby, the bright Atlanta sun shining through the tinted glass and giving him a bluish hue. "Despite what Erica said back there," he starts.

I cut him off, still holding that smile. All I'm missing is the petroleum jelly on my teeth. "It's fine. Really." Again, lies. All lies. *It's fine! I'm fine! Everything is fine!* "It's been great, Dan. Maybe I'll see you around!" I chirp, then back into the door to open it.

Dan hustles to hold it for me, his hand smacking the glass pane above me with a *thwack* as the muggy heat settles around me.

I duck beneath him. As I straighten back to my not-insubstantial height, I catch a beat of hesitation on his face.

"Sorry," he says, his eyes darting to my waist before returning to mine. "But I—erm, well..." he stammers. "Your card."

I blink. "My key card? Seriously?" It's got a really good picture of me on it, and besides, I thought I'd get to keep at least one thing from this godforsaken place.

It's not like I kept those cheap sunglasses.

"I know. It's just..." He sighs. "It's procedure."

It takes everything in me not to roll my eyes. *Tell him to fuck off, Elodie.* I nearly laugh at myself. I would *never* say those words out loud, let alone actually say them to some-one's face. "Okay, Dan. Hang on." I set the box down, unclipping the key card from my skirt as I straighten—a skirt, I even *dressed* nice for this place!—before handing it over.

He pockets it. "Thanks."

I don't bother saying anything as I bend to grab my box.

An hour later, I'm off the MARTA and unlocking the door to my tiny duplex, letting out a grateful sigh that the only roommate I have is of the four-legged kind.

My calico Cleo, short for Cleocatra, looks up from her spot on the couch and stares at me with a distinctly feline expression.

"Yeah, I know," I sigh, letting the box fall with a thud on the parquet floor and kicking off my shoes before padding over to her. I drop onto the cushion beside her and let myself sink, both physically and metaphorically. "I got fired today. Me. Fired." Cleo regards me, and just when I think she's going to give me some pity with those lime-green eyes of hers, she throws a back leg into the air and bends down, going back to cleaning herself.

"Love you, too," I mutter, then shoot an SOS text to Kari.

When the knock comes on my door not even half an hour later, I smile. Leave it to my bestie to drop everything and come to my rescue. I peel myself off my couch and cross the room, already talking.

"I'm thinking nachos and—Mr. Brown?"

My landlord and neighbor stands before me, his shoulders hunched, his mouth drawn into a tight, rueful smile. "Heard you over here. Early day at work?"

I fight the lump in my throat. "Something like that." No need to tell him I was canned. I'll have something sorted out by the time rent is due—and besides, Fore Gone promised a six-month severance.

He nods. "Well. Figured I better come and get this over with."

I battle the sinking feeling in my chest and force yet another smile onto my face. "Would you like to come in? Where's Mrs. Brown? I can make some tea." I open the door wide and gesture.

The old man simply looks at me. "My daughter's coming home."

"Tyra? That's amazing!" I gush, genuinely happy for him. "Gosh, how long has she been gone?"

"She needs the place."

I blink rapidly, unwilling to accept what I'm certain he's saying. "Do you want some help with a welcome home party? I bet she'd love that. Streamers? Balloon art? I know the perfect person—"

"She's going to move in here, Elodie. To your place." His voice is kind, but firm.

No. *No.* This can't actually be happening. There is no way that I am losing my job *and* my home on the same day. I have done everything right. I was an honor student. I played flute in the band. I did pageants until I wanted to scream, because my mom wanted it. I went away to school on a scholarship and came back home. I got a job. I *kept* that job. I met a man and planned a future, and when that went to hell, I got my own place. I have a pet. I am thirty years old. This isn't happening.

"Here?" I squeak. I sound like a mouse.

He swallows. "Here."

"But—but my lease—"

"Expired last year, and you've been month-to-month ever since," he interjects. "Which means I only have to give you a month's notice."

My mind whirls. I can't call my parents. I won't face the crushing weight of condescending disappointment on my mother's face at yet another of my perceived failures and carefully neutral expression on my father's. They may live within the greater Atlanta area, but I'd rather walk naked down I-20 in the boiling heat at rush hour before asking them for anything.

So. I'd like to scream now.

Right now.

Like, open my mouth and let out the most ear-piercing scream that anyone has ever scrumpt. And I don't even care if that's proper English. *That's* how much I need to scream.

I begin to close the door in Mr. Brown's face, my body on a mission, even if my manners are not.

"Elodie?" he asks.

"Mm?" I keep shutting it.

"You understand, right?" Only an inch of his face is visible now, his eyes narrowed in what might be concern. "You have one month."

I flash him a smile. A nice, bright one.

Then I slam the door.

And I scream.

Chapter 2
Ansel

THE ROAR OF the crowd is deafening, powering me on as I grip the ball. I run, lungs heaving in the final seconds of the game, looking for someone, *anyone*, to pass the ball to.

There's no one.

I'm not even supposed to have the damn ball right now. But sometimes that's how it goes. Tucking it tighter against my body, I double down. I'm almost there.

I already can't hear shit, and the packed stadium gets even louder.

Too late, I realize why: one of the other team's players is diving at me, angling his body perfectly towards my waist. There's another at my back.

Where the *fuck* is River? Carter? I'll take anyone.

There. Coming into view on my left is our number eight, Lennox Campbell, and not a moment too soon. I toss the ball in his direction, praying he catches it as I'm taken down. It's an effort to keep my eyes open, straining to watch the ball as my body hits the pitch.

We go down in a heap of grunts and curses, me first,

then three other players on the opposing team. There's not enough time. I scramble up and scan the pitch, hoping like hell that Lennox caught the ball and made the try. But he's booking it in the opposite direction, chasing the Hounds' winger like a man possessed.

Fuck.

I turn and sprint, knowing I can't make it in the three seconds we have left and hauling ass like I'm going to anyway. All our guys are running hard, doing everything they can to break through the Hounds' defenses and make it to their number eleven. Holy *shit* that guy is fast. We knew he was. We trained to stop him. We have to stop him. If we don't, we lose the fucking championship.

And there he goes, flinging his body toward the try line with two seconds to go, ball gripped tight in one hand, arms outstretched, legs nearly covered by our guys.

The crowd roars, increasing in volume when the winger pops up and nearly gets tackled again by his teammates.

They made it.

We lost.

The yell that comes out of me is loud, primal, and pissed. "Fuck!"

THE SOUNDS in the locker room are muted, and I can't tell if it's that everyone is subdued, or if it's my own rage drowning them out. I rip my shirt off and toss it in my bag, momentarily considering skipping the shower but knowing that Lennox will give me ten kinds of shit for it.

Besides, I played the entire eighty minutes. I stink.

Coach shoots me a glance from across the room, and I know what he wants. I'm the captain; I should probably say something to the team. Lucky for Coach, I don't have it in me. We lost. We worked our asses off, we left it all on the pitch, and we lost anyway. I've got nothing to say, so I shake my head and start unwinding the tape on my wrists.

Coach taps his cheek and raises a brow. *"You're bleeding,"* he mouths.

I shrug. I know. But it happened on that last hit, so I ignored it. Pretty sure I took a cleat to the face. Wasn't the first time, and it won't be the last.

He narrows his eyes.

I turn my back on him and sit on the hard bench, unlacing my boots with quick jerks of my fingers. Behind me, Coach calls the room to order.

"I'm not going to say anything you don't already know," he starts.

I peel off the tape around my ankles.

"But remember that last year, we were last place in the league. Last. Place."

A chorus of grunts and grumbles responds.

"And this year, we damn near took the championship. Am I disappointed? Hell yes, I am. But we almost won."

I stand and face Coach. "Almost isn't good enough."

"No shit, Miles," Coach fires back.

"So quit saying we *almost* won," I growl in return. "We lost. We played our asses off. But we lost. That's the end of it." I look at my teammates. For so many of them, this is a part-time job, never mind that we're Major League Rugby. The pay isn't great.

"Not really the inspiring speech we're looking for," Cash mutters from the bench beside me. He's our hooker. Great guy. Does the job. Huge heart.

I look at him. "Since when have I been known for inspiring speeches?"

He grins. "Good point."

"When is our next practice?" I ask Coach.

He gapes at me like I've grown a second head. "Today was the championship game."

"That we lost."

The locker room is deadly quiet as Coach and I have a staring contest.

Finally, he dips his chin in the barest acknowledgment that I might actually know what the fuck I'm talking about. "Two weeks."

Noise erupts as I nod my thanks to him and head to the showers, ignoring the protests from my teammates that we were supposed to get the summer off.

The bus ride home is brutal. The team rarely puts us on planes—not even the economy ones, not that our bodies would fit in those seats, but still—so if it's an eight-hour or less drive between cities, we're making the trek in a chartered bus.

It's not the bus that's the problem. It's Lennox, who won't shut up.

"Are you a fecking gowk, Ansel? I thought there was more in your brain than that. Or did that last hit knock the sense off you?" It's late, and his Scottish burr is really coming through.

I take the good-natured swat to the head that he delivers from the seat behind me before raising up to look back at him. "Define 'gowk,' Len."

He huffs. "You know what it means, you ass."

I do. But I love making him explain things because it drives him crazy. "If I'm a gowk, then you're a lavvy heid."

"I regret the day I taught you anything about my language."

I laugh, then grow serious. "We have to practice, Len. You know these guys need it."

He shrugs his massive shoulders. "I know. But I wanted to visit home."

Glasgow. "So go. If anyone doesn't need the practice, it's the guy who's been playing since he could walk. It's the Americans who need the help."

"You're American."

I flash him a shit-eating grin. "Yeah, but I'm not normal."

"Ye can say that again," he says with a chuckle. "What about you? Thought you had plans to work."

"I'll be fine." But I don't know if that's true. Then again, I never know if that's true. For the past five years, ever since Rosalie landed in my life like my own personal flower bomb, I've had to take things month by month. Hell, sometimes week by week and day to day.

I wouldn't change a thing. Not one second of it. I mean, yes, it's shocking to open your door and find your neighbor asking why the hell there's an infant on your doorstep, but once I got through that initial surprise, I dove into fatherhood without hesitation. I needed help—a lot of it at first—and my mom jumped in, teaching me everything I needed to know. Once I got my feet under me and Mom was certain I could do it myself, she went back to Charleston, with promises to visit with Dad. And they have. Rosalie has a wonderful relationship with them.

But being a professional rugby player and single dad isn't for the faint of heart. I'm the best-paid player on the team, and I definitely have the best sponsorship deals, but living in the suburbs of Atlanta means everything is expensive—especially childcare. Which is why I was beyond thrilled when Mom and Dad offered to take Rosie for the entire summer this year, starting next week. I'd planned to use the time to find some construction work or even use my finance degree in some way. Admittedly, I was a little behind on locking something down, but given the way I opened my big mouth earlier today, I guess that isn't the worst thing.

Lennox gazes at me with those all-knowing eyes of his, and I stare right back. "I'm talking to Coach, then. I miss the cold."

I roll my eyes and slump in the seat. Hours later, we've made it back to our own stadium and I'm in my SUV heading home. It's the wee hours of Sunday morning by the time I'm sliding my key into the lock and walking in the front door, unwilling to open the garage door and risk the sound of it waking Rosalie.

The house is quiet, but the smell of fresh coffee wafts from the kitchen. I make my way there and find Sharon, my neighbor and personal saint from heaven, waiting for me. "Figured you'd be here soon," she says, pushing a freshly poured mug across the island to me.

"You're a goddess among women," I tell her, taking a grateful sip. "My coffee never tastes this good."

She smiles, but it's pinched. "I have news."

My body stills, all my senses focused on the woman in front of me.

"Your mom called last night. Everything is fine," she hurries to say, holding up a hand and meeting my eyes.

I exhale, shoulders drooping in relief. "Jesus, Sharon. Don't do that to me."

"She didn't want to bother you while you were playing, and asked I deliver the news."

Still feeling a little wobbly, I ask, "Which is what?"

She hesitates, then dives in. "That your dad needed emergency knee surgery because he fell off the ladder. And that it was his good knee, meaning they're going to operate on the other knee in a month or so, once he's mobile again."

As she speaks, a sinking sensation takes over. I know where she's going with this. My parents are proud people, never wanting to accept help if they can handle things on their own. But proud or not, Dad's accident means there's only so much they're going to be able to handle this summer. An energetic five-year-old is not on the list.

With a final, sorrowful smile, Sharon says, "They can't keep Rosalie this summer."

Chapter 3
Elodie
Two Weeks Later

"COME ON," KARI wheedles as she grabs my hand and tugs me across the parking lot toward the Atlanta Granite's offices. "It'll be fine. I promise."

"I still don't think this is a good idea." Even still, I let her pull me out of the scorching mid-July heat and into the nearly Arctic-level air of the building.

"Rugby players are *always* a good idea," Kari shoots back. "Well. Most of the time."

I raise an eyebrow. "You been keeping something from me?"

She waves me off with a flip of her black bob. "Just trust me."

I'm still not sure. But my best friend has been awfully insistent that this is the way to go, so here we are. Despite how it makes my stomach hurt.

After Mr. Brown's pronouncement that I wouldn't have a place to live on the same day that I lost my job, I might have...well, I might not have lived up to my "nice" reputation for a few days. It was more like "unwashed" and "feral." But I can't stay angry or sad for long, so after a solid seventy-two hours, I was upright and focused once more.

I needed a plan.

Kari was more than happy to help, and that's how I find myself being dragged into the Atlanta Granite's corporate offices on a Saturday afternoon. Offices that are situated at the top of the stadium, where the team practices and plays. Like me, Kari landed what she thought was her dream job right out of college, but unlike me, she hopped around until she got the position here as the senior public relations specialist. Which is a fancy title but really just means she still has a boss. And that she still does a lot of grunt work, but she does it while kicking butt.

Plus, she has her own office. Which I, in my jobless state, am more than a little envious of.

But it's fine. Remember? Everything is *fine*.

I shove down the rising anxiety. I can do this. I have a plan. It's paper-thin, and I'm pretty sure I've thrown up almost every day at how ridiculous I feel about it, but it's a plan.

Kari roots in her oversized tote for the swipe card she needs to get us to the top of the building, then lets out a whoop of triumph as she yanks it into the air. "Success!" she crows. As we exit a moment later, she turns to me with a mischievous grin. "You ready to watch some practice?"

I shrug. Even though Kari's been here a couple of years now, I know only the barest facts about rugby. I know it's kind of like soccer, and kind of like football, is super popular all over the world, and is starting to get popular here, too. Also that the guys wear shorts and no padding to speak of. After that? It's all a bit of a mystery. "Is asking them to help me move after they've practiced all day really a good idea?"

"Trust me," she says. "They'll be more than happy to do

it. Besides, we only need four of them, max. You don't have much stuff. It'll take one trip. We offer to pay in beer and pizza."

"We're not in college anymore," I admonish. "Beer and pizza can't really still be a form of payment."

She snorts a laugh. "Oh, you sweet, innocent woman. You clearly haven't met a rugby player." She swipes her card another time, leading us into a lush VIP lounge that stretches almost the entire length of the building and overlooks the field below. Wait: pitch. Not field. The term is *pitch*. I've really got to get better at learning the right words. After pulling out my phone, I make a note in my to-do app. *Learn rugby*. There. Done.

"Miss Kari!" a high-pitched voice exclaims from the row of tables set up against the windows.

I look up in time to see a little girl barreling toward us with a smile nearly as big as her face. She practically tackles Kari, who takes two steps back and pretends she's almost been knocked down.

"Now *that's* a hit your dad would be proud of!" Kari says with a laugh. Then she kneels for a hug before standing back up and introducing us. "Rosalie, this is my friend, Elodie. Elle, this is Rosalie."

"Hi! Our names rhyme. I just turned five. Everyone asks, so I'm telling you so you don't have to."

I grin. "Hi, Rosalie. Our names *do* rhyme, like a melody."

Her face lights up even more, her braided ponytails bouncing with the movement. "You're fun. Wanna color?"

Okay, honestly? Yes. Seems better than asking a bunch of enormous strangers for help. I beam. "That sounds amazing. Lead the way."

I follow Rosalie back to her table. The biggest box of

Crayola crayons that I've ever seen sits open, surrounded by stacks of coloring books. Girlfriend has nailed this coloring thing. "Wow. So many choices!"

She shrugs. "I had to promise my daddy that I'd stay put. Figured I could use the opportunity to get more coloring books."

I snort out a laugh. "Smart girl." Big words, too, but I'm not pointing that out.

Kari looks out onto the pitch while Rosalie and I settle in at the table. I follow her gaze, and almost immediately have to fight to keep breathing.

Holy fluffing airballs.

There are easily two-dozen men below us, all in close-fitting shorts and shirts, skin of all shades glistening with sweat in the mid-morning heat. Admittedly, their legs are, erm, really nice to look at. Thick as tree trunks with muscles so defined I can see them from up here. As I watch, a bunch of them seem to get in two lines where they're facing each other and crouching down. It's almost like they're preparing to tackle. Then, on a command I can't hear, they surge against each other, each row tightly bound up and trying to push the other row back.

"That's a scrum," Rosalie explains, noticing my focus. "They practice that all the time. Daddy says it's so they can get stronger. They have to scrum a lot in games."

"Where's the ball?" I look around, but don't see it.

"On the pitch between them. The hooker's gotta get it with his foot and kick it out. Then another player takes it and runs, and all the guys in the scrum explode across the pitch and start playing." She pauses. "Once the ball comes out of there, the whole game moves really fast. You've gotta focus or you won't keep up."

I grin at her. "You know, that's the first time anyone's

made sense describing rugby to me. You're officially my new rugby teacher."

A cute blush stains her cheeks as she dips her chin.

"Are you up here by yourself?" Kari asks.

Rosalie plucks a crayon out of the box and studies the half-finished page in front of her. It's a scene from Beauty and the Beast. "Yep. I was supposed to go next door, but Miss Sharon is helping another friend today. And Daddy says it's not a good idea for me to be down on the pitch when they're practicing. Lots of swear words." She sighs dramatically. "As if I don't know them already."

I laugh again, but I don't miss the concern that passes over Kari's face. Something tells me she's not a fan of Rosalie being left alone up here, and I tend to agree. But I don't know this little girl or her circumstances, and am not about to judge.

Kari looks at her watch. "They should be finished any time now."

I nod absently, opening up a coloring book, grabbing a green crayon, and going to town on a certain Scottish princess's dress. I've always liked her best. Probably because she has hair problems like me.

A while later, the boisterous sound of laughter drifts into my consciousness, and I blink back into reality. I'd lost all sense of time while coloring, but now, some of the men are coming into the lounge. Kari looks over at me. "Ready to meet some rugby players?"

Chapter 4
Elodie

THE FIRST MAN to enter the room isn't even human. He can't be. He's tall, easily over six feet, and I'm not a tiny woman by any stretch of the imagination. His muscles have muscles, straining the teal and black Atlanta Granite T-shirt he wears. His shorts are longer than the ones they wore on the pitch, but not by much. His wavy brown hair is wet from the shower, and I'm hit with a fantasy of him *in* that shower, water sluicing down his face and neck, gathering in the small divots of his shoulders before traveling south.

I swallow and shake myself out of it, but there is nothing in this world that can keep me from staring. He sports a closely trimmed beard that does little to cover a square jaw. If anyone's looking for a new superhero, I found him. There are no words to do him justice. He's both beautiful and rugged, carrying himself with the precision and confidence of someone who's used to commanding a room. The floor shakes as he leads a handful of men into the room, his dark eyes instantly catching on mine and flaring.

But it's not a flare of anything other than pure suspicion.

"Daddy!"

Immediately, his expression changes, the intimidation falling off his face as he breaks into a delighted smile. "Rosie Posie," he responds, his voice deeper than I expected, delivered with a slight Southern twang that also throws me. He crouches to catch her, scooping her into his arms and standing a moment later.

Rosalie smiles happily. "Miss Kari is here, and I made a new friend!"

"Oh yeah?" He turns to Kari and me, his expression still guarded, but more curious now.

"Rosalie Miles, my rugby princess!" another man exclaims in an accent I can't yet place, making Rosalie giggle. He's just as big as Rosalie's father, with dark red hair and ruddy cheeks. "Get out of that ogre's arms and give me a hug."

Rosalie wriggles down and gets a hug from the man while her dad's gaze turns back to me.

Kari finally remembers her manners, stepping forward to introduce us. "Ansel Miles, this is my best friend, Elodie Cole."

"Nice to meet you." I extend my hand, and it disappears into Ansel's in a powerful handshake.

"Hi," comes the response. Polite, but distant.

"I thought Rosalie was going to be with her grandparents?" Kari asks, her voice low.

Ansel sighs, his face tensing. "Long story."

Kari raises her eyebrows. "Leaving her up here—"

"Won't be happening again," he finishes. "I just have to figure things out."

"So who's watching her?"

"That's one of the parts he hasn't figured out yet," the man holding Rosalie says. Then he holds his hand out, delivering a devastatingly flirtatious smile along with it. "Lennox Campbell."

"Elodie Cole." I smile back, finally placing the accent. Scottish.

"We were hoping to get y'all's help with moving some furniture." Kari elbows me. "Right?"

"Oh. Right." My cheeks flame, and I'd rather count the tiles on the floor in here. Asking strangers for help is ten kinds of wrong. It's a burden. I should be able to do this myself. Or if not do it myself, then pay someone to do it. And I have the money—for now, at least—but Kari wouldn't let me consider it.

"Och, the old 'let's ask the ruggers to toss around my belongings' move," Lennox says. "We know all about that, don't we, Rosie?"

Rosalie nods seriously. "We require pizza and beer as payment."

Lennox's smile could lay waste to an entire continent. "Exactly."

"But juice for you," Ansel states, one lone eyebrow rising as if it's got a mind of its own. The move highlights the scar that runs through it, making him look more intimidating than ever.

"It's not a big deal," I blurt, my worries getting the best of me. "I'm sure y'all are busy. This was a silly idea." I turn to Kari. "We should go. I can call a moving company or something."

"Are we moving the contents of a mansion?" Lennox asks.

"We're moving things?" another guy pipes up.

"Just, um, just a duplex."

"A *small* duplex," Kari offers. "Easy peasy. Literally one trip. And I'll supply all the pizza."

"When?" comes a chorus of inquiries.

I force my voice to stay steady. Remind myself that I'm not asking for the world. "Two weeks."

"Why?" Ansel's question is gruff.

I wince. It's embarrassing to get fired at thirty. And besides, it's none of his business.

"Her job downsized her, and now her landlord is kicking her out, so she's moving in with me while she figures out what to do next."

"Kari!" I hiss at my former best friend. Is she serious right now? "They don't need to know all of that."

Lennox leans in. "You need a job? You like kids?"

"Lennox," Ansel warns.

Kari's head swivels between the two men. "Wait—what's going on?"

"Rosalie." Ansel nods at his daughter. "I'm...in a bit of a bind."

And suddenly, it all makes sense. Rosalie mentioned she was here because her dad couldn't find anyone to watch her, but I'd assumed she meant only for today. Does he need someone to watch her for the entire summer?

Do I want to do that?

"It's a great idea," Lennox continues, turning to me. "So?"

"Um." I stare at the floor.

"Will everyone calm down for a minute?" Ansel turns to me, and I wish he hadn't. Because something about his voice makes me look back at him. And, whew boy, the intensity of his gaze is enough to make me squirm. As though I've done something wrong. I haven't, of course, but tell that to the fight-or-flight response currently taking place inside my body.

But then his eyes soften, and the brackets on either side of his lips disappear. He keeps his focus on me as he continues, "You two are a lot. Give Elodie a moment to adjust to the idea and consider it. Most people aren't dying to be nannies for a summer."

The way he says my name gives me shivers. Then again, it's ice cold in here.

Lennox snorts. "And live in your pool house? My man, if I weren't going home to Scotland, *I'd* do it."

Ansel doesn't bother looking at him, his expression all business. I get the feeling he'd be just as comfortable in a suit as shorts and a T-shirt. "He's right. If you want the job —and if you pass the background check and interview we need to have—then yes, you would be required to live in the *guesthouse* on my property."

"Oh, excuse me," Lennox interrupts. "The *guesthouse* on his *property*. My sincerest apologies, me laird." He gives an exaggerated bow, winking as he straightens.

Rosalie giggles.

Just the summer? In a guesthouse? With a *pool*?

A wave of nausea hits. Do I really want to put myself in a situation where I'm around the very thing I can't have? The very thing my fiancé broke it off with me for? I exhale, looking around for a chair. *I thought I was past this.*

Apparently not.

"Hey." Ansel's voice breaks through the noise as his face comes into focus. His warm caramel eyes flit over my face with concern. "Come sit down. You okay?"

A warm, calloused palm encircles my elbow and steers me to the padded bench against the windows. Heat ripples out from the glass, but it does little to dispel the chill that's draped itself over me.

This is too much. I cradle my stomach and squeeze my eyes shut in a feeble attempt to keep the memories at bay.

Jeremy's expression is carefully blank, reminding me so much of my father that it opens up a pit inside me. "I love you, but I want kids. I'm moving out. Keep the ring."

"Miss Elodie?" Rosalie's sweet voice comes softly from my right. "Want some water?"

I look down and blink, seeing that the little girl has brought me a cup of water. I take it, grateful she's not filled it too much, and hoping no one can see the way my hand shakes.

"There," Rosalie says. "Drink up. Sometimes I get light-headed, and Daddy says it's because I'm so busy talking that I forget to eat or drink." With a motherly pat on my leg, she scampers off.

My mouth twitches. She's painfully adorable.

With a soft snort, Ansel lowers himself to the bench, crossing a powerful leg on the cushion so he can face me. "I'm sorry about Lennox...*and* Kari. They're quite the duo when they get something in their head."

Shaking my head, I force the rest of the cobwebs away and pull myself together. No one wants to watch me have a mini breakdown over a sudden job and housing offer. It's not Ansel's fault that he unknowingly put three of my fantasies on a platter and offered them to me. Or, maybe Lennox offered. Either way. And my inability to have kids is *certainly* not his issue to sort through.

"It's fine," I murmur, making myself meet his eyes and immediately wishing I hadn't. Because now the sun is hitting him just right, highlighting the swirls of light caramel within his deep brown eyes and the faint traces of auburn in his beard. He's human after all, it seems, and the look of concern on his face makes him that much more devastating.

On a blink, he seems to come to a decision. "Just forget about them. You clearly aren't interested—"

"I'll do it." The words are out of my mouth so quickly that I barely register what I've said. "I mean," I stammer, "if you're actually offering. But I have a cat. And people are weird about cats."

"Cats are fine."

I keep going, blowing forward. "You don't know anything about me, but I'm really nice, and I was a killer babysitter when I was a teenager. I mean, not killer, that sounds bad. But good. Great. I was *great*. I even have first-aid training. It's been a decade or so, but—" I stop, caught off-guard by the brilliant smile he's giving me.

"So, you're interested."

"Uh, yeah." I wince. *Uh, yeah?* I'm a thirty-year-old woman. "Sorry, I mean yes. I'd love to talk more."

"How's now?"

"Now?"

The smile barely dims. "Yes. Now."

A nervous laugh bubbles out. "Do you make a habit of interviewing people on the spot?"

He looks down, the beginnings of a blush forming just above his beard. It might be more adorable than the grins his daughter has been throwing my way. "Nah, but I've had to learn to trust my gut. Make decisions quickly. And you seem nice."

Nice. Of course. Of *course* the hot rugby player thinks I'm nice. Some sexless creature with a one-dimensional personality who will play Barbie with his daughter for a couple of months.

Then I check myself. Don't I want him to think I'm nice? I mean, I *am* nice. So why am I suddenly anti-nice? *Get it together.* I throw on the pageant smile. "Hit me."

He raises a scarred brow, and there's something in his expression. As though he sees right through me.

Impossible. "I mean, you know." I wave my hand, forcing myself to claw back to metaphorical standing and to get my act together. I've faced much, *much* more intimidating situations than this hulking set of muscles. Besides, the prospect of living rent-free for a few months in a place that doesn't involve Kari's couch is too good to pass up, even if it does come with a daily reminder of everything that I can't have. "Ask me the questions."

He pulls his phone out, opens an app, and pushes it to me. "Fill that out."

The phone may as well be a snake for the look I give it.

Ansel chuckles. "Remember the background check I mentioned?"

I fix him with a look. "You run background checks so often that you have an app at the ready?"

He sighs. "I...have trust issues."

I snort a laugh, then immediately cover my mouth. "Sorry. That was rude. I just—" I hesitate, trying to figure out how best to say this. "First you tell me you trust your instincts, then you say you have trust issues."

"Hey," he protests, the veneer he's constructed falling for a moment, "I'm multi-faceted."

It makes me laugh even more. "Gotta say, Mr. Miles, I've never met a guy who readily admits his shortcomings." Especially one who looks like him.

"Ansel," he corrects. "Mr. Miles is my father."

"Ansel," I repeat, trying his name out.

He clears his throat. "And don't worry. There's plenty I get wrong." He glances at his daughter, who's returned with a sheet from one of her coloring books. "Right, Rosie?"

She nods seriously. "Right." Then she climbs into his lap, the paper crinkling between them as she settles in. "What am I right about this time?"

I pick up the phone and start entering my info, wondering where her mom is. I can't ask—not right now, anyway. But it seems like she'd be an obvious choice for summer Rosalie duty. I'm sure Kari knows. It's her job to learn all there is to know about the players, so I'll get the scoop later.

But...no. I won't ask her. That feels like an intrusion.

"Do you like kids?" Rosalie asks after I finish with the phone and slide it back to Ansel.

My gut twists painfully, but I plaster on my trusty smile and answer, "I do."

"Do you have any?"

I fight to keep my expression steady. "I don't."

"Rosalie," Ansel warns. "We talked about that question."

"It's revelant," Rosalie protests, her little voice full of indignation.

"Relevant," Ansel corrects, a smile playing at the corners of his lips.

My heart melts. Something about a newly minted five-year-old using big words is just too much for me to bear, even if the question hurts. "It's okay," I assure them. "Do you have more questions for me?"

Her hazel eyes light up. "I do!"

It's a solid half hour before I've answered all of Ansel's,

and a fraction of Rosalie's, questions. Her questions are definitely more fun than her father's: favorite place to visit, favorite color, childhood pets, current pet, is my hair always this curly, favorite rugby team, favorite sport, did I know who Bluey was, can I count to ten in Spanish, and so on. But in the end, Ansel nods decisively. "The job's yours if you want it. Assuming you pass the background check."

"Right," I tease him. "Trust issues. Got it."

Rosalie slides off her dad's lap and gives me a hug, smelling of sunshine. "I hope you get it," she whispers loudly.

We stand, and Ansel towers over me once again. I move back, having forgotten just how big he is.

He clocks the move, making his own retreat by a couple of steps. "I'll be in touch. Should only take a day."

Kari and Lennox join us. "Took you long enough," Lennox says. "I'm starving."

"You ate all Rosalie's snacks," Kari points out. "How are you starving?"

"Woman, have you looked at me?"

Kari shrugs, pretending to be thoroughly unimpressed with Lennox's hulking form. "I've seen better." Then she turns to me as Lennox protests behind her. "Come on. I've sorted out who's helping you move already. I'm allergic to this place on the weekends."

I laugh and lean forward to kiss her on the cheek. "You're the bestest best friend."

She smirks. "I know."

Hooking my purse over my shoulder, I begin to follow her without a backward glance.

"Elodie," Ansel calls.

My feet stop of their own volition, and I turn back to him.

He holds Rosalie's hand, keeping her steady as she hangs from it and lets her body go limp to dangle inches from the floor. It's clearly a move he's used to. "I'll be in touch."

I smile. "You said that already."

Chapter 5
Ansel

ROSALIE IS VIBRATING with excitement. Today's the day we move Elodie into the pool house, and you'd think my daughter was preparing for a visit from the queen.

I still can't believe my luck. Having Elodie practically drop into my lap was the second luckiest thing to ever happen to me, without question. The past two weeks have been...overwhelming. Even more overwhelming than usual, and that's saying something.

I knew my stubborn parents probably needed help, even if they weren't saying anything, so Rosie and I drove the four hours to Isle of Palms to see them. Sure enough, Mom was hours from losing her mind with Dad, who swore up and down he didn't need to take the painkillers, but then whined about how much pain he was in. So I spent my days with the mule of a man while Rosie soaked in the sunshine on the beach with her grandmother. Then there were the projects around the house that neither had gotten to, so if I wasn't making Dad do his physical therapy or helping him up and down from the makeshift living area we'd created in the living room, I was crawling on the roof or fixing the pump or making sure the generator had gas.

At home, it's not been any better. I've spent every moment I can back in the guesthouse, getting it deep cleaned and ready for a semi-permanent resident. And that's been on top of the usual day-to-day things. Laundry. Calling the preschool to see if, by some miracle, a slot had opened up for Rosalie. Dentist appointment. Making sure that Rosie wasn't rotting her brain in front of the television for the entire day. Cooking. Shopping. If I'd had to work another job these past two weeks, absolutely nothing would have gotten done.

Then again, if I'd kept my mouth shut, I *still* wouldn't be going for practice on Monday. The entire team, including me, would have had two glorious months off. As it is, we'll be practicing four full days a week instead.

"Daddy, do you think Elodie will like this one?"

I look at the paper Rosie holds up for my inspection. It's a drawing of the guesthouse and pool, with Elodie standing outside the house. I'll be the first to admit that Rosie is no genius with the crayons just yet, but it's obvious enough who the subject of the drawing is. "She'll love it," I promise, pulling on one of her pigtails.

I think back over the conversation we had. The background check. The brief story she gave about growing up in Athens, just seventy miles away. Everything about her is normal. Perfectly, wonderfully *normal*. Nothing about her stands out. She's just...a person. A person who was in pageants, sure, but as long as she's not going after my daughter with a makeup kit and hairspray against Rosie's wishes, what does it matter?

All I have to do is pay zero attention to the fact that she's drop-dead gorgeous, and I'll be fine.

I scrub my eyes in an effort to remove the memory of her legs when she tucked them beneath her on the bench as we chatted. The tiny geographies of freckles against creamy skin.

Nope.

No way. Not happening. I have neither the time nor room in my life for anyone other than my main girl Rosie. Anyone else is a waste of time. Not that there aren't opportunities—there are plenty. One of the many "perks" of being an athlete in a city filled with them, I suppose. And I've had flings here and there, but once they realize I have a daughter, every single woman bounces. Which is wild, because it's not like I keep Rosalie a secret. Even the sports press knows all about her. But for them, it's more of a "if you take pictures of my daughter, I'll smash your face in without a second thought" thing.

It's just past lunch when Rosie squeals from her perch on the couch, jumping up and down on the cushions and pointing out the window. "She's here!"

Sure enough, four cars have pulled up in front of my house with the smallest of moving vans tucked into the line of vehicles. *That's all she has?* Though the guesthouse is furnished, so I don't know why I'm shocked at this. Maybe they made a pit stop to put the rest of her things in storage.

Rosalie flies to the door, looking back at me with a half-crazed smile. "Can I go?"

I nod, and she's bolting outside before I can blink, cries of "Miss Elodie! You're here!" floating back as she goes.

I take a slightly less manic pace, shutting the door behind me before heading to meet everyone on the street.

Elodie slides down from the driver's seat, surreptitiously pulling a wedgie out of her cut-off jean shorts. Shorts that do absolutely everything for her, showing off a far more luscious set of curves than I even realized. Her eyes find mine, and she knows she's been caught, because she blushes redder than the sunset before quickly turning away from me. Her hair's up in a bun, the same as when we first met, and her shirt falls off one shoulder to reveal a black sports bra.

"Hi," she says.

"Welcome to your new digs," I reply. "Is this it?"

She gives me an incredulous look, as though I'm either stupid or clueless. Maybe both. Probably both.

In the face of her? Definitely both.

"The rest is in storage. We stopped there first."

"Figured that might be the case," I say as Kari rounds the van.

"Can I carry the cat?" Rosie asks. "I'll be very careful. I'm strong."

Elodie smiles at her, then nods. As Rosie cheers, Elodie walks around the van to the passenger side.

I join the guys, grabbing two boxes from the van and leading the way up the side of the house and through the wooden gate.

Most of the guys have been here before, so they're used to the scene: a backyard mostly occupied by the pool, half of which is taken up by a huge unicorn float and a He-Man float. Rosalie insisted we get the floats last year, and both of them are in heavy rotation once again this year. There's a slim patch of lawn, just big enough to require an actual mower, and situated between the house and the pool is a massive entertainment area. It's the reason I bought the place, hoping to fill it with memories of good times and laughter. There's an outdoor grill and small refrigerator, and leading out the back door of the house is a screened-in area with seating and an enormous flat-screen television.

I got the property for a song during a real estate downturn, when I was just out of college and had no business buying something like this. Seriously. What does a twenty-two-year-old need with this much house? But I'd gotten a hefty contract from the league, and thanks to an undergrad academic scholarship, I never used the college fund my parents had saved. Between those two things, plus my father's enthusiastic financial guidance—basically, he told me if I didn't buy it he'd seriously consider disowning me—I snagged it.

I'd never been more grateful for it than when Rosalie's piece-of-shit mother left her on my porch. And now? I'm grateful for it once again.

I know how privileged I am. Hard not to when my mom won't ever shut up about how nice it must be to be a tall, good-looking, straight white man in America. She's not wrong. I mean, I don't know about the good-looking part, but the rest is true.

"Wow, Ansel—how much they paying you to be captain?" Xavier's voice is full of wonder. He's new to the team and fresh out of college, eager as hell. Big kid, too, and his whole persona makes me think of a mastiff puppy.

"Bought it a long time ago, Xave," comes Cash's answer.

"You were probably in middle school," I say, shifting the box I'm carrying into one hand while I open the guesthouse door with the other.

"How old *are* you, Ansel?" Kari asks, following me in with Elodie right behind her.

I glare at her. "Thirty-two. Of which you are well aware."

She grins and pops her gum. "Yeah, but I love making you feel old."

"Don't start with me," I warn. "You forget that I know how old you are and I'm not afraid to say it."

"You wouldn't *dare*," she hisses.

I move behind her, snickering, and set the box on the bar that separates the kitchen and living area.

Beside us, Elodie stands quietly off to the side with a box in her hands, worrying her lip as she takes the place in.

I step forward and take it from her, and the movement doesn't quite seem to register at first. When it does, she blushes again and blinks up at me.

"Thank you. This is—wow," she gushes, looking around. "When you said it was the pool house—"

"Guesthouse," I correct with a smile.

"Guesthouse," she says and nods. "I figured it was going to be small. Not...whatever this is."

"Can I let the cat out?" Rosie asks.

Elodie kneels to get on Rosie's eye level. "Not yet. Let's wait until the door is shut. Do you want to help set up some food and water for her?"

"Yes!"

Kari calls her over to do just that, and I look back at Elodie as she stands. "Want the tour?"

"I should probably help get the rest of my things," she protests.

"You shouldn't." I gesture for her to follow. "These guys can earn their pizza."

"Oh, shoot!" She hits her forehead with her palm. "I forgot to order it! How many should I get? Is anyone gluten-free?"

I bite back a smile. It's sweet of her to think about something like that. "I've already ordered. It'll be here soon."

Her eyes widen, the green—blue? No, hazel—irises flaring in the sunlight streaming into the living area. "Oh, no! No, no, no, I can do it. I can afford it—especially with what you're paying me, which is still—"

"Entirely acceptable for a live-in nanny," I finish, then hold up a hand and blink away from her blue eyes. Or hazel. Whatever. In fact, it doesn't matter what color they are. I shouldn't be paying attention to their color, period. "I promise, everything is fine. I know everyone's favorite order, and feeding five rugby players isn't for the faint of heart."

"It isn't?"

I give up on fighting the grin. "It most certainly isn't. Come on. I want to make sure you like the place."

She follows me as I walk her through. "The bathroom only has a shower stall, but—"

"Oh, that's fine. I never, well, I *rarely* take baths. I mean, look at me." She laughs self-consciously. "I'm huge. Not huge like you—not that you're huge, I mean you *are*, but not in a bad way—not that being huge is bad. Ugh." She blows a breath, puffing the frizzy strands of hair around her head into motion. "What I'm trying to say is that I don't fit in bathtubs. There." She looks away, muttering something that sounds like, *smooth, Elodie.*

I decide to ignore the entire thing. Too many traps that Elodie's best friend has drilled into me, ironically enough. *"Never comment on someone's size. Especially a female's. Especially a female reporter's."* Plus, I am not thinking about the size of her body. Or her body, period.

I'm also not going to mention that I have a master bath with a tub so big it could easily hold three of me, or that Rosalie literally began her swimming lessons in it because of how big it is, or that she takes a bath in it every night. Because Elodie will figure that out the second she needs to take Rosalie through her nighttime routine.

"The bedroom is here." I scoot past her and down the

short hallway to open the door. It's modest, with a dresser on one wall and a queen-sized bed flanked by built-in corner bookshelves on another wall. A teal-blue reading chair and stool are in the other corner. "You're welcome to redecorate if you want to," I start, then stop.

Because she looks like she's about to cry.

"Um, are you okay?"

She sniffs hard and wipes at her eyes, then looks back at me. "I'm good. Really good. Sorry. Just...holy smokes, I can't believe I get to live here!"

Holy smokes? She's not only sweet; she's adorable. "You're welcome," I say warmly. And I mean it.

She turns, still taking it all in. "Built-in bookshelves? Am I Belle? I'm Belle. That must be it."

Rosalie skids through the hallway and crashes into me, wrapping her arms around my waist and looking adoringly up at Elodie. "I love Belle! She's not my favorite, though."

Elodie's entire demeanor changes, going soft and fuzzy at the edges. "Yeah? Who's your favorite? Wait—don't tell me."

Rosie giggles. "You'll never guess."

Elodie pretends not to notice the *Brave* T-shirt that Rosie's in. "Hmm. It's...Snow White!"

Rosie makes a face. "No way. She's not self-reliant at *all.*"

I may or may not preen at this declaration.

With a laugh, Elodie dips her chin. "Good point. But it's okay to rely on your friends, too. And Snow White was friends with everyone, wasn't she?"

Rosie nods seriously. And all I can think is, *well, shit.* Because I should have seen that lesson in the movie, too. All I ever think about is how shrill her voice is when she sings. Am I the asshole here? Probably.

"Cinderella," Elodie declares.

Rosie giggles again. "Nope! One more guess."

"Hmm." Elodie taps her lips with her finger. "I bet... it's...Merida!"

"You got it!" Rosie says. "Daddy says I'm brave just like her. *And* that my hair is just as wild."

I smile ruefully down at her. "That's true." But believe me, I can wield a detangling spray and brush along with the best of them. It's why Rosie's hair is in two slicked-back braided pigtails...and why it usually stays in those. I learned that trick pretty quickly.

"Hey, Ansel? Think the pizza's here!" Cash calls from the front.

"Come on, Rosie Posie," I say, picking my daughter up and relishing the sheer solidity of her. "I ordered your favorite."

She wraps her arms around my neck and squeezes, then mashes her forehead to mine. "You look funny like this."

"You look funnier," I counter.

"Pineapple and ham?"

"That's still your favorite, right?" I start the walk to the front of the guesthouse, moving slowly so I don't trip over a rogue box.

"Ooh, yay!" Elodie cheers from behind us, pumping a fist in victory.

"Let me guess: you also love the worst pizza on Earth?" I ask over my shoulder.

"Watch yourself, Ansel," she warns. "You're on thin ice with a statement like that." Then her cheeks flush, as if she can't quite believe she's just let herself utter the words.

It might be the first real thing I've heard her say. Until now, she's been in interview mode. But declare a certain type of pizza a terror, and suddenly the real person emerges.

I laugh. "Is that so?"

Rosalie cups my cheeks with her hands and pulls my attention back to her. "Be nice to her, Daddy."

I give Rosie a zerbert on her fat little cheek, delighting in the squeal I get in response. "Or what?"

"Or we'll both have to tickle you!" She holds her hands up like claws.

"I'll be nice," I promise, holding my pinkie up and glancing at Elodie, who's watching us. Rosie loops hers with mine, and we both kiss our pinkies.

Our ritual complete, I put her down and direct everyone back outside to the screened-in area, then hustle to the front to take care of the driver's tip. After I get the pizza set up and everyone's getting their slices, my phone buzzes.

Figuring it's Lennox, lamenting he's missing us even while he's visiting family back home in Glasgow, I don't hesitate to pull it from my shorts pocket.

UNKNOWN

I messed up.

I stare at the text, willing it to make sense, yet terrified that I know precisely who it might be.

Before I can think too much about it, I type back.

ME

You know exactly what you did. Lose this number.

Chapter 6
Elodie

FALLING ASLEEP IN a new place is never easy for me.

Falling asleep in the next-level guesthouse that belongs to my new employer, who also happens to be incredibly hot...is much, much harder.

It doesn't matter that the air conditioner works flawlessly, that the mattress is incredible, that Cleocatra has settled in perfectly, or that I've got my own pillows and satin pillowcases. None of it matters.

Because I can't get him out of my head.

The easy way he was with his daughter, and how he didn't hesitate to pick her up and shower her with love and affection?

So fluffing sexy.

The way all the other guys looked up to him, not hesitating to do whatever he asked. The smiles he delivered without hesitation. His treatment of me as an equal.

And that's throwing me for such a loop. Because apparently, I've spent years *not* being treated like an equal at work. Always getting the coffee and printing copies and taking notes and setting appointments, even though there were people more junior than me who should have done it. Always doing the lowest level of work even as I pitched brilliant event idea after brilliant idea. Never allowing myself to get too worked up over any of it, though, because *that's just the way it is.*

It's only now, lying in the dark and staring at the ceiling, that I think maybe—no, *definitely*—I was taken advantage of. For years. Years that I spent being nice. So very, very nice. Of doing whatever was asked of me, even if it wasn't my job. Of smiling and gritting my teeth when my boss took credit for my ideas after watering them down. Of staying in that stupid cubicle.

Getting fired was a gut punch.

Realizing that I should have walked away a long, long time ago? Devastating.

Today, none of the guys looked at me with anything but respect. None of them made crass jokes. I never caught them looking at my body with disgust or in a way that made me feel like I existed just for them to gaze upon. And somehow, I knew they behaved because of Ansel. Or maybe that's not quite it. Ansel set the example, and they followed suit.

And that...that is sexy.

Did I mention the glasses? Because he was wearing *glasses*. He didn't have them on the first time, but today he did, and ugh, I don't know why it made him so good-looking. But it did.

It's probably bad that I think he's hot. Actually, it's not *probably* bad; it's *definitely* bad. So bad. I haven't even officially started the job—I do that tomorrow—and I'm doing the very thing to him that I was thrilled not to have done to me today.

Great.

I'm not remotely a good person.

I sigh, flip my pillow to the cool side, and finally manage to fall into a fitful sleep.

MY ALARM BLARES me awake with a jolt. It's six, and Ansel told me that Rosalie doesn't wake up until eight most days—a rarity among littles, as I understand it—but I thought I'd make a breakfast casserole and have it ready for when she wakes up. Start us off on the right foot and all that.

It's a quick twenty minutes of showering and dressing, then feeding Cleocatra and filling my travel mug with a K-cup before I head to the Piggly Wiggly a couple miles down the street. My beat-up Honda CR-V has seen better days, but Atlanta traffic is so horrible that I'd rather have a car I don't care to get dinged up.

Which is good, because it has absolutely seen its share of dings. But it's safe and dependable, even if it barely held up to Ansel's standards. Then I reminded him that my driving record spoke for itself, and he begrudgingly admitted it was fine. I snort a laugh to myself as I breeze through the aisles, making my way through the produce, then dry goods to stock up on my absolute favorite cereal and grab some other essentials, then into the dairy section for the rest of the ingredients.

I'm back before seven, shocked at how light the traffic was in Ansel's neighborhood. Guess that's what happens when you live in one of the suburban zip codes. Humming to myself, I press the buttons to turn the oven on and begin whisking eggs into a stainless-steel bowl, before realizing that the oven didn't actually start. So I peer closer—I probably need glasses, but if I could make it farther into my thirties than, well, the thirty I am before succumbing to them, that'd be amazing.

Sure enough, it isn't turning on.

"Fluffing fluff nuts," I mutter.

Well...surely he won't care if I make them in the main house, right? Who says no to a breakfast casserole?

I gather everything up, tossing the ingredients into a travel grocery bag and hooking my coffee over one finger so that I can have a hand for the whisked bowl of eggs, then step outside. In no time at all, I'm making my way through the screened-in porch to knock on the door.

"Come in!" a tiny voice answers.

"It's open," a much, *much* deeper voice follows.

I try the handle with the few free fingers I have, and sure enough, the knob turns easily.

"We're in the kitchen," Ansel says.

How has his voice gotten deeper overnight? Is this a morning thing? Or is this an Elodie-needs-to-get-her-life-together-and-stop-fantasizing-about-her-new-boss thing?

Shaking my head, I do my best to breeze into the room like I meant to be there, then I flash a smile.

Which I nearly almost choke on.

Because there's Rosalie, perched on the stool at the kitchen island, smiling up at me from the coloring book she's been working on, cute as a button.

She is not the issue here.

Not even close.

No, it's her father. Who stands behind her, wearing the same glasses he was in yesterday, with a rubber band tucked between his lips as he works one of Rosalie's ponytails into submission. Exactly when I became a puddle of a person at the sight of a dad braiding hair is beyond me, but to be fair:

he is a hulking giant of a man, and the look of concentration on his face—he's biting his lip and his brow is furrowed—might be the hottest thing I've ever seen. The other side of her hair is a frizzy mess, forming a brown halo of unbrushed curls that reminds me so much of my own hair as a little girl.

My knees might shake.

Because apparently I have a thing for hot guys who take care of their daughter's hair? Is that happening right now?

There's a word for that, right?

Oh. Oh yes, there is.

DILF.

Dad I'd like to...ohmygosh.

"Hi, Elodie!" Rosalie singsongs.

I cough and re-paste the smile on my face, praying my cheeks aren't as flaming red as they feel. "Good morning, sunshine!"

"What's in the bowl?"

I look down, surprised I'm still holding anything, let alone a bowl with a half dozen eggs whisked in it. "Oh! Um. Right."

Ansel's eyes flick up to mine, and I freeze, a baby deer caught in the big bad wolf's gaze. Is that a thing? Do wolves eat deer? They probably eat anything.

"Elodie?" Ansel prompts. "Are you okay?"

I spring back into life, lurching to the island before doing a one-eighty and aiming for the counter beside the sink. "I'm fine. Um, but the oven in the guesthouse doesn't work?" I wince. Why am I saying it like a question? I swallow and palm the surface, letting the coolness of the stone ground me back into the reality where *I am a strong woman*. Taking a breath, and far happier to be facing away from Ansel than looking right at him, I try again. "I wanted to make a breakfast casserole, but the oven won't turn on. Can I use yours?"

"Of course."

"I don't like breakfast casserole," Rosalie declares.

I whirl around, horrified. "Oh no. Really? Well, um, that's okay..."

But Ansel just smiles down at her. "Rosie Posie, you don't even know what it is." He looks up at me. "It sounds delicious."

My heart squeezes. There's so much here to unpack, and I have no business unpacking it. Instead, I put my focus back on the bowl of eggs.

"Do you have a Pyrex?"

"A what?"

"A glass pan, like a casserole dish? Usually clear?" I explain, holding my hands out to show the size as I do.

"Ah. Yes. It's...well..." He shrugs. "I can grab it as soon as I finish here."

"Just tell me where it is; I can get it."

With a relieved smile, he directs me to it. "Sorry if it's a little cluttered," he apologizes. "I have a system of where things go, but it keeps getting changed."

"It's because every new nanny has a different spot for things, Daddy."

A pained expression crosses his face. After a beat, he nods and gestures for the rubber band next to Rosalie's hand. She gives it to him, and a moment later, one side of her hair is tamed into a sleek braid.

Then, with horror, I realize I've been watching him instead of doing the very thing I came in here to do.

Get it together, woman.

Dumping out the cheese, chives, and two potatoes, I prep the rest of the casserole. Behind me, Rosalie hums and chatters about the scene she's coloring from *Brave*, all while I force myself to keep my eyes on my work. By the time I have the dish in the oven, Ansel, who'd left the kitchen after finishing Rosalie's hair, is striding back in.

And I...I might black out.

Because it's the first time I'm seeing Ansel up close in his workout shorts.

Um.

Is it hot in here? It's hot in here.

This isn't fair. In no way, on no planet, is any of this fair.

First, he had the glasses, and that's bad enough. But now? He...he has a tattoo. On the outside of his thigh. The most intricately done roses that I have ever seen. They're mostly deep red with shades of pink woven in as well. How did I not notice that first day? Or yesterday?

Bless those rugby shorts. Bless, *bless* them. So very much.

"Elodie?"

I snap out of it, jerking my gaze up to Ansel's, my cheeks heating furiously once again. "Hmm?"

He grins, as if he knows exactly what I was looking at and is very aware of the effect it's having on me.

Is there an escape hatch anywhere?

"I was saying that I'll call an electrician to come look at the oven. And Rosie has been asking to go to the library, so you might need my library card."

Is he serious right now? He takes his daughter to the library to check out books?

"Are you okay?" His mischievous smile morphs into one of genuine concern, and he begins to close the distance between us.

"I'm fine!" My voice hits a pitch I have never hit before. "Sorry. Just, ah, lost focus there for a second. Not that it happens a lot. Me losing focus. I don't. I never. Well, I mean, I've never lost it before now." *Really?* I take a deep breath. Force myself to meet his caramel-brown eyes, full of warmth and no small amount of amusement, once more. "I would be happy to take Rosalie to the library. I have my own card, though; we can use it with no problem."

He adjusts the duffel on his shoulders—a duffel I had no idea he'd been carrying until this exact second, because I have been memorizing the green leaves and thorns that surround the roses *on his thigh* instead of talking to him like he is my boss.

He is my *boss*.

I can't lose this job. Is it what I want? No. But is it perfect while I decide what my next move is going to be? Absolutely.

Which means I need to keep whatever *this* is under control. By a lot.

A lot a lot.

No more gawking at leg tattoos.

I can't look.

I won't look.

His daughter is literally in the room and he is my boss and I am making an egg casserole and therefore I can. Not. Look.

"I should be home around four," Ansel says.

"Great!" I really, really hope that I don't look as deranged as I suspect I might.

"Bye, Daddy!" Rosalie chirps, sliding off her stool and running to him, wrapping her arms around his waist and gripping with all her might.

He scoops her into his arms. I can't handle it. I look away, busying myself with the dishes in the sink.

After he's left, Rosalie climbs back onto the stool, swinging her legs and studying me thoughtfully.

I run a bowl under the water, rinsing the suds and watching them swirl down the drain, feeling her attention on me. I keep to my task, knowing she's just curious.

"What happened at your old job?" she finally asks.

"They let me go."

She cocks her head. "What's that mean, let you go?"

I give her a sad smile. "They fired me."

Her eyes go round. "Were you bad? Did you get in trouble?"

Laughing, I shake my head and finish rinsing the dishes. "No. They decided they didn't need me anymore. But you know, I'm beginning to think that it was a good thing."

"Why?"

"Because it means I get to hang out with you this summer," I grin. "And that means..."

"Swimming and libraries and stories and movies and *fun*!" Rosalie finishes.

I laugh. "Exactly."

We eat our breakfast, and afterward, Rosie gives me a tour of "all the important places" in the house. Meaning her room, the bathroom, the living room, and of course the outside area by the pool. Then we start a load of her laundry, water the many plants that I'd have sworn were fake, and head to the library. After that, it's home, snack, half an hour on her iPad, a brutal game of checkers, lunch, meeting all her dolls and stuffed animals, dress-up, drawing, and I think my brain checked out at some point while I colored.

By the time Ansel makes it home that afternoon, I'm completely beat. I look up from where Rosalie and I are sprawled on the couch, watching none other than *Brave*, and offer a weak wave. Even the sight of him, comfortably dressed in black sweatpants and a loose T-shirt, isn't enough to cut through the haze of exhaustion.

He laughs, a deep belly laugh that tells me he knows exactly how I feel. "Wore you out, didn't she?"

I nod. "I didn't think—"

"No need to explain," he chuckles. "Been there many, many times before. I'll make you dinner."

My brain must be hallucinating, because I swear this man just offered to cook dinner. After *he* was the one working his butt off all day. "Sorry, what?"

His smile grows, and I am done for. "Let me feed you."

Chapter 7
Ansel

ELODIE BLINKS UP at me, clearly trying to make sense of the words coming out of my mouth. I let her brain glitch, knowing that it'll put itself back online. It's hard not to be pleased she's just as thrown by me as I am by her. But I won't be doing anything about it. I can't risk it. Can't risk the tightrope balancing act that is my life with Rosie. And there's no time for a relationship anyway. When would I fit that in? I'm barely hanging on as it is.

"I'm cooking anyway," I remind Elodie. "Nothing fancy. Just stay." I turn away before she can protest anymore, letting a grin widen across my face for the briefest of moments. Her reaction is something I'd honestly forgotten about, but was once supremely used to.

Once upon a time...for a very brief time, that is. My looks don't make sense to me. I mean, they're part of who I am, clearly, but as a child, I was short and chubby. It wasn't until I was a teenager that I started to grow and pack on the muscle, and even then, the girls I'd grown up with seemed determined to keep me and any ego that threatened firmly in check. None of them were interested in me, ever. My prom date was the same girl I'd once traded Pokémon cards with. To say there was no spark would be a drastic under-statement.

My name wasn't any sort of help. Being a huge photography buff, Mom had idolized Ansel Adams and thought giving me his name would be the highest honor she could possibly bestow on me.

Yeah.

Did I mention the horrific glasses? And braces?

I'm not sorry for any of it, though. Being raised the way I was, surrounded by the same kids all through grade school and high school who were all generally *nice* to each other—a rarity, for sure—was a comfort. Something about it gave me this ridiculously wholesome sense of self that I carried into college.

College, however,...well. That's where it all went to shit. In a manner of speaking. I joined the rugby team, and it turned out I was good. Really good. All those years of middle and high school football finally paid off, and I took the ball and ran with it. Literally. Rugger huggers were everywhere and ripe for the taking, so I took. And took and took.

It was a great four years.

But I stopped it all after college. I'd planned on using my accounting degree and figured I needed to grow up. Then Major League Rugby came calling, and it was a dream come true.

The point here is that I know what I look like, but I also know it doesn't matter. It's surface-level. It's how a person acts that really matters. Some of the guys on the team say I sound like a complete douche when I talk like this, that it's something only a good-looking guy would say, but I still believe it with my very soul.

Besides, who cares what I look like when there's a miniature dinosaur attacking me as I walk into the kitchen?

"Rawr!" Rosie snorts as she latches onto my leg, unhinging her jaw and pretending to bite me as we move.

"Are you a Rosasaurus Rex?"

"I demand food!"

"Yeah, yeah," I chuckle, pulling her up and smothering her soft face with kisses.

"Your beard tickles," she giggles, but even as she says it, she leans in harder.

"Love you, Rosie girl." I set her on the island stool and begin making dinner. Nothing too involved tonight: some pasta and turkey sausage with frozen peas thrown in for color, topped with a jarred sauce I doctor up. Some pre-made garlic bread for Rosie and Elodie—I love it, but it's not on the approved food list—and boom, dinner.

"Wanna call Nana?" I ask Rosie, pulling my phone out and getting my mom's number ready.

Rosie nods excitedly. When Mom's face comes onto the screen, she's already smiling.

"My two favorite people in the world!" she exclaims.

Rosie giggles. "What about Papa?"

"That old coot? No way." Mom makes a face and Rosie cracks up. To me, she says, "How are you?"

Better than I expected. "Good, good. Figured we'd call and see how Dad is."

"She's mean to me!" Dad calls from the background.

Mom rolls her eyes and looks back at him. "Because I'm making him do his physical therapy and won't let him wallow in misery."

Watching them lets something ease in my chest a bit. I

worry about them, even though they're still fairly young and surrounded by friends where they live. Mom insists they can take care of themselves, and they can. But being the only child means I'm ultimately the one responsible for them, and there's no telling me any different. We catch up for a few more minutes, Rosie launching into a story about the day before we finally disconnect.

"Can I help?" Elodie appears a few minutes later, looking decidedly beat. Her shoulders droop and her energy is low, especially compared to any other time we've interacted. Rosie must have put her through the wringer—and they didn't even get in the pool. I almost feel sorry for her, except for the part where I'm paying her to do this job.

"Nah." I wave her off with what I hope is a friendly smile. "You're off duty. Go relax."

She hesitates, her top teeth worrying her bottom lip in a maneuver I'm already deeply familiar with, clearly torn.

I laugh. "Fine. You want to help? Set the table. Rosalie can show you where everything is." No matter Elodie probably already knows where things are; it doesn't take long.

Brightening, she launches into action. "Got it!"

Conversation over dinner is easy. Turns out that Elodie knows just about zero about rugby, so Rosie and I take turns explaining the basics of the game.

"So, a touchdown—" Elodie starts.

"Isn't called a touchdown," I finish, spearing a bite of pasta.

"It's a *try*," Rosie says in an exasperated tone.

Elodie grins. "I'm teasing. I really *did* know that. But not much else."

Watching them, it's hard to believe it's only been one day. There's an ease between the two of them that I've never seen with any other nannies. Granted, that might be because they've all been ladies closer to my mom's age, but still.

Elodie finally seems to get comfortable with being in the same room as me right as dinner ends. Gone is the immediate blush every time she looks my way, which is good. Great, even. I don't need a nanny who's distracted. Not when I'm distracted enough for the two of us.

She insists on helping to clean up, and I stay at the table for one more minute to luxuriate in being still. My gaze snags on the way she places her hand on Rosie's shoulder, gently guiding her to the sink. As she bends down to position the step stool for my daughter, I allow myself to wonder —just for a second—what it'd be like to be with someone like Elodie. To feel the soft caress of her fingers on mine after a long day. To let myself look into those beautiful hazel eyes and just...breathe.

I shake my head. I can't lose myself in a fantasy.

In the kitchen, Elodie hums a Disney song with Rosie, their movements as easy and intimate as though they've done it Rosie's whole life. Watching them, I swear I feel a physical weight lift off my chest.

Finally, I pull myself together and stand to take my plate to the sink. Rosie holds soapy hands out for it, and when I turn, I run straight into Elodie.

"Oh!" she exclaims, her eyes widening.

My hands go out on instinct, as do hers. She's soft. Soft hands on my forearms, and a soft, generous body pressed against mine. The whole moment lasts all of a second, but my body comes alive at the contact. As though it, too, can't remember the last time it was touched by anyone who wasn't trying to tackle me—Rosalie included.

Also, she smells incredible. The scents of vanilla and brown sugar waft around me, like my own personal dessert.

"Sorry," I murmur, releasing her and stepping to the right.

Only she steps in the same direction.

Her laugh is so genuine that her entire face lights up. The smile she gives is beautiful, wide and lush, and its very presence seems to thaw a piece of my heart that I didn't know was frozen.

My own chuckle is more reserved, but I hope she sees how undeniably grateful I am. For...everything. I step backward, nearly toppling into Rosalie in the process, and it makes Elodie laugh even more.

"Sorry." She wipes tears from her eyes. "I don't know what's come over me. I'm just..." She trails off, then meets my gaze. "Thank you. For everything."

Her words are like an arrow, hitting a mark she has no idea is even there. The fact that she echoed my own thoughts makes it that much sweeter. "You're welcome. But the thanks is all mine."

Surprise flashes across her face, and I think if I were any other person, Lennox perhaps, I'd make a joke here, ease the thickening tension and reset us into the more easily navigable roles of boss and employee. But I don't know what kind of joke would work, and...I'm tired. Tired of, well, everything. I don't have the will to fight a damn thing tonight.

So I smile, and move out of the way, and we finish cleaning up. She leaves shortly afterward, once the final Clorox wipe has been discarded and the kitchen is clean and tidy once more.

Closing the back door on Elodie's retreating form, I turn to my daughter. "Head upstairs and get ready for a bath. I'll be right up."

"Okay, Daddy." Rosie flashes a smile and darts away.

My phone buzzes on the counter. Thinking it might be my mom with an update on Dad, I grab it and glance at the screen.

UNKNOWN

Did you get my last text? We need to talk.

The breath whooshes out of me as my body tenses with adrenaline, my grip tightening on the phone. Before I can decide how—or even whether—to reply, another message comes through.

I know you're reading these. Don't ignore me.

Cursing, I blacken the screen and barely manage to contain the urge to throw the phone against the wall. Violence never solved anything, but it sure would make me feel a tiny bit better.

I know exactly who's texting. And there's no way in hell she's getting what she wants.

Chapter 8
Elodie

IT TAKES A couple of weeks, but finally, on the third Monday of my job nannying for the world's hottest rugby player, I'm able to sustain an air of "why, no sir, your beefy tattooed thighs and slightly crooked smile and scarred eyebrow and chest muscles and love for your daughter actually *don't* affect me" whenever I see Ansel.

I'd like to say that it's because that whole idea of being repeatedly exposed to something can make you immune to it is right.

Except that's not it at all.

Not even close.

There's no denying how scaldingly hot he is. Or how he makes each and every particle in my body scream *"holy FLUFF he's hot"* every time I see him.

No, it's simply that I've stood in front of the bathroom mirror and literally practiced keeping my face from reacting.

I'm not proud of it.

I'm also not proud of how I've watched, um, hours— *hours!*—of rugby highlights with him in it, trying, I swear, to get immune to him. All it's done is made me hyper-aware of the way his body moves. Also, whoever does the slow-mo reels featuring him and his ridiculous butt on social media should be awarded a medal. Or jailed. I'm not sure yet.

And it's not as if he's deliberately showing off his hotness when I'm around. If anything, he's kind of...a dork. It feels wrong to say, but I'm pretty sure that Ansel would be happiest surrounded by spreadsheets instead of sprinting down a rugby pitch.

Which, of course, makes him that much hotter. A beast of a man on the rugby pitch who turns to absolute goo for his daughter and talks about financial solvency like it's the most interesting thing in the world.

I guess what I'm attempting to say is that I'm *trying*. And lo and behold, I think I've finally succeeded, because this morning, I'm able to smile and meet his warm caramel eyes without blushing. I mentally give myself five points—same as a try is worth in rugby—as I say, "Good morning, Ansel."

He smiles back, and I *still* don't blush. It's tempting to award myself another five points, but no need to get ahead of ourselves. "Rosie's putting on her new swimsuit. She's decided to wear it all day."

"As she should," I agree. "It's disgusting outside already. You didn't do her hair, did you?"

His answering grin, slightly crooked as always, does things to my insides, but I keep chanting *keep cool keep cool keep cool,* and I swear, I think it's working. "No. Still in yesterday's braids."

"The ones she did herself?"

"The very ones." He strides across the kitchen and plucks the keys to his Land Rover off the hook on the wall.

"Thank you for teaching her. I don't know why that never occurred to me."

I keep my eyes firmly on his back. Not his back*side*. And you know what? That's another five points.

I'm winning.

"Stay for dinner tonight?" he asks. It's casual, delivered with the same nonchalance as asking if it's one hundred percent humidity outside.

It's not the first time he's asked. And every time, except for that first night, the one where he said, and I quote, *"Let me feed you,"* I've turned him down. I've either gone out with Kari for our weekly girls' night or—once the oven got fixed—made something myself in the guesthouse's tiny kitchen. Which has been incredibly strategic. Because, for one thing, he's my employer. For another, he's my landlord. Never mind his aforementioned gorgeousness. And I don't want Rosalie to get used to having me around constantly, because I'm only going to be here for three months.

That's the plan, anyway. I should probably be looking for another place to live after this, but any free time I've had has been devoted to working on my business plan. I'm done working my butt off for other people. It's time to focus on myself.

Which is a lot harder than it looks. I was strong enough to stop talking to my mother after my break-up with Jeremy, but there's no erasing her voice from my head. It's infuriating. The longer I've been away from Fore Gone, the more I realize just how poisonous the place was for me. How I never stood up for myself. And for a long time, I think I stayed because I had Jeremy. We were happy, or so I thought, and when we got engaged, I was the happiest I'd ever been. It wasn't until we started trying for a baby that things went sideways. And I was so numb in the aftermath of our break-up that it's a wonder they didn't "let me go" at that point.

Who knows? Maybe the universe decided to throw me a bone after all these years, because somehow I've landed here: nannying for the most genuine and brain-meltingly hot man in the world, and he's asking me to stay for dinner.

I may be working to put myself first, but I can't be rude, and saying no to his repeated offers is starting to feel, well, rude. Besides, I've successfully managed to keep my body in check for five whole minutes this morning. I can do a dinner. I'm positive. I believe in myself.

"Sure," I answer, being certain to sound just as nonchalant as him.

Then I make the mistake of looking up. And his expression—he's *beaming*—is enough to send heat right to my cheeks. Drats.

"Perfect," he says. "I didn't ask the first time, and I'm sorry for that, but do you have any allergies? Preferences? Intolerances?"

I swallow, forcing myself not to be affected by his consideration, then smile brightly. "Nope! None at all."

Relief washes over his face. "Perfect," he repeats. "I mean, great. I'll see you a little later than usual, then. I've got to run by the store—"

"We can go," I interrupt. "Just tell me what you want us to get."

"No," he answers, his brows knitting in a scowl so brief that I can't decide if he's irritated or if it's just an extension of him being considerate. "I'll take care of it." Then he swivels away, the duffel I once again failed to notice swinging off his shoulder. "Tell Rosie Posie I said goodbye. And—" he turns back, his expression so totally parental it can't possibly be confused with anything other than that, "Fresh sunblock is in the bin with the towels outside."

I press my lips together, wondering if he's telling me that because he thinks I've not been applying it to Rosalie every time we've been outside for longer than half an hour. "Of course. Thanks."

He leaves, and I nearly puddle from the five-minute interaction. It's my own fault, this ping-ponging of feelings.

But I don't get to think any more about it, because Rosalie chooses that moment to bound into the kitchen, excited to show off the new suit that arrived yesterday from her grandmother. It's adorable, pink with little red strawberries and white piping.

"And she sent a matching suit for Violet!" Rosalie exclaims, holding her doll in the air with both hands.

"Beautiful!" I agree. "Let's get the two of you breakfast, and then we can go play."

"May I have French toast with that yummy white powder again?" she asks, clasping her palms beneath her chin and blinking up at me.

I laugh. "It's called 'powdered sugar,' and sure. But only if you help."

"Yay!"

The day passes lazily, with multiple trips from the pool to the shade and back again. Around three, when the sun has baked me within an inch of my life, I finally give in to Rosalie's demands and agree to join her in the pool. But I'm not in my suit, so first I get her safely inside the screened-in porch. Then, I extract a pinky promise that she'll stay there while I change and hustle to the guesthouse.

I grab the first suit I come to, a royal-blue two-piece that would have been perfectly at home in the fifties, and throw it on. The bottoms are high-rise and the top holds me in tight, ensuring the girls don't go anywhere. It's perfect for playing in the pool with Rosalie.

Back outside, I call to Rosie, who squeals at the prospect of me finally joining her. It's not that I haven't wanted to get in, it's just that somehow, it's felt like a boundary I don't need to cross. As though by doing so, I'm taking one more step toward a relationship with her that I shouldn't. But maybe that's silly. Maybe I'm overthinking the whole thing and Rosie just wants someone to play with. Besides, she's dug herself so firmly into my heart already that I can't fathom not doing just about anything for her. Getting in the pool is an easy decision.

Once my eyes are on her, she climbs up the ladder to the slide and situates herself at the top. "Ready?" she calls. When I nod, she scoots off, throwing her hands in the air and sliding down the hard plastic into the deep end of the pool. She emerges with a gasp and grins while she doggie paddles to the shallow end, strands of hair plastered to her forehead. "Your turn!"

I open my mouth in mock surprise. "You want me to go down the slide? Me?"

She giggles. "Yes, you!"

I don't hesitate. To be honest, the slide's been one of the more tempting aspects of the entire thing. It's tall, rising easily fifteen feet into the air, curving twice before emptying into the pool. Strategically placed jets keep water flowing down the slide. Ansel undoubtedly installed it once Rosalie learned to swim, because it doesn't really match the aesthetic of the rest of the pool at all.

I climb the stairs and find Rosalie. She's grabbed a pool noodle and has her arms hooked over it, her little body stretched out in the water behind her. "Ready?" I ask her.

"Ready!"

I push off, raising my arms just like Rosie, not bothering to stop the huge grin or giggle that comes out of me as I go down the slide and into the pool.

The water is perfect, a little warm on top and getting cooler as I descend, letting myself fall so my toes touch the bottom before bending my knees and pushing off. I break the surface to the sound of Rosie's cheers, then wipe my eyes and tread water.

Why in the world have I denied myself this amazing pool for two weeks?

"Isn't it *fun?*" Rosie asks, kicking to close the distance.

We spend the next hour in the pool, playing Marco Polo and sliding and racing and splashing. Finally, I haul myself onto the giant He-Man float to judge Rosalie on the different faces she can make while jumping into the deep end.

"What's going on out here?" The deep voice startles me, and I jerk my head around, shielding my eyes from the brutal sun to see Ansel standing just off the edge of the pool. He's smiling down at his daughter. "Have you been in here all day? Are you a prune yet?"

"No," she giggles. "Come swim, Daddy!"

He tilts his head in the direction of the kitchen. "I need to start dinner."

And it has to be the heat that's addled my brain, because before I know what's happening, I'm opening my mouth and saying, "We can wait. Come on in—the water feels amazing!"

He turns his attention to me, his eyes narrowing as they travel the length of my body.

My breath catches. Was it wrong of me to say that? Should I have worn a one-piece? Is he mad that I'm on his float?

Then our gazes collide, and I stop breathing. His eyes are dark, darker than I've ever seen them, and it warms every part of me.

He's definitely not mad.

I swallow and wet my lips, and his attention dips to watch the movement before darting back to his daughter.

Whoa.

"You sure you want your old daddy in there with you? I'm stinky."

I doubt that very much, but I keep my mouth shut. I'm practically hyperventilating at this point, wondering what's about to happen.

When Rosie answers in the affirmative, he nods and goes inside.

I try to breathe. To remind myself that I'm only the nanny, and that this is not a big deal. That the look he gave me wasn't filled with...well, that it was just a look.

I slide off the float, needing the water to cool down my overheated body. And I stay there, hoping that maybe he isn't coming. That maybe he'll simply choose to start cooking dinner. Dinner that I stupidly agreed to join him for.

Them. Join *them* for.

But it seems that luck is not on my side, as moments later, he emerges.

And I can't take it. Can't take how devastating he is. I simply cannot. So, like the perfectly mature thirty-year-old I am, I duck under the surface before I can get a good look and push off, swimming underwater from the shallow end to the deep. I go until I feel the wall against my palm, and even then, I consider turning and swimming back. Unfortunately for me, my lungs aren't even remotely suited for that kind of thing, and I pop up, resolutely turned away from Ansel and his muscles.

I know I'm being ridiculous. But I can't stop my body from reacting to his, and it's embarrassing. I'm too old to act like this, yet my hormones absolutely refuse to agree with me. I exhale and steel myself. There's nothing to do but face it. Face *him*.

Suddenly, a shadow appears on my right and Ansel surfaces not even a foot from me, grabbing the edge with one hand and wiping the water from his eyes with the other.

And I...am transfixed.

Light bounces off the flurry of waves around us, reflecting onto his tanned skin and dragging my attention to the way every muscle on his arm seems to bunch and ripple as he moves. Water sluices off his hair, drawing my attention to his corded neck. His collarbones. The dusting of hair that dips below the surface.

He is unfair.

Entirely, completely, wholeheartedly unfair.

He whips the hair out of his face in that distinct move that, God help me, every good-looking man seems to be born knowing how to do, then focuses on me.

I might be hyperventilating. That's not normal, right? Right.

"Are you okay?" There's legitimate concern in his eyes.

Reality slams into me with the question. I am *the nanny*. Whatever brief moment of insanity that I had a few minutes ago, where I considered that maybe he might have, I don't know, thought of me as anything other than the help, burns away. Beneath his searing looks, he's a legitimately kind man. And apparently, I'm so starved for the male gaze that I'm willfully creating fantasies in my head now?

I need to get laid. Not by Ansel.

I blink, hoping against all hope that my very expressive face didn't just convey that particular thought. "I'm fine!" I chirp. I've waited too long to answer, and I hold my breath as he studies me, his gaze roaming over my face and dipping to my shoulders before flicking to my lips and back to my eyes.

He must come to some kind of conclusion, because he nods and says, "Okay."

I exhale. Flash the pageant smile.

Without another word, he takes a breath and ducks beneath the water, pushing off the side with those powerful legs of his.

Chapter 9
Ansel

UCK. ME.

Two weeks. Two weeks was all it took. I went from thinking I could totally manage my attraction to her to suddenly jumping in the pool at the slightest suggestion from my daughter in an attempt to, what, be close to Elodie? Touch her?

I don't really know how it happened. It was slow, a frog boiling in water, because I was completely and totally fine until this morning. Truly.

I've known the effect I have on her. It's impossible not to, with the way she blushes the second her eyes land on me. She's gotten better at it, and this morning, there wasn't a hint of red to be found. Not even the tips of her ears were pink.

I should have been grateful. Relieved. But no. No, instead I was disappointed. Which makes no sense, for all the reasons I've gone over in my head. Over and over. Chief among them? My daughter. Rosie needs her. Hell, *I* need her. The little things she does around the house that no other nanny ever bothered to do and I sure as fuck never find time to do? Jesus, I'm damn near tempted to beg her to stay forever based on that alone. I'm talking about organizing junk drawers and sorting clothes and toys that Rosie's outgrown type of stuff. Little stuff that piles up. Bigger stuff that's a huge mental load that I know I need to deal with, but can't manage to find time in the day. Stuff that I can't possibly keep track of on top of everything else. I'm over here fighting for my life to keep Rosie and me fed, watered, clothed, and up to date on all our shots, never mind dentist appointments and haircuts, and here comes Elodie, who's done some kind of Mary Poppins voodoo on me.

But if I'm grateful for her, then I'm pretty sure Rosie is obsessed with her. God knows I've heard all about Elodie these past two weeks. In fact, I probably know way more about her than she's comfortable with. But that's what happens when you have an inquisitive daughter who doesn't think twice about sharing what she's learned at the dinner table.

Then I come home and see them through the kitchen window, Elodie's plush body laid out on the He-Man float as though it were made specifically to display her every dip and curve. Of which she has plenty. Never mind the blue bikini she was in, wrapped around her like a modern-day pin-up. As I watched, she laughed at something Rosie said. There was nothing but pure joy on her face, and I saw how carefree she was when I wasn't around. How fucking gorgeous and kind she was. How she treated Rosie with respect and love. And suddenly...suddenly a switch flipped.

So now I'm here, treading water in the pool and trying desperately to make the switch go off.

It's not working.

She's keeping her distance, and I don't know if it's because I make her uncomfortable or if it's something else entirely. All I know is that Rosie's not having it, and it's not long before she's cajoled Elodie to join us for a game of Marco Polo.

And Elodie chooses to be the one to try to find us.

Again: Fuck. Me.

Because now her eyes are closed and she's standing fully upright in the shallow end, her torso out of the water and *right fucking there* for me to look at. I shouldn't look at her like this. I know that. Even so, there's absolutely nothing in this world can keep me from feasting on her. I repress a groan. She smiles, turning toward the squeals and giggles of my daughter, and before I can stop myself, I call out. I need her to face me. To come close.

She turns, eyes still clenched, but her smile seems to stutter. She calls again, "Marco!"

"Polo!" Rosie answers.

"Polo." I'm breathless in the face of her. Her skin is apparently resistant to the sun, resolutely pale except for the faintest tinge of pink on her shoulders. Shoulders that are, God help me, recklessly painted with freckles and dotted with water falling from her hair. Even wet, her hair is thick and wild, the curls springing up and around her face like curlicues.

I step toward her.

"Marco!" she calls.

The blue bikini top crisscrosses her chest, drawing my attention to yet another series of freckles, these beginning at the dip of her collarbone and snaking down to disappear into the top. A line leading to heaven, I'm certain of it.

She's closer now, and I should move, keep playing the game, but I stay in position.

When her fingers brush against my chest, her eyes fly open.

For a split second, the world stills. She's motionless, the tips of her fingers touching me, branding me. Dark lashes, wet from the pool, frame wide hazel eyes that meet mine. And I see it—the raw, clear need that flashes across her face.

Then the world spins forward, the expression gone, her touch a memory.

"Caught me." My voice is hoarse.

Red stains her cheeks as she dips her body into the water and pushes away. But she holds my gaze, tipping her chin up slightly. *Brave girl.* It takes everything in me not to say the words out loud, to offer the praise. Need coils within me. There's so much more I want to know about her.

I shouldn't. Obviously. I come with a pretty big set of complications and restrictions.

I duck underwater, my daughter's squeals of laughter audible even from down here. When I surface, I tell myself that my momentary blip needs to be just that—momentary. A passing phase.

I tag my daughter easily, and then she's the one with her eyes closed while Elodie and I have nothing to do but look at each other. She keeps her gaze firmly planted on Rosie, but I don't bother. And every time she glances my way, I meet her eyes. She grows more and more flustered, her cheeks blazing red by the time I launch in front of Rosie to get caught.

I need to stop. Tossing Rosie into the air and catching her, her delighted squeals following as I tickle her and she wiggles in my arms, I say, "I'm going to start dinner. Maybe you and Elodie can make dessert?"

Her eyes light up. "Strawberry shortcake?"

I nod, confirming one of her favorite summer treats. "You know it."

I force myself to get out of the pool, taking the steps and

grabbing the towel I'd brought out. I dry off, and it's only when I'm heading inside that I allow myself a backward glance at Elodie.

She's turned away, gathering up the pool noodles.

Dinner is straightforward: citrus grilled chicken, baked potatoes, grilled asparagus and tomatoes, and for Rosie and Elodie, a side of mac and cheese. I busy myself with the food on the outside grill while Rosie takes Elodie through the strawberry shortcake process. It's safe enough: I let Rosie use a plastic knife to cut the strawberries, and then it's a simple matter of washing them and mixing a bit of sugar in. I've got some cantaloupe set aside for me.

We eat out on the screened-in porch, and just like our first meal, conversation flows easily. It's impossible to keep my eyes off Elodie, impossible not to notice how the white T-shirt she's thrown on highlights the faint pink of her skin, a bit burned from a full day in the sun. Or notice the smattering of freckles on her nose and cheeks, and how bright her eyes seem in contrast to the flush of her skin.

I can't remember a time I've been so affected by anyone. And to have it happen in what feels like the blink of an eye.

"This is delicious, Ansel," she says, finally meeting my eyes again. "Thank you."

God damn. Her sincerity might be the very thing that tosses me into the deep end. I clear my throat and throw on a teasing smile. "See what you've been missing by not accepting our dinner invitations?"

She smiles a bit, averting her gaze and reaching for her water glass, not answering me but humming noncommittally in response.

Needing a topic change, I ask, "Any ideas for what you plan to do after the summer?"

Her gaze flicks to mine, widening almost imperceptibly but delivering a punch, nonetheless.

"Not trying to kick you out," I grin. "Promise. I'm just... interested." And that's true.

She fiddles with her napkin before answering. "I'm working on a business plan at night. It's an idea I've been mulling over for a couple of years now, but it wasn't until, well." She takes a deep breath. "It wasn't until I got fired that I realized the only guarantee of safety was to do something myself."

Safety? Interesting word choice. "What's the idea?"

Elodie takes a bite of chicken and swallows before answering. "It's not fully baked yet," she hedges.

I hold my hands up. "No judgment here, I promise. You're talking to a professional rugger, for goodness' sake."

She grins. "Good point. How many knocks to the head have you had, anyway?"

My own smile widens. "Too many to count."

A breath huffs out of her. "Fine. I'll tell you, but you can't laugh at me."

I make the sign of an X across my upper left torso. "Cross my heart."

"I want to run a honeymoon planning company," she says. "Like, I'm who the couple calls. They give me the gist of what they're after and the budget, and I plan the entire thing from start to finish."

"Seriously?"

She nods, her lips pressed together nervously.

"That," I declare, "is the coolest thing I've ever heard."

A pretty blush stains her cheeks. "No, it's not."

"It is," I insist. "That's really cool. What made you think of it? How did it come to you?" I'm leaning toward her now, legitimately invested. I wasn't kidding when I said it was the coolest thing I'd ever heard of. My head whirls with possibilities. "Do you need an investor?"

Her eyes really do widen now. "A—an investor?"

"Seed money. Someone to get you started," I continue. "Because I'm interested."

She stiffens. "I don't need help."

"That's not what I mean."

"I don't need help," she says again, in a tone that tells me she's serious. But then her body relaxes, as if she wants to apologize for telling me to go to hell. "My old boss...she was always going on about how my ideas were 'too much' or 'too silly' or whatever. And maybe they were."

"Your old boss was an idiot," I interrupt.

Elodie smiles, tilting her head in consideration. "Maybe. But then, I don't know, I was watching some reality show where the couples are all on this pre-wedding vacation thing, which was weird, but it doesn't matter. It got me thinking about how there's so much emphasis put on the wedding itself, right? And there's so much stress involved in it, and all the details and energy go there. Which makes sense—for most people, anyway, that's the big moment. The huge party. The celebration. But what about the honeymoon? Who's putting the detail and thought and love into that? I mean, sure, there are probably people on those giant island resorts who do this as part of an overall wedding package, but I'm talking about making it happen anywhere in the world. Not just a relaxing island vacation, either. Whatever a couple wants. Wherever they want. That's what I want to give them." She's flushed again, but this time, it's because she's bursting with excitement. And it's incredible to see.

"Can you plan *my* honeymoon?" Rosie asks, her mouth full of mac and cheese.

I point a finger and give her my best fake scowl. "No way. You're staying with me forever."

She gets the joke and delivers her own fake pout in return, before smiling brightly. "Okay! As long as I get the guesthouse."

I pretend to think about it. "Deal."

"Deal!" Rosie pops another forkful of food into her mouth and chews.

I look back at the remarkable woman to my right and blurt, "Elodie. It's an amazing idea. Truly." I reach over to grasp her free hand and squeeze it, the movement so natural that I don't realize I've done it until I feel her skin beneath my own. And when I look up, Elodie's expression belies a jumble of emotions.

I pull away right as she does, both of us reaching for our waters. I down mine in a giant gulp. I have got to get a grip.

After a beat, Elodie recovers. "Right. Well, thank you," she says with a shaky laugh. "Anyway, that's my plan. I don't think I'll have it up and running in a mere six weeks, though, so...I don't really know what I'm going to do after the summer." She delivers the last bit of information as a mumble.

"Then stay here." The words are out of my mouth before I have time to catch them.

"Oh, I couldn't—"

"Why not?" I interrupt. "I won't charge you rent, and the guesthouse will be empty otherwise. I'm not asking you to watch Rosie; I'll have figured something else out by then." As I talk, it's as though I'm having an out-of-body experience. Watching myself look and sound like an absolute nutter while Elodie slowly retreats into herself. I take a breath. "Just think about it. The offer stands."

She smiles, but it's strained. "Thank you. Truly. It's a generous offer. But I can't accept."

Well, that stings. "Why not?"

Her lips curve up. "Because I can do it myself."

"Just because you can do it yourself doesn't mean you have to."

She studies me, and after a beat, she says, "You're right."

Right. I'm right.

Wait. Is she saying—? I squint at her. "You say I'm right, but why does it feel like I'm actually wrong?"

Rosie giggles.

Elodie bites her lower lip, considering. "I mean that you're right. And...that you should probably tell yourself that, too."

Oh. *Oh.* I shrug. "Living the single dad life makes things pretty straightforward," I say. "If I want something done, then I'm the one who does it. No one else."

Her eyes soften as she regards me. "It's funny."

"What is?"

She wipes her mouth and lays her napkin on the table. "Just...I'm the same way, kind of."

"How so?" I lean back in my chair.

She slides a glance at Rosie and shakes her head. "Doesn't matter. Anyway," she sighs, "I'm still trying to figure everything out about the new adventure."

I nod. It's clear she's giving me the stiff-arm, and just like on the pitch, there's nothing to do but respect it. So I stand and say, "Sounds good," like an absolute goober, before grabbing my plate and glass in a desperate need to breathe without taking in her vanilla and sugar scent.

Later, after Elodie is long gone and Rosie is asleep upstairs, I let myself back outside to the dark of the screened-in porch, a small glass of whiskey in my hand. It's loud outside, with all the nighttime crickets, cicadas, and frogs calling to one another. It's one of my favorite sounds. I settle onto the couch, glass balanced on my knee, and take a deep breath to relax.

Or at least, attempt to relax. Once upon a time, I could count on this time of night to provide a sense of contentment. Of a day well-earned. But these days, the best I can hope for is for the constant swirl of anxiety to recede a bit.

I force my thoughts away from Elodie and the endless to-do list that surrounds my daughter, and focus instead on the team. We're working hard, pushing ourselves on the pitch and in the weight room to within an inch of our lives. No one's happy to be practicing this intensely in the sweltering heat of an Atlanta summer, but the improvement I'm already seeing tells me I was right. There's been some chatter about updates to the roster, but that's nothing I can concern myself with. My job as captain is to set the example, keep everyone focused, and execute the drills that Coach gives us.

I take a sip of whiskey, feeling the familiar burn course down my throat, and run through the list of plays we'll do tomorrow.

A few minutes later, a light blinks on in the guesthouse bedroom.

My breath catches. I should turn away, but I'm rooted to the spot, watching Elodie move around the room through the gauzy curtains. She's left the blinds open, leaving me easily able to see her from where I sit in the dark. She's in a tank and skimpy sleep shorts, and as I watch, Cleocatra leaps gracefully onto the bed, her tail swishing as she arches her body beneath Elodie's outstretched hand. After a moment, Elodie leaves the room, but returns with a glass of water that she places on the bedside table. She reaches up and pulls her hair out of its customary bun, and I whimper. Her hair is its own fantasy, thick and waving down her back. But my joy is short-lived, because she pulls it back to the top of her head and binds it loosely before climbing into the bed. With a languid stretch, she reaches over to the bedside lamp, throwing the room into darkness.

It's only then that I realize what an absolutely horrible thing I'd just done. Spying on the nanny? What if she'd been naked?

Then that would have been amazing.

I shake my head. No.

After tipping the rest of the whiskey back, I stand and head inside.

Chapter 10
Elodie

It's been a week, and Ansel hasn't invited me to have dinner with him and Rosalie again. It stings a little, if I'm being honest. I know it's for the best, I do, but that doesn't mean I don't wish he'd offer. On the plus side, I've almost managed to keep from obsessing over how ridiculously incredible he looks clad only in swim trunks, so there's that. I'm not constantly thinking of the way his eyes darkened as he looked at me in the pool and said, *caught me.* And I'm definitely not considering taking him up on his offer to stay in this perfect little guesthouse like a modern-day suburban Disney princess, waking up each morning to birds chirping outside my window and literal deer strolling on the edge of the woods across the street.

Silver linings, right?

I finish putting the finishing touches on my makeup and step into the short pink dress I've laid out for dinner with Kari. It's my favorite style of dress, the short hem and bias cuts serving to highlight my curves instead of hiding them. I'm a tall girl, 5'10", so I usually stand out, anyway. I hated it as a teenager, but now that I'm thirty? Nothing to do but embrace it, and short dresses with cute tennis shoes make me happy. After a close examination of my hair, and subsequent giving in to the chaos that is my head of curls, I spray a tiny bit of perfume onto my wrists and get ready to leave.

Cleo follows me to the door, meowing her discontent at me leaving her alone for the night. She's gotten utterly spoiled these past few weeks, thanks to Rosie's insistence on daily visits. I've settled into an easy routine, but I refuse to let myself get comfortable. Not when I'm finally focused on doing something good for myself. Something that even my mother might be proud of, if I were brave enough to tell her.

I give Cleo a scratch beneath her chin, make sure I have everything in my purse, and step outside. Only to make my way across the yard and see Ansel and Rosie sitting down at the outside table for their Saturday night dinner.

"Oh, you look so pretty!" Rosie hops up and bursts through the screen door to give me a hug. "Mm, you smell good, too!"

I laugh and wrap my arms around her, reveling in her sweet smile. "Thanks, bug."

"Where are you going?" Ansel asks lightly. His tone is the same conversational one he's had all week. It doesn't sound right, but who am I to tell a man his *tone* sounds wrong?

I smile brightly. "Out with Kari. She's been busy the past few weeks, but Saturday nights are usually when we tear up the town...or at least pretend to." My phone buzzes, and I hold it up. "Ride's almost here. Have a good night!"

I swear I feel Ansel's eyes on me as I leave. I probably shouldn't, but I swish my hips just a little more than usual. The bottom of the dress kisses my upper thighs while I imagine Ansel groaning behind me.

A grueling thirty minutes through Atlanta traffic later,

I'm walking through the doors of our favorite Mexican restaurant and beelining for the table where Kari sits.

"I'm *so* sorry," I begin. "Traffic...drivers being drivers. Ooh, what's this?"

Kari grins as the server appears. "A mojito! Figured I'd go ahead and take control of the situation. And tonight felt like we needed to start with mojitos."

We cheer and drink, then she leans forward. "Now tell me how it's going with my spreadsheet superhero."

I laugh. "Your what?"

She waggles her eyebrows. "That man is a literal freak *with* the sheets. You know that, right?"

"I mean, he likes spreadsheets, but..." I'm about to make her tell me more when someone approaches the table. She's gorgeous, exuding an effortlessly cool, just-stepped-off-the-beach vibe. Blonde hair hangs nearly to her bottom, and aqua blue eyes look out from a makeup-free face.

"Kari?" she asks, with what sounds like an Australian accent.

At the sound of her name, Kari breaks into a huge smile. "Holy crap—Samantha?" The women embrace, and Kari introduces me. To Samantha, she says, "What in the world are you doing here?"

She holds up a to-go bag. "Had a desperate craving for chips and guac and no desire to make it myself, so..." She grins.

"Samantha," Kari deadpans. "The last time I saw you was the semester of college I spent in Melbourne. Twelve years ago. Running into you at a Mexican restaurant in Atlanta makes no sense."

Samantha's smile doesn't quite reach her eyes. "It's a boring story."

"I doubt that." Kari pushes a chair out. "Sit down and spill."

I nod. "Guac and chips by yourself sounds tragic, if I'm being honest."

She hesitates, then grins. "Fine. But only if you stop with the Samantha shit. You know it's Sam."

Kari rolls her eyes. "*Sam*, will you please join us?"

With a satisfied grin, Sam sits and pulls out the guacamole. "If you insist." After popping a chip in her mouth and chewing, she says, "It looks like my brother's going to join the Atlanta Granite."

Kari's face morphs into a grin. "No. *Way!* Your baby brother? The one who was—"

"Chubby and played video games the whole time you knew him? Yeah. Turned out to be quite the rugger but wanted to get out of Australia for a while. He was looking at Canada but couldn't pass up the possibility of playing in the States. He's convinced he'll be the best on the pitch. So, he's here, training with them for a couple of weeks to see if he likes it."

Kari smacks her forehead. "I should have put it all together. I knew there were some guys here from overseas trying out but never thought that Ollie Nash was your brother."

Now it's Sam's turn to look shocked. "Hold on. You work for the Granite?"

Kari nods. "I'm on the PR team."

They spend a few minutes getting caught up as we order a pitcher of margaritas, quickly realizing that individual drinks are a waste of time. Kari nods at me. "Elodie here is living with number ten."

My face burns at the suggestive sentence, and Kari absolutely catches it. She smirks in triumph.

Sam turns to me, eyes bright. "Ooh, the fly-half? That sounds fun. Tell me more," she urges, shimmying her shoulders.

"It's not like that," I protest. *But I think I want it to be.* "I'm his nanny—"

"His nanny!" Sam cackles. "I've read that book. Spoiler: they end up together."

My face burns even brighter. "I swear, I live in the guesthouse behind his house."

"She lives in the *pool* house," Kari intones, and the pair of them laugh.

"Shut up," I mutter, taking another sip of my drink.

"Okay, okay, I'm sorry," Kari says. "But you'd make a pretty great couple. He's the nerdy rugby player in the slutty short shorts, and you're the sweet-as-pie Disney princess. The happily-ever-after practically writes itself, Elodie."

"Except this is real life," I remind her. "And in real life, thirty-year-old women are let go from their jobs and find themselves nannying, which is super ironic, given their fiancé dumped them because they can't have kids."

Sam's mouth snaps shut.

Kari makes a choking sound.

"Did I...say that out loud?" I whisper.

"Babe," Kari says, reaching for me.

I wave her off. "It's okay. I promise." And it is. Mostly. I've had a couple of years to get used to the idea. I shake it off and laugh. "Clearly, the margaritas are a little strong."

"That they are," Sam says, her eyes softening with something that looks oddly like...solidarity?

"So, Sam, tell us what you're up to while your brother tries out for the team," I say, desperate to shift the conversation away from me.

Sam sighs. "Honestly, I'm not sure what I'm going to do. Tour around the country a bit, take in the sights. I promised Mum I'd get Ollie settled, but he's twenty-two, not a child."

"You're just visiting, then? No plans to stay if he makes it?"

She shakes her head. "I'm on break from my job for the summer. We'll see what happens."

"What's your job?"

"Physical therapist. Sports therapy, specifically."

"Ooh, maybe the Granite is hiring," Kari says playfully.

Sam rolls her eyes. "Mum would love that, honestly, but I'm not sure. I've been Ollie's therapist for a few years, but it's not like he can't have a different one."

The rest of the night passes in a pleasant blur of drinks and laughs. By the time I step out of my rideshare, it's a little after eleven. I let myself through the back gate and am passing by the fenced-in patio when I hear his voice.

"Elodie."

I freeze in my tracks, the sound of my name in Ansel's husky timbre sending shivers across my skin.

The door hinges open to my right, and there he is, leaning casually against the frame and backlit by a solitary candle burning on the table behind him. He's in low-slung shorts and a T-shirt, the same outfit he'd been in earlier—not that I make a habit of noticing his clothes. Except I do. I always notice.

And those glasses. He never wears them to practice, but it seems they stay on at any other time. Thin wire frames rest perfectly on his face, highlighting his already stupidly handsome bone structure and bringing even more attention to his gorgeous eyes. Eyes that saw a little too much last week.

I swallow. "Hi—hello," I stammer.

His lips quirk up the tiniest bit. "I thought you were finally immune to me."

And there it is. The way he says it, the open, loose way he stands. He's put the ball in my court. Whatever I say next can change everything. And maybe it's the alcohol running through my veins, or maybe I'm just done being shy, but I'm done. It's not worth hiding the truth from him. Not worth being nice for the sake of it. Because nice girls don't ruffle anyone's feathers. Nice girls make themselves small. They smile and look at the ground and do whatever is needed to keep the peace, even at their own discomfort.

I don't want to be nice anymore.

Squaring my shoulders, I meet his stare in the dim light. "I don't think I'll ever be immune to you."

A soft laugh escapes him, and the sound of it, unguarded and pleased, sends another wave of shivers across me. He lifts a glass I didn't notice before and toasts me with it. "Glad to know I'm not alone in this."

I tilt my head. "Alone in what, exactly?"

He doesn't answer.

After a beat, he gestures toward the couch behind him. "Nightcap?"

I shouldn't. Without question. It's a terrible idea. "Sure."

Chapter 11
Elodie

H E DOESN'T ASK what I want. Instead, he waves his hand at the couch in a clear command to sit and picks up the bottle and rocks glass on the table a few feet away. He pours two fingers, then plucks three ice cubes from a small cooler that sits next to it.

Was he *waiting* on me?

The thought is dizzying. When was the last time anyone did that for me? The realization is another gut punch: never.

I study him, his form casting long shadows as he tops his own drink off before turning to close the distance. I expect him to sit on the couch opposite me, but he doesn't. He lowers his massive form to the one I'm on, not even a cushion away.

I reach for the glass as he's handing it to me, and our fingers brush against each other when he releases it into my grasp.

It's the lightest of touches, but my body wakes up, electricity coursing through me. I literally felt a zing when we touched. That's...that's not real. I imagined it.

I *definitely* imagined it.

Shaking it off, I lift the glass in thanks and bring it to my lips. It doesn't smell like anything I've ever had before, a little sweet but still leaning toward whiskey.

Ansel's gaze never leaves my face, even as he brings his own glass to his lips for a drink.

I take the smallest sip, then another. It's delicious. Almost sweet.

His lips quirk at my expression. "It's a liqueur made from Irish whiskey."

I grin. "One of the Irish rugby players introduce you to it?"

He smiles. "Guilty as charged." He takes another sip, then places his glass on the side table. "How was your night?"

It occurs to me that this is the first time we've been alone together—*really* alone—and the realization sends a burst of heat through my body. Or maybe it's the drink. "Good," I answer. I lick my lips nervously, and he tracks it before snapping his gaze back to mine. With a deep breath, I ask, "What did you mean before?"

"By what?"

"When you said you weren't alone in this." I want him to tell me he feels this, too. This pull. This desperate, undeniable need to touch me, to feel my lips on his, the same way that I feel it.

His eyes darken behind his glasses, then shift away. His chest expands and contracts as he breathes, and I shouldn't watch him this closely, but I can't make myself stop. Eventually, he grabs his drink and looks back at me. "It doesn't matter."

I wait to see if he'll elaborate. When he doesn't, I set my liqueur down and fold my hands in my lap. Still nothing.

But his eyes...they stay on me this time. Studying. Memorizing. Unlocking something inside me.

It feels cellular, whatever it is this man's attention is doing. As if here, in the dark of the night, when the rest of the world sleeps, I'm waking up. My heart kicks around, a Mustang free on the plains.

Eventually, I find my words. "Do you know what everyone says about me?"

Twin lines appear on either side of his mouth as he frowns. "No."

"That I'm nice."

He furrows his brow, easily catching the disdain lacing the word *nice*. "And that's...a bad thing?"

Instead of answering, I take another step into the unknown. "Do you know what I realized tonight?"

He shakes his head, his gaze still firmly on mine, unlacing every rope I've ever lashed across my life. Ropes I didn't even know were there. Restraints he's plucking off, one by one, by simply listening.

I can't remember the last time I held someone's attention so thoroughly. Not like this. Mom would inspect me before a pageant, but this kind of intense review, as though he's seeing deep below the surface and is reading the neon signs that blare. Never. I have never had this. Not even Jeremy gave me this kind of undivided study. It's intoxicating, and it's impossible to fight the feeling of lightheadedness it brings. Because it's not the drink. Not even close.

Ansel waits. Like he's content to listen to the cicadas and frogs while I find the courage to say the words that are clawing their way up my throat.

I swallow. I could stop all of this. Stand up, tell him thanks for the drink, and then take my nice little self to the nice little guesthouse for a nice little sleep.

But I don't want to do that anymore.

So I take the metaphorical leap. "I realized that I'm tired of being nice."

He nods, a subtle dip of his chin that encourages me to keep going.

"Like tonight." I wave my hand around. "I went out with my friends, and when I came back, you were here. The nice girl in me—the girl I've been my entire life—she says it's because you just want to be sure I got home safe. That your *nanny* got home." I swallow and glance away from him, needing a break from the intensity of his gaze.

Still, he says nothing, one hand loosely steadying his drink on his thick thigh while his other arm lies across the back of the couch. Dark hair covers his forearm. There's even some on his wrist. And if I tipped my head just right, I could know what it's like to have his palm on my cheek. Would I feel another burst of electricity like I felt when our fingers touched?

Do I *want* that?

Yes.

God, yes. So much yes.

I shift, trying and failing to relieve the pressure building between my legs.

Ansel's gaze lowers, and I swear he's looking right... *there.*

Inhaling a shaky breath, I continue, "But the other part of me thinks that maybe you waited for a—a different reason."

His lashes lift, his gaze searing into mine once again, and my heart pounds so hard that I can scarcely believe it's not beating right out of my ribcage like an old cartoon.

If this is what it feels like to be brave, I don't know if I can survive it.

Ansel's beautiful dark eyes roam over my face, seeming to catalog each part to tuck away and study later. His jaw clenches, barely noticeable in the dim light beneath the beard, but I see it all the same.

I shiver, unable to control my reaction to his attention.

"Elodie." His voice is low, so low that I have to strain to hear it over the sound of my pulse roaring in my ears.

I wait. It's my turn to let him have the space to talk. I take another breath, forcing myself to do it slowly, but it's hard to be quiet when it feels like I've sprinted up ten flights of stairs. If I could even make it up that many. Twin bursts of adrenaline and panic flood my system, but underneath it all is this wild sense of need I've never felt in my life.

I blame that part—the needy part—for the way I'm behaving.

Nice Elodie would definitely not be in this situation.

Nice Elodie wouldn't have stopped at the sound of Ansel's voice in the first place.

In the famous words of Taylor Swift: *I'm sorry, the old Elodie can't come to the phone right now. Why? Cause she's dead!*

"Elodie," he repeats. Only this time, it sounds like he's asking a question.

He lifts his arm off the top of the couch, and the very fingers I'd studied are hovering beside my face, as though he isn't quite sure.

I don't know who moves first, but one moment his hand isn't touching me, and in the next, it is. The pads of his fingers, rough and calloused, trace along my hairline, down my temple, and over the shell of my ear. Goosebumps fly across my body, betraying me once again, and Ansel palms my cheek in response.

He shifts closer, bringing his body so close to mine that I swear I feel the heat coming off him.

I breathe even faster. Is he going to...?

I might pass out.

"Sweet Elodie." He chuckles, his eyes softening as he nears. He brings his other hand to my face, cradling me gently. It's cool from holding his drink. "Will you let me kiss you?"

Oh, my God.

Am I dreaming? This is happening? He's...he's asking to kiss me?

"I need your words, Elle," he says.

Elle. Why do I want to melt at that? "Y-yes," I stammer.

His thumb caresses my temple. "Are you sure? That sounded—"

"Yes." I say it more forcefully this time, bringing my hands to his forearms, needing to touch him, scooting even closer. Our bent knees rest against each other on the cushion. His skin is so warm.

"Yes?" His eyes crinkle behind his glasses, and I might swoon.

"Definitely."

With a smile, he closes the distance and brings his mouth to mine.

Everything stops.

Goes quiet.

His lips are soft and gentle against mine. As though he wants me to be absolutely certain.

And *hoo boy*, am I certain. A final tether falls away, and I increase the pressure, slanting my mouth and licking at the seam of his lips.

He opens with a groan, and the sound of it—needy, soft

—it's unholy, sexy and impossibly sensual. He pushes his hands into the curls at my nape, tugging me close.

It's not enough.

I rise, and he instinctively knows what I'm going to do, bless those rugby skills. In two seconds, we've shifted, him resting against the cushions and me straddling his hips. His hands slide beneath my dress to the underside of my thighs, gripping the soft flesh and digging in. I whimper, deepening the kiss.

It's everything. His tongue slides across mine before pulling back for a lighter touch, then deeper once again. He seems to know exactly what I want before I want it. His hips press up beneath me, and if I shifted just right, I could feel him. *All* of him.

Still kissing, I thread my fingers through his silky hair, then let myself touch his chest. It's rock hard, the muscles flexing beneath my touch. He keeps one hand on my thigh, but the other circles to the top of my leg, then out from beneath the dress to palm along my waist. I deepen our kiss once more, silently communicating that he can touch whatever he wants.

But he doesn't go farther. Eventually, he eases up, nipping at my lower lip before meeting my eyes once more. We're both breathing hard.

"Why'd you stop?" I ask.

"Who says I'm stopping?" he counters. His thumb moves back and forth on my upper waist, tantalizingly close to the side of my breast. Judging by the sly grin he wears, he knows precisely what he's doing.

I'm still on my knees, hovering above his hips, half scared and half desperate to let myself relax onto his lap. I lick my lips. They're already swollen.

He watches me, his irises as dark as I've ever seen them. "Is this okay?"

I lean in for another kiss in answer. As our mouths meet, he lets out another erotic groan. It's too much, and I surge against him. His arms band around me, holding me in place, my knees locked against his hips, my core pressed against his chest as he takes me deeper. I'm in control of the kiss, but he's in control of my body, and I swear it would only take one touch in the right place to send me soaring.

I don't know how much time passes while we kiss. I don't know how many ways his hands move across me, never going where I'm desperate for them to go. I don't know how I manage to keep my own hands to his chest and arms when half of me legitimately wants to sink to my knees and bite his thighs. He smells so good, soap and comfort and a hint of whiskey, and I don't want any of this to end. But eventually, my legs start to shake from holding me up, and Ansel notices.

"Gotta work on those muscles," he teases softly, his eyes following my every move as he guides me off him, seeming to know I need to sit back on the couch.

"You've got enough for the both of us," I toss back.

He chuckles. "Part of the job, that's all."

I let my gaze roam over him appreciatively. "And thank God for it."

He gives a surprised laugh in answer, his lips stretched wide and his eyes alight behind the glasses. I drink him in. The deep rumble and sharp bark of sound, the way he holds his hand against his stomach, the way his head angles up for the briefest of moments.

Have mercy.

He stands and reaches out. "Come on."

I take his hand, my stomach fluttering. I will literally follow him anywhere, but this admittedly seems...fast.

His eyes crinkle again. "Not to worry—I'm walking you to the guesthouse, Elodie."

"I knew that," I say as I join him.

He smirks. "You are a terrible liar."

Heat stings my cheeks as I mumble, "Am not."

He threads our hands together, the move as natural as if we'd done it a thousand times, and turns me so that we're face-to-face. "Look at me."

I tilt my head to meet his warm gaze.

"I like you, Elodie. But this..." He trails off.

I nod and look away, my stomach sinking.

Well, at least I had a great make-out sesh with him.

"Hey." His voice is soft.

I drag my attention upward, stumbling a bit when he pulls me so close our chests touch.

"I was going to say that this is hard for me. Letting someone in. Rosalie—"

"It's okay," I hurry to say, the words coming out in a rush. "It's fine. Really. We'll forget all about it."

He frowns. "No."

"No?" I blink, confused. "Then what—"

"Will you let me finish?" he asks, a hint of amusement playing across his features.

"Sorry." I bite my lower lip.

His eyes darken again as they flick to my lips, then he clears his throat and shakes his head. "My first priority is Rosalie."

I nod. "Of course."

"And you're...Shit, Elle, you're the nanny." He runs a hand over his face. "A nanny who has consumed every spare moment of my thoughts."

"Then I quit."

He barks another laugh. "Please don't. Just...be patient with me?"

I stare up at him. At this man who, mere moments ago, had his hands all over me. Who is hands down the best kisser I have ever known. Who has unknowingly set me loose into the world. And he wants patience?

"You can have anything you want, Ansel," I tell him truthfully. "You want me to be your side piece? I'll do it."

He balks. "No, *Jesus*, that's not—"

I put a finger on his lips, hardly recognizing myself, but knowing beyond a shadow of a doubt that this is right. "Hide me or don't. Tell Rosalie or don't. Come see me in the guesthouse at night or don't. I will give you whatever you want. Whatever you need."

He kisses my finger, and I pull it away with a smile. Then cups my face, kissing me, once, twice, three times. "I do not want you to be a hidden side piece, Elodie. That's not what I'm after. It's never been anything I've ever wanted, and I'm certainly not starting now. But for now, Rosalie—"

"Doesn't have to know," I finish for him. "I get it."

He looks pained. "I'm sorry."

I straighten. "There is absolutely nothing to be sorry for. She's your daughter. She will always be the priority. I promise you, I understand."

His features smooth, and he places the softest of kisses on my forehead. "Thank you."

Doesn't stop me from dreaming about biting those thighs, though.

Chapter 12
Ansel

I'M TACKLED TO the ground for what feels like the twentieth time, and it's getting old.

"Oh, come on! Get your head in the game!" Coach is easily two-thirds down the pitch, but there's no mistaking his words were meant for me. When I stand and look back, he's waving a binder in one hand and glaring at me. He is pissed.

As he should be, honestly. I leap up and run, doing my level best to re-focus. I've spent more of my time with my head in the Elodie-shaped clouds than with a ball in my hands, and it's less than ideal.

Gabe skips past the try line and presses the ball to the ground, then turns around and blows a kiss at me.

Fucker. In a real game, that would have been five points.

I give him the bird, and he laughs while pretending to flip his hair. "Gotta get up faster than that if you think you're going to catch me."

"From the lineout," Coach barks. "Move!"

We run back to the sidelines and get in position: two lines of opposing practice teams facing our hooker Cash, who's on my team and holds the ball on the sideline. On each line, the two props prepare to lift a third man into the air.

Coach bellows, and the play starts. Cash angles the ball toward our line as Jake and Chandler are lifted by the guys. They're both tall as fuck, but Chandler's got maybe two inches on Jake, and his reach is on full display as he leans to snatch the ball from Jake's fingertips.

"Here!" I yell so Chandler knows where I am, and he tosses it in my direction as he's lowered to the ground.

Ball firmly in my grip, I haul ass. I get a full five seconds with it—damn near an eternity, and I make every second count, eating up the yards as fast as I can—before Xavier appears in my periphery, his only goal to take possession of the ball. I have to throw it, sending it backward to my wing, Carter. He catches it with a wink, pivoting away from a tackle effort by one of the rookies and sprinting down the pitch.

I keep running, ready to take it if needed. Sure enough, Carter throws it behind him, and I catch it, flinging it back to Sam, who tosses to Xavier while Carter performs some kind of miracle maneuver, spinning away from yet another rookie to get right where Xavier needs him. He catches it, then runs the remaining yards to the try line.

And he almost makes it, too, before getting slammed at the waist by the other team's flanker. The ball rolls a couple of feet, and it's a race between me and the full-back to get it. He beats me to it, turning and drop-kicking the ball way the fuck down the pitch and away from the try line.

"Mother*fucker*," I curse, turning and running.

After the three-hour practice, I shower and throw on a tee with my favorite pair of black mesh shorts. They're loose and comfortable, which is welcome after wearing the tight shorts the sport requires.

Carter's heading out when I catch up to him. "Great job today," I tell him.

He grins, pure cockiness oozing out of him. "That's the name of the game, old man. Those football guys got nothing on my fast feet."

I laugh. "Should I get our PR team on that? You versus a receiver on the Falcons?"

He snaps his fingers and points at me. "Do it. I'll crush that dude."

"I love your enthusiasm."

"You mean my *youth*," he says.

I roll my eyes. "Get outta here with that shit." He's probably in his early twenties, along with a good half of the team. "Don't let Lennox hear you say that stuff."

Carter laughs. "Facts. He'd kick my ass just to remind me he could. But speaking of the Scot, how is he? Heard from him?"

"Good. Happy to be home for a bit but also wishes he were here training with us."

Carter opens the door of his Jeep and winks. "Tell him I'll kick his ass when he gets back."

I chuckle. "Will do."

The second I'm alone, my thoughts turn to Elodie. I

have no idea what I'm doing, but for once in my life, I'm going to try to relax about it.

Which, in all honesty, is laughable. There's no way I'll relax. I don't *do* relaxed.

Although I was happy to relax last night with Elodie. That woman's lips are sent from heaven. And the little noises she made? The gasps and whimpers? Fuck me. I spent an extra five minutes in the shower this morning just so I could be certain I wouldn't immediately get hard the instant I saw her.

It almost didn't work.

She'd breezed into the kitchen like she always does, fresh-faced and beautiful, a wild mess of wavy curls piled on top of her head, one shoulder bare from the oversized tee she wore. A shoulder I'd had beneath my lips for a glorious moment last night. Then I caught her vanilla and sugar scent. It was the same scent I'd breathed last night, the same scent she always wears. Probably something simple like a lotion, but *damn*, it gets me every time.

Thankfully, I'd been making breakfast for Rosalie, so I simply focused on sprinkling cheddar cheese into the scrambled eggs and pretended everything was fine.

Everything is *not* fine.

"Get a grip, Miles," I murmur, merging onto the interstate and beginning the thirty-minute drive home. Atlanta traffic is, hands down, the worst. The only bonus is that, even though every person on the road drives like a crazed lunatic, most of them pay attention, so the experience is *just* this side of chaos. A shot of adrenaline to start and end your day.

That's what I tell myself anyway. In reality, I'd love to pull the city planners to the side and shake them.

When I exit the interstate, I head to the grocery store to

pick up some things for dinner. I've never asked Elodie what she likes; for all I know, I've been stocking the house with things she's allergic to, or at the very least, despises. I pull my phone out before I think too much about it.

"Hello?" Elodie's voice sounds fucking delicious over the phone.

"What do you like to eat?"

She huffs a surprised laugh. "Um, food?"

I hear a splash in the background. She must be by the pool.

"If this is about dinner, Rosalie is demanding pizza. I haven't committed one way or another, but figured you'd want to know."

"Good to know," I say, steering a cart out of the line at the front and making a mental note to get the ingredients for pizza. "But I mean in general. I'm heading into the grocery store, and I don't know what you like."

"Oh, I don't care. Besides, I have food." Another splash. "That was a six," she calls out.

"A six?" Rosie's voice is distant, but clear as a bell in its indignation. "That was at *least* an eight."

"No, that was barely a medium-sized splash," Elodie shoots back. "Sorry," she says to me. "I'm judging her cannonballs."

I laugh. "I know that game well. Back to food. What do you like?"

"It doesn't matter, anything is good," she says.

Well, this won't do. What was it she said last night—that everyone always says she's so nice? This is a classic *nice girl* move. "Quit being nice, Elodie."

"I'm not being nice; I'm just saying that..."

I grin as she falters. "I heard you last night, Elle."

She's silent on the other end.

Shit. "Did I say something wrong?" I ask.

"No!" she blurts. "No, it's only," she exhales. "Sorry."

"Nothing to apologize for."

"Right. Sorry. I mean—*crap*—I'm not sorry. I mean that I say sorry too much, and I'm sorry for saying sorry?" Her voice rises as she speaks.

"Breathe, Elle." I chuckle. "It's okay. This is day one of not being nice, remember?"

She exhales. "Right. But I've actually been working on it longer than that."

"Fair enough."

"Excuse me?" A voice pipes up on my right.

I look down and see a little boy, probably about ten years old, staring at me. He's wearing an Atlanta Granite shirt, and his mother stands a few feet away, grinning. "Hi," I say.

"Are you Ansel Miles?" he asks.

I smile. "I am." To the phone, I say, "Hang on one sec."

"Whoa," he breathes.

"You like rugby?"

He nods furiously. "You're my favorite."

"Really?"

"He's got a poster of you in his room," his mother says.

"That's pretty cool," I say. "Do you play?"

"I want to, but there aren't any teams my age in town," he answers, his disappointment clear.

"Well, that's no good," I say. "We need to fix that."

He nods again, his eyes still wide as saucers.

Behind him, his mother asks, "Mind if we get a picture?"

The boy whirls to his mother and back to me, but all I do is nod and grin. "Of course."

We take the picture, and they disappear down the aisle.

I pick the phone back up and hear Elodie call out, "So close! That was a nine!"

"I'm back," I say.

"That was downright adorable," she gushes. "How often does that happen?"

I think about it. "Eh, depends. When season is in, it's fairly common. But I've never been recognized in the grocery store."

"Wait, are you famous?"

I laugh. "I'm a professional athlete, Elodie. So...sort of? Nothing like the pro footballers or basketball players in the city, but I'm known enough."

"Huh."

I can't decide if I'm insulted or charmed that she's utterly clueless. "Anyway, back to me being in the grocery store. I need you to tell me what you want to eat."

"You."

I skid to a stop in the canned food section. Holy shit. "Did you—"

"Oh my God," she mumbles. "I didn't mean that."

I grin. "I don't know," I tease. "I think you did. You find out I'm famous and suddenly—"

"I'm hanging up now."

"No!" I laugh, starting to walk again. "Please don't. We'll move past that." Even though I most definitely do not want to move past that.

"Pasta." The word comes out as if she still has her hand over her mouth. I can picture how red she must be right now. Fucking adorable.

"You like pasta?"

"And shrimp. All seafood."

"Look at you go—now we're getting somewhere. What else?"

"Isn't that enough?"

"Are you squirming?" I tease. "I bet you're squirming."

"Shut up."

I bark out a laugh, startling some of the other shoppers. I lower my voice. "Tell me what else you like, Elodie."

She starts to cough.

"You okay?"

She gives a strangled "Yep!" Then coughs more.

I keep going, moving through the store as quickly as I can. "Seriously, are you okay?"

"Fine, I'm fine." She takes a deep breath and lets it out. "Are we done here? Don't you need to focus on shopping? Price comparison and all that?"

I toss a box of Honey Nut Cheerios in the basket. "Uh, no? I just want to know what you like."

Something between a choke and a whimper comes through the phone.

"Seriously, are you okay? Do you need water?" I prompt.

"Nope, we're good!" she chirps. "But, ah, I gotta go. Hard work judging cannonballs, you know."

"But—"

"See you when you get home, bye!"

I pull the phone away from my ear and look at the screen. Huh. She hung up on me. Was it something I said? Shrugging, I finish the shopping and head home.

My phone buzzes as I'm pulling into the driveway. I grin as I throw the engine into Park, figuring it's Elodie. But the second I pull my phone from the outside kit pocket, my system floods with anger.

UNKNOWN

Ansel, you can't keep ignoring me.

Yeah? Watch me. I pull up my lawyer's number and dial.

"Ansel?"

"Hi, Jennifer."

"What's up? You only call me when things are going to shit."

My laugh is strained. "Yeah, well, you *are* my lawyer. No need to call you when things are rosy."

"Fair enough," she concedes. "But it's been years."

"Five years, in fact."

She hums. "You're lucky I still have your contact in my cell. Must mean I like you. Tell me what's going on."

I hesitate. The second I say the next words, this whole thing gets very, very real.

"Listen, if it's a criminal defense lawyer that you need, I'm not your woman," Jennifer says, "so if that's what this is about, spit it out and I'll get you a name."

I turn the air conditioner to Arctic. "It's Rosalie's mother. She's back."

Chapter 13
Elodie

I'M STILL OUTSIDE, sitting beneath the pool's lone umbrella in my bathing suit and preparing to judge what might literally be the fiftieth cannonball of the day when Ansel appears, the screen door clacking shut behind him.

"Daddy, watch!" Rosalie bounces up and down on the diving board, her little face scrunched in concentration.

"I'm watching," Ansel reassures her, hands on hips and eyes firmly locked on her tiny form.

I study him. He's wearing an Atlanta Granite T-shirt and black mesh shorts that, praise the Lord, rise well above his knee. I don't know when shorter hems came back into style for men, but I am absolutely one hundred percent here for it. I will never get over the man's legs. His thighs flex as he shifts position, bringing my attention to the rose tattoo that adorns the outside of his upper thigh. I haven't seen all of it—I might pass out from excitement if I did—but the glimpses I get are enough to make me salivate. The tattoo works with his leg, the deep red of the roses seeming to highlight the way his muscles move.

"Tell me what else you like, Elodie." Holy fireballs, that was hot. It's all I can think about.

Well, that and how I told him I wanted to eat him. My Lord. I can't believe I said that. Honestly, it might be those thighs. They muddle my brain.

A giant splash draws my attention back to Rosie, who pops through the surface of the water and grins like a maniac at her dad.

"Well?"

"A solid ten out of ten."

"Yay! Elodie *never* gives me a ten."

He flashes me a mischievous grin, his eyes dragging down my body as he walks to the edge of the pool and kneels down beside it. To Rosie, he says, "Get over here, you."

She swims to him and holds her arms out. He pulls her to him, standing as she wraps around him and absolutely soaks him. His grip on her is tight, and his eyes are shut as he turns from the pool, taking a few slow steps.

I blink and look away, feeling like an outsider as I swallow the emotion down.

Rosie giggles. "I'm getting you all wet, Daddy."

"Doesn't matter, Rosie Posie," he says. "Wanna know what we're having for dinner?"

Her face lights up. "Pizza?"

He smiles. "Pizza." Then he finally looks over at me, giving me his attention for the first time since arriving home. His brown eyes are warm as they settle on me. "Stay?"

The request is impossible to resist. "I'd like that." I stand and jerk my thumb to the guesthouse behind me. "I'm gonna shower and change first."

His gaze darkens as his jaw clenches, but his voice stays the same as he answers, "Sounds good."

"Daddy, can Cleocatra come over, too?"

He raises an eyebrow at her.

"Please?" she wheedles. "I've barely gotten any time with her today and she probably misses me."

He laughs, then looks over to me. "If Elodie says it's okay, then that's fine with me."

Without missing a beat, Rosalie whips her pleading eyes to me.

"Of course," I say with a grin. "See you in a bit."

I shower and throw on a casual cotton dress that falls to my knees, needing the loose fabric after being in the bathing suit a little too long. I let my hair stay down to air dry, throwing a silk hair tie around my wrist for later. Grabbing Cleo in one hand and my phone in the other, I make my way back to the house.

Rosie immediately takes the cat, hugging her tightly, and I laugh as Cleo's tail swishes in resigned irritation. "Be gentle," I remind her.

"I know," she responds, placing a kiss on Cleo's head.

It's not long before the three of us are huddled around the island, putting our individual pizzas together. Ansel's is light on cheese but heavy on the veggies; mine is a solid mix of cheese, pepperoni and mushroom; and Rosie's is very, *very* pineapple heavy. It's easy being around them, watching the way they are together. The love, the teasing, the gentle lessons he manages to weave into everything. As I watch him show her the buttons to press on the oven, I'm struck by the knowledge that it doesn't hurt to be here. To be with a man and his daughter, even though they represent the very thing I'll never get to have. And shouldn't it hurt? Shouldn't it, I don't know, make me sad that I'll never get to have the experience of being pregnant?

It doesn't. Holy crap. It *doesn't*. I want to jump up and

down and shout with the realization. It's a cool balm, a relief against the scorching desert of heartbreak that I've waded through for so long.

I'm not sure when it happened, this acceptance. But, my goodness, does it feel amazing. The contentment of it is something I never thought I'd experience. And who knows? Maybe it's not permanent, but for now? I'll take it.

When the pizza is ready, we eat at the small table in the kitchen, each of us sharing bites of our pizza with everyone else, and Rosalie declares both my and Ansel's creations to be disgusting.

Ansel just laughs. "Hey, at least I'm not the one eating pineapple like a monster."

Rosie harrumphs and crosses her arms. "You're just jealous mine is better."

After the kitchen is cleaned, Ansel looks at his daughter, still clad in her swimsuit. "Time for a bath."

"Can I keep my suit on?"

He shakes his head. "Not this time."

"It'll be like the pool, only inside the tub. Please?" she begs, blinking big eyes up at him. When he doesn't so much as give an inch, she deflates. "Fine. But can Elodie give me a bath?"

"Elodie's probably ready to relax," Ansel says.

"I don't mind," I say. And I don't. "Show me the way, Rosie girl."

Rosie bounces on her toes. "Yay!" She runs to me and grabs my hand, leading me to the stairs and then letting go as she climbs. "Come on! You haven't seen the bathtub yet. It's *huge!*"

I look back at Ansel for permission. He nods, a small smile on his face, and I take that as my cue. Turning to

Rosie, I crouch and raise my hands into the air, forming claws. "You'd better run!"

She squeals and runs up the steps. I follow at a leisurely pace, the sound of Ansel's warm laugh at my back.

I head in the direction of Rosalie's voice, going past her bedroom and to the end of the hallway, where Ansel's room is. I pause at the threshold before walking in, knowing I'm crossing into what feels like the final frontier of the house.

The room is undeniably masculine, but not overly so. The walls are painted a dove gray; the king-size bed framed in glossy black wood and covered with a white down comforter. Light blue pillows are on top, and there's an over-stuffed light blue armchair in a makeshift alcove beside the window. The comforting scent is unmistakable: Spice and soap, clean and warm. Ansel.

"Why are you just standing there?" Rosalie asks, poking her head out from the bathroom door. "Come on! Daddy always turns the faucet on, but then I get to put in as many bubbles as I want. And I use a *lot* of bubbles."

I grin. "Do you now?"

It is, in fact, an unbelievable amount of bubbles. And the bathtub is, just like she said, huge. She wasn't kidding. It could hold three of me and still be comfortable.

Is it wrong to be jealous of a five-year-old's bathtub? Because I am.

It's easily half an hour before she gets out. She pulls on her nightgown and I brush her hair to pull it into loose space buns at the top. Naturally, she talks me into reading her a bedtime story, so she runs down to get Ansel's permission first. Three reads of her favorite three books later, we're done.

"G'night, Elodie," she says sleepily, rolling onto her side and tucking her legs into her chest. She kisses her bear's head, then leans down as if to hear what he's saying. She nods, then looks back up at me. "Kata says g'night, too."

I smile. "Good night to you *and* to Kata."

She beams, and with a loud yawn, closes her eyes and wiggles under her comforter.

I retreat, clicking off the bedside lamp and turning on the small fan that rests on her chest of drawers. She's already instructed me to crack the door, so I do as requested, then make my way downstairs.

Ansel's voice floats up as I go. "Are you sure? Well, no, but I thought—*fuck*." A long pause. "You can't be serious." Another pause. "Well, I'd like to see her fucking try."

Who is he talking about?

"Okay. Yeah. Bye." He curses and throws the phone, sending it flying into the couch at such a high speed that the sound is audible.

I freeze halfway down the stairs, certain he'll see me. But he doesn't. He turns in circles, clearly at a loss.

"Fuck!" he whisper-shouts. "Fuck, fuck, fuck!" Then he sinks into a crouch, running his hands through his hair.

I don't know what to do. Do I go to him, ask him what's wrong?

Nope. I'm all out of bravery. Used it up last night. Not ashamed of it, either. Whatever is going on, it's not my business.

I back up the stairs quietly, then start over, being loud and hoping he hears me.

It works, because by the time my feet hit the hardwood of the downstairs floor, he's straightening beside the couch, pocketing his phone, and attempting to look like all is well.

"How'd bedtime go?" he asks, a strained smile on his face.

I give him one of my pageant smiles, the one I use when

I'm trying to make sure everyone is having a good time. Mom drilled it into me for years, and for the first time ever, the smile leaves a bad taste in my mouth. Forcing my voice to sound normal, I answer, "Great! Three reads of three books."

He huffs a laugh, and it's almost genuine. "Sounds like my Rosie."

We stand there, looking at each other, for what feels like an eternity. And I must be the dumbest woman on the planet, because I actually say, "Are you okay?"

Surprise coats his features. "Me?"

Something about that—the way he's surprised—hits a tender part of my heart. "Yeah," I whisper. "You." Does anyone ever ask him how he's doing?

He sticks his hands in his shorts pockets, rocking back on his heels. "I... No." With an audible swallow, he looks away from me.

It stings a little, but I swat the feeling away. He owes me nothing. "Do you want to talk about it?" Instantly, I want to scoop the words back in my mouth, but there's no going back now. I know one thing: I am not telling him what I heard.

"Talk about it?" he repeats. "Um." He coughs, then runs his hand through his hair again. "It's... No," he breathes. "Thank you. Truly. But..." He grimaces. "It's nothing. I mean, it's *not* nothing, but, ah, no."

I hold my hands up in surrender. "No need to feel weird about it. It's totally fine."

He exhales loudly, his shoulders visibly drooping. "Thanks."

Be patient with me. He said that last night. Well, this definitely counts as being patient.

"I'm going to go," I say, hitching my thumb up and over

my shoulder. "Curl up with my laptop and do some research."

His brow furrows. "Research?"

"Yeah. For my business."

He brightens, clearly relieved at the topic change. "Of course. How is that coming?"

"Good. Turns out all those years of internet dives and Pinterest boards are really coming in handy," I joke. But they really were. I have entire digital folders full of ideas based on country, city, vibe, activities… Honestly, I'm proud of myself.

"That's really wonderful," he says earnestly. Then he closes the distance between us in three long strides and reaches for my hand, threading his fingers into mine. He smiles down at me, the worry I'd seen moments ago nowhere to be found. "Let me walk you home?"

I nod. "That'd be nice, thank you."

The walk is two minutes, and he holds my hand the entire time. At the door, he stops, studying me in the near-dark. "Did you like the tub?"

I laugh, totally caught off guard by the question. "Yeah," I answer. "It's nice. Big."

His lips quirk up. "That it is." Then he lifts his hand and cradles my face, his thumb caressing my jaw. "Can I kiss you again?"

With a smile, I wrap my hands around his neck. "You don't have to ask, you know."

He winces. "I do. It's been drilled into me."

"Because you're a fancy pro athlete?" I tease.

His lips quirk up. "Because my mom wasn't about to have her boy be an asshole. Her words, not mine."

I laugh. "Sounds like an amazing woman."

His eyes are warm as they study me. "She is."

I hum and tap my lips with my finger, delighting in the way his gaze tracks the move. "How about this: you have permission to kiss me from here on out. Does that help?"

His voice is deep when he answers. "It does."

And with that, he leans down as I tip up on my toes. My body lights up as our lips touch, and I can't help the sigh that escapes.

His hand moves down, fingers caressing my neck and making me shiver in delight. "So responsive," he murmurs.

You have no idea, I think, tugging him closer. His mouth opens, and our tongues meet. God, he's such a good kisser, attentive, deepening and easing back, exploring and tasting, then pulling away to kiss my neck, nipping my bare shoulder and following it with a lick.

My hands clench at his waist, and he walks us to the door, pushing my back against the wood and lifting me a second later. My legs wrap around him instinctively, and his cock presses against my core. Ohmygod.

I whimper, and he growls. "Fuck, Elle, you..." He trails off, exhaling roughly before taking my mouth again. There's no more hesitation as he plunders it, claiming it as his with every stroke and nip.

I writhe against him, and he groans, his hands digging into my bottom so hard that I think they'll leave bruises.

God, I hope they do.

My core pulses with need, and I swirl my hips. I need...I *need*.

"Elle," he murmurs again, kissing down my neck and sucking softly at the delicate skin. "You taste so good." He eases the pressure of his hands on me, and I slow my rocking. I don't want to stop, but he's not ready. That much is clear.

He lowers me to the ground, then cages me with his arms, his eyes blown with lust.

Well, at least it's not just me.

"Let me take you on a date," he says.

I stare. "A...date?"

"On Friday. I'll get Sharon to watch Rosie overnight. She's been asking to see her anyway, so this would be perfect." He clears his throat. "I mean. Not—not that I'm expecting anything by saying she'll watch her overnight. I just—"

I press a finger to his lips. "Yes."

He raises his eyebrows. "Yes?"

Removing it, I give him a kiss. "Yes."

He smiles. "Good." Then he starts to back away. "See you in the morning?"

I laugh. "Sure hope so."

His smile grows. "Great. Excellent. I'll—see you tomorrow."

And then this ridiculously hot man, who is, in all likelihood, a total beast on the rugby pitch, turns and trips over his own two feet.

I stifle a giggle as he stabilizes, watching as he walks away.

Chapter 14
Elodie

I WAKE UP with a huge smile on my face. It's Friday, and I get to go on a date. With Ansel.

The past week has been a dream, honestly: stolen kisses with Ansel before he leaves for practice, then more kisses when he shows up at my door after putting Rosie to bed. He's taking it slow, and while part of me is screaming to get my hands on...*all* of him...I appreciate the slow-burn situation.

Kind of.

But to be super clear, I'd like to do more than kissing. Except, short of actually telling him to strip me naked and have his way with me, I can't figure out how to make him understand that he can literally do whatever he wants. Well, maybe not *whatever* he wants, but like, a *lot of* whatever he wants. Pretty please with whipped cream and a cherry on top.

Also? It's hard not being Nice Girl Elodie. Kari didn't just laugh at me when I told her I was working on being not so nice, she flat-out guffawed. Snort-laughed and nearly choked on her iced coffee kind of laugh.

Rude.

Then she had the audacity to tell me to say a cuss word.

And...I couldn't.

Which made her laugh more.

"You're the living embodiment of a Disney princess, Elodie," she'd said. "Just embrace it."

I stuck my tongue out at her and told her to be nice.

Which made her laugh so hard she started crying.

I wash my face and brush my teeth, then throw on some lounge clothes to head across the backyard to the house. Inside, it smells like bacon and eggs and pancakes, and sure enough, Rosalie is chowing down at the counter.

"Good morning, Elle Belle," she says, syrup dripping down her chin. The nickname is new, and cute, and she was beyond excited when she came up with it.

Did she reference a certain Disney princess when it occurred to her? Of course. Am I telling Kari about this? Absolutely not.

Ansel has his back to me, and I take a moment to appreciate the absolute specimen that he is. Tight, round butt inside short shorts, a trim waist expanding up to broad shoulders, and deliciously defined muscles that flex beneath the form-fitting sleeveless practice shirt he wears. Goodness, he's pretty.

Then he turns, and he's wearing his glasses, and he winks and smiles, and I swear my knees get weak. I grip the island for support.

"Good morning, Elle Belle," he repeats, and his eyes freaking *twinkle* with delight because he knows exactly what he's done to me.

I am convinced he does it to torture me.

"Good morning," I answer with a *you're being incred-*

ibly mean smile, then tear my gaze away from Ansel to beam at Rosie. "Did you have a good night?"

She nods. "Daddy got me some puzzles. Can we put one together today?"

"Of course!"

"Grab two plates, will you?" he asks.

I do as he requests, nearing his spot behind Rosalie. He pulls me to him, nuzzling my neck and palming my side as I barely suppress a squeal, biting my lip and smiling as I push him away. "*Stop,*" I mouth.

He waggles his eyebrows and tries to grab me again, but I sidestep him. He smacks my bottom in retaliation, and my cheeks burn as I gape at him. Rosalie could have heard that.

"*Quit it!*" I mouth again.

"*Never,*" he mouths back. Aloud, he says, "What's taking so long with those plates, Elodie?"

I glare at him. "Sorry. Got *distracted.*"

Chuckling, he pulls the skillet off the stove and scoops scrambled eggs onto the plates, a much larger portion for him than for me. "I made extra bacon if you want it. I know you're not big on pancakes. Want some avocado toast?"

I stare at him. "I…"

"I'm making some for myself," he clarifies.

I'm about to say no, but the reality is that yes, I *would* like some avocado toast, and in the spirit of chipping away at Nice Girl Elodie, I smile. "Yes, please."

He grins, thoroughly pleased. "Grab the Everything Bagel seasoning from the cupboard," he says. "That's my go-to when I don't have time to chef it up."

"This isn't 'cheffing it up'?" I ask, putting the seasoning beside him as he plucks two avocados from the bowl on the island.

"Nah," he says. "If I really wanted to go all out, I'd put

some pickled onions on here, a bit of olive oil, some arugula, then some yellow and red tomatoes." He pauses. "On some good bread, maybe with some eggs over easy on the side so you can run the bread through the yolk."

My stomach growls.

He laughs and nods. "Exactly."

"You're a really good cook," I tell him.

"Not really." He waves off the compliment. "I just do what the trainer tells me to and then add things around the edges to be sure a certain five-year-old will eat it."

He finishes slicing the avocado and places it on the toast, then sprinkles the seasoning. I go to take a bite, but he stops me, grabbing a fresh lemon slice from the bowl he keeps in the fridge and squeezing it on top. "There. *Now* you can eat it."

I laugh. "I would have just slathered the avocado on the toast and eaten it like that."

He blanches. "But why, when another minute can make it so much better?"

I take a bite. Dang it, it's *good*. And he barely did anything to it. "You know what? You're right. Never again."

Satisfied, he turns to his meal. He makes quick work of it, and I have to practically shove him out the door to keep him from doing the dishes. The man would do everything himself if it were up to him.

"Beat it, mister." I accept a quick kiss in the foyer and barely manage to keep myself from smacking his rear as he opens the door. "I'll handle this."

"Bye, Daddy!" Rosie calls.

Later, after Rosie and I have gotten the outside of her puzzle put together and she's watching *Brave* for the millionth time, Kari FaceTimes me. Because I know she's prone to all kinds of inappropriate language, I leave the room.

"Hey, girlie!"

"Hey yourself," I say, then squint. "Are you up in the lounge at the stadium?"

She smiles and flips the camera, zooming to the pitch. "I am. Figured you might want to see your man in action."

"He is not my man," I protest.

"Sure," she deadpans. "Now shut up and watch."

I find Ansel immediately. He's not the biggest man out there—that honor seems reserved for the forwards—but he carries himself in a way that communicates he's one of the guys to listen to. I've learned that his position, the fly-half, is one of the more crucial ones on the team. They're all crucial, I guess, but the fly-half is one of the more strategic. I'm still figuring it all out.

The men aren't actively playing a game right now. Instead, they're all in a handful of lines with their backs turned to me, and as I watch, they all raise their arms and bend at the waist, swan-diving to the ground.

"Oh my," I breathe.

Kari laughs. "Thought you'd like that."

"I demand you call me every day at this exact time," I joke, my eyes glued to the screen as the men go through a series of lunges that would have me begging for mercy. As it is, I'm begging for mercy, all right, but it's more in the "bless these men and their physiques" category.

Kari zooms in on Ansel. "This is for you, not me," she says. "I mean, he's good-looking and all, but he's not my type."

I snort. "And what's your type?"

"Not rugby players," she fires back. "Especially ones who annoy the shit out of me even when they're out of the country and refuse to listen to reason when I explain that they need to keep their dick in their pants or bad things happen."

"That sounds awfully specific," I tease. "And keep the phone steady. I'm trying to ogle Ansel."

He's breathing hard, sweat pouring down his face as he jogs back to the sidelines and grabs a water bottle. He tilts it up and squeezes, and never have I thought the act of drinking water was sexy, but...here we are. Then he squirts the water on top of his head and uses his other hand to rub it in, shaking his head and wiping his face when he's through.

Suddenly, it's very hot in here.

"You still there, or did you pass out from the view?" Kari asks.

"Hanging on by a thread," I croak.

She flips the screen back to her face and situates herself on the couch.

"Put it back," I pout.

She laughs. "I actually had a real reason to call."

"That wasn't reason enough?"

"One of the players is getting married. He mentioned that his fiancée Allyson wanted to go on some kind of adventure honeymoon, but that he had no idea where to start. Said that she was so busy planning the wedding that he felt he needed to help, but the poor man is clearly out of his depth."

"Kari," I start, "you didn't."

She grins mischievously. "So of course I called Allyson because I'm good like that, and I mentioned that my best friend had a honeymoon planning business and would be happy to talk with her and Jake about options."

"But I'm not even up and running yet!"

"So what? Nothing like the present to dive in. She's out

of town for the next little bit, but when she's back, we're all meeting up for coffee."

"We're—*what?* No, I'm not—"

She points at the camera. "Yes, you are. Don't pretend you're not already thinking about ideas."

I purse my lips, caught. "I am."

"Ha!" She pumps a fist in victory. "See? You can do this. You just need a push."

"Feels more like a shove," I say wryly. "But...thank you." Her faith in me sends tingles of happiness through my body, like little bits of sunshine streaking through me. "You're the best."

She winks. "I know. Now, what are you wearing for your date tonight?"

Chapter 15
Ansel

WHY AM I so nervous?

I take a deep breath and let it out, shaking my hands and checking I have everything: keys, wallet, cash for valet. Teeth are brushed. Freshly showered. House cleaned and living room devoid of any and all evidence that a five-year-old is in there every night, even though I'm taking that five-year-old's nanny on a date. Dropped said five-year-old off at Sharon's next door with promises to pick her up late tomorrow morning for our weekly brunch of blueberry and banana pancakes.

I lock up and walk to the guesthouse in the backyard, taking a moment to situate the He-Man and unicorn floats in a way that ensures they won't roll across the yard in the storm we're forecasted to get tonight. At the door, I take another breath and knock.

Relax, Miles. It's Elodie.

Yeah, exactly: It's Elodie.

She opens the door. "Hi." She smiles shyly up at me.

I'm struck dumb. She's...my God, she's so fucking flaw-less it's not even funny. How did I get this lucky? She's wearing a short black dress that shows off every single curve she has. The top is cut in a square, showing off all those freckles of hers and merely hinting at what's beneath. Gold, gladiator-style sandals wrap up her legs to stop just below her calves, and her hair falls in soft curls all the way down her back. Her hazel eyes are greener tonight, highlighted by a hint of makeup. Her lips are glossy and pink, and I'm overcome by a desire to kiss her senseless.

"Hi." My mouth is suddenly very dry. "You look incredible." I lean forward to brush a kiss against her cheek, guessing that she doesn't want that pretty lipstick ruined just yet, and take in her warm vanilla-sugar scent. "And you smell delicious."

She makes a show of looking me over. "You're not so bad yourself," she says with a wink. "Let me grab my purse."

I'm taking her to my favorite restaurant in Atlanta, a low-key French countryside place with impeccable service and the best Croque Monsieur sandwich I have ever had in my life.

When we get there, I put my hand on the small of her back, guiding her through the tables to a corner booth I specifically requested. The design is such that you can't help but sit next to each other, which is exactly how I want it.

"I've never been here," Elodie says as we scoot in, her eyes scanning the restaurant. The tables are small, as if designed for seating in a European restaurant and not an American one, and the waitstaff is impeccably dressed to exact specification. Sure, they may sport plenty of tattoos and piercings, but their shirts are crisp and white, their black ties are lined up perfectly with their black pants, and even their shoes are clean and shined.

"I come here as often as I can," I admit, "though I haven't brought Rosie along just yet."

The corners of Elodie's eyes crinkle as she studies me. "You bring all your dates here, Ansel?"

"No!" I sputter. "I don't date. I mean, I don't bring dates. When I date. Which is rare." I sigh and grin at her. "You make me nervous, you know that?"

Her smile widens, but before she can say anything, a server appears to take our drink orders.

Once we've ordered—a vodka and water with a splash of cranberry for me, and a crisp Pinot Grigio for her—I settle into the booth and let my eyes roam her appreciatively while she reviews the menu.

She pulls her lower lip into her top teeth when she's focused, the tiniest of furrows forming between her brows. Finally, she seems to come to a decision and sets the menu down. "Do you already know what you're getting?"

I'd like you, spread out before me. The fantasy of her laid out on one of these wooden tables comes to me, unbidden, and I struggle to blink it away. "Mussels with fries to start, then the Croque Monsieur with a salad. It's far too much food, but I want the tastes of each. Do you like escargot?"

She makes a face. "Snails?"

I chuckle. "Let me try again: do you like butter and garlic?"

Her face smooths. "Do you see this body? It's safe to say I'm a fan."

"Oh, I see it alright." I waggle my eyebrows suggestively and laugh at the pretty blush that spreads across her cheeks. But...yeah. I see the way the dress is giving me just enough of her breasts that I want to bury my head in them. I have seen it clad in a swimsuit and wanted to sink to my knees in gratitude for its curves. But I bite all that back and nod decisively. "Then you'll like the escargot. Trust me."

The night is absolutely perfect. She loves the snails, no surprise, and conversation flows from topic to topic. The food is delicious, but my date is far more delicious, and I can't keep my eyes off her. After paying the bill, we step outside and find it's storming, so she steps back into the restaurant while the valet brings the car.

The rain pelts us as we rush to get in the car, and visibility is shit as I drive. It's not quite dark yet, a quirk of it being summer *and* that Atlanta is right on the edge of where the Eastern time zone begins, but it's darker thanks to the storm.

Elodie looks over at me as I pull onto the interstate, the wipers working overtime to give me a prayer of seeing where the hell I'm going. "I had a wonderful time. Thank you for dinner."

I glance her way. "You're welcome. It's not over yet."

She gives me a soft smile. "Good," she says quietly.

The drive is mostly silent, but it's a comfortable silence. No pressure to make small talk, which is good, because I need all my focus to be on driving. When I finally pull into the driveway, the sky opens up, dropping what seems like actual buckets of water onto the car.

Elodie laughs as I squint through the windshield. "Guess we're making a run for it."

I twist and reach for the warm-up jacket I keep in the back seat, but it's not there. Grimacing, I say, "I can run and get an umbrella for you—just stay here."

She reaches for my hand. "No need. I won't melt." Then she grins. "On three?"

I chuckle. "On three."

Her eyes bright, she grips the door handle. "One... two..."

"Three!"

It's a scramble out of the Land Rover, and I curse my lack of garage space as we run. It's not even that far, but the rain is coming down so hard that we're both soaked by the time I get the door open and we tumble inside. Shutting the door behind us, I laugh as I turn to her.

"You're *drenched*," she says, giggling. Rivulets of water run down her face and neck. Then a shiver wracks her body.

"You too," I note. Another tremor takes over her, and an idea hits me. I grab her purse and set it on the small table in the entryway, then take her hand to pull her farther into the house.

"I should go change," she says.

A massive clap of thunder goes off above us in answer, and the sound of rain intensifies.

I grin. "I have a better idea."

She squints, and as with everything she does, it's fucking adorable. "Like what?"

"Like let me draw you a bath."

Surprise washes over her face. "A bath?"

I nod, pulling her close to warm her when she shivers. "Come upstairs. I'll behave, I promise."

She lifts her chin, a bit of defiance glinting in those beautiful hazel eyes of hers. "What if I don't want you to behave?"

It's as though the world stops. Or maybe I black out for a second, because no way did she just say what I think she said.

Stepping close, I pull her to me and lean down. Her lips are so soft, and they open without hesitation. The softest of whimpers comes out of her as I take the kiss slow, keeping a hand cupped around her face, thumb stroking her temple.

Elodie increases the intensity, her hands gripping my waist as though she wants more. When I break the kiss, her eyes are glazed and blown with want.

"C'mon." I turn and lead her upstairs, her hand in mine. Her skin is soft and clammy with cold. In my bedroom, I lead her to the reading chair. "Sit," I say, grabbing the blanket from the chair and wrapping it around her shoulders.

"But I'm wet," she protests.

My dick immediately perks up at that. "Please." I guide her down, then press a kiss to her forehead. "Give me a few minutes. Okay?"

She looks up at me and nods, and my heart fucking *squeezes.*

In the bathroom, I close the door and start the water, then find the bubble bath I'd set aside on the hope that I might one day get her in here—something a bit more adult than Rosie's usual fare—and dump a ton into the water. The scent of lavender fills the air as I grab the candles I'd stashed beneath the sink and set them around the room, turning them on as I go. They're not real; I'm way too much of a worrier to have real ones in the house with a five-year-old. I find a silk hair tie of Rosie's and put it on the edge of the tub for Elodie, then look around. Satisfied with my setup, I turn the lights off as the water still runs, and step back into my bedroom.

"Ready," I say. Elodie's eyes snap to me. "Go on in."

She rises and comes toward me, and try as she might, there's no hiding the way she trembles as she leaves the blanket behind. "But—"

I put a finger on her lips. "Once you're in the tub, I'll

check on you. Promise." Then I step back and gesture for her to walk in.

A gasp escapes her as soon as she steps inside. "Ansel." Her eyes glitter, soft and surprised in the candle-lit room.

"You like it?"

She laughs softly. "This might be the most romantic thing anyone's ever done for me."

"Well, that's bullshit," I retort, making her laugh louder as I pull her to me for one last kiss. "You deserve far better romantic moves than this."

"Thank you," she whispers.

"Get in," I tell her, backing out and shutting the door behind me.

A few minutes later, the water shuts off, and I swear I hear a soft moan.

Fuck. She's in there, naked, and I'm out here like an absolute idiot. After taking my shoes off and changing into dry clothes, I find the robe I never use and knock on the door.

"Come in," she calls.

I step into the lavender-scented bathroom and am nearly taken to my knees by the sight before me. Elodie lounges in the tub, covered by the bubbles. Her hair is piled on top of her head, exposing her neck and shoulders, and as she smiles up at me, all I can think is how right it feels to have her here. This whole night has felt like that: *right.* As though Elodie is what I have been missing. And I don't know if it's as easy as all that, because I still have to be so careful, but now? Now, there is a naked woman in my bathtub, and I'm stuck in place, staring at her.

"Hi," she says softly, a smile playing on her lips.

"Hi." Any game I thought I might have had—any possible bit of smooth-operator moves in my arsenal—flies totally out of my head. "You're beautiful," is all that comes out of my mouth.

She giggles and blushes, her eyes darting away from mine.

I hold the robe up. "I brought you this. I can put your stuff in the dryer, unless that's weird?"

Another sweet giggle as she meets my gaze. "That's not weird. But no."

"No?"

"Get in with me."

The world stills and my head empties. "Get—get in with you?" I repeat dumbly.

She nods. "I'll close my eyes." Then quirks a grin. "Promise."

I'm about to tell her no, but a smarter part of me whacks the stupid part in the head with a muttered *I swear to God if you don't get in that tub, you asshole.* So I swallow and nod. "Um. Okay."

A broad smile erupts on her face. "Okay. I'm closing my eyes."

I step to the other side of the enormous bathroom, more grateful than ever that I bought this house, and lay the robe on the counter. I pull my shirt off and shuck my bottoms, then catch a glimpse of myself in the mirror. I'm hunched over like some kind of bridge-dwelling troll, with a look of utter shock on my face, and I have to laugh at myself. *Get it together, Miles.* I straighten, take a deep breath, and step out of my underwear. After folding everything and setting it neatly into a pile on the sink, I risk a glance at Elodie. Seriously, how lucky am I?

"Keep those pretty eyes of yours closed," I admonish as I step in, lowering myself in on the other side from her. The tub is truly enormous, but not so big that our legs don't touch as I get situated.

She giggles again, pulling her knees above the water and opening her eyes. They roam over me appreciatively, even though all she can see is my upper chest. "Hi," she says again.

I let out a breath, my gaze locked on the bubbles sliding down her bare knees.

"Warm?"

Burning up. I look at her. "Yes. You?"

She bites her lip, sucking it into her mouth a little and letting it slide out from her teeth. I can't hold the groan back, and a soft sound of appreciation leaves her. "This is nice," she says. "But it could be nicer."

"Oh, yeah?" I sound hoarse. And that internal voice from earlier, the one that slapped the back of my head, is back. *You. Are. An. Idiot. Get the fuck over there.*

"Mm-hmm," she says, her gaze searing into mine.

Got it. "I have an idea."

Her brows rise hopefully. "You do?"

"I do."

"And what's that?"

"A way for both of us to stretch out."

A corner of her mouth quirks up. "How might that work?"

"I think I should get behind you, and you can lean against me." And I'll just pray that this semi I'm sporting underwater doesn't get any bigger.

"That sounds perfect," she says, scooting forward a bit.

Here goes nothing. Is it weird that it sounds like stadium cheers are going off in my head?

It's weird.

Whatever.

I pull my legs up and shift in the tub, both of us snick-ering a bit as we get into position. But after a moment, we've got it, and I'm leaning against the back of the tub with her between my legs. The warmth of the water is finally seeping into my muscles, forcing me to relax. Time slows. I study her back, the patterns of freckles and the way the bubbles are scattered across her wet skin. I try to keep thoughts of where else I might find those freckles out of my head. I fail.

She turns to look back at me, her arms covering the tops of her breasts, then grins. "Your glasses are fogged." She reaches to take them off, her touch soft and sure, then stretches to set them safely out of the way before settling safely back against me. "Are you sure this is okay?"

"I can confidently say that I've never been more sure of anything in my life," I state, finally getting my shit together. Whatever existential moment I've been having is gone, and I pull her to me with no hesitation. She settles her back against my chest, her bottom half not quite pressed against me. Which is good. Great, even. Because I am not...soft.

"Lay your head back," I whisper. She does, her weight dropping onto me as she relaxes.

I pull a hand up and trace her skin, moving from her neck to her shoulder, then tracing her arm down into the water. Back and forth I go, keeping my moves damn near saintly, until she sighs and raises her body a bit. It's enough to tell me she wants more, so I give it to her. My fingers trace along the tops of her breasts, right at the waterline, until I move just a little below.

She inhales.

"Good?" I murmur into her ear.

"Yes," she answers quietly.

I go farther, tracing the outside of her breasts, circling tighter and tighter. She raises an arm and wraps it around my neck, and the move lifts her even more out of the water. I keep circling her breasts, then going out, down her arm, and then back up, until her back arches, her nipples tight and hard, as my fingers finally move over them.

Her breath hitches. "So good," she says. Then, "More."

I'm so hard, it's ridiculous. But she doesn't seem to care, and in fact, I'm pretty sure she likes it. I press my palm flat against her chest, running down her generous belly until I move to the side and squeeze her leg.

She whimpers. "No, Ansel."

I chuckle. "Tell me what you want, Elodie."

She whines. "You know I don't talk like that!"

I bring my hand up to her stomach, then go to the other leg and squeeze. "Say the words, gorgeous. Just say the words and I'll give it to you." Fuck, *please* say the words.

She whimpers again. "Ansel..."

I trail my fingers up one thigh, then down and over her stomach to the other thigh. "Tell me, Elodie." My voice is rough, dark.

"I want your fingers between my legs," she says, breathless.

"Good girl. And when they get there? Then what?" I prompt.

"I—" she exhales roughly. "I want you to touch me. Make me...make me *feel*."

"That's a good start," I croon, and then I give her what we both want.

Chapter 16
Elodie

O H MY GOD.
Oh my God.
Oh. My. *God.*

Ansel's thick fingers push between my legs, and I nearly combust right then. Never have I ever had a man touch me like this. Not with such expertise. Such...certainty. My grip tightens around his neck as my other hand scrambles for purchase on his thigh.

His *thighs.* I'm bracketed between them, hard and muscular and absolutely everything I want to have wrapped around me always. The bubbles are disappearing, leaving me with a delicious view of those thick legs as they move in the water, spreading to ensure my own comfort as his fingers—

Holy shit, his fingers. I moan and arch up, needing the friction.

"Tell me, Elodie," he demands, his rough voice sending shivers down my spine.

"Harder," I pant. "Faster."

"Good," he praises, giving me exactly what I've asked for. "There's my girl. Telling me what she wants."

A delicious sweetness starts to build between my legs as his fingers press and swirl around my clit. I'm lost to everything. Lost to the thunderstorm raging outside. Lost to the worries, the what-ifs that plague me about this thing happening between me and Ansel. Lost to worrying about the million things I need to do for my new business. None of it matters except this man's talented fingers between my legs. His hand on my breast. His voice crooning into my ear and urging me to come.

"Ansel," I gasp, my hips bucking in the water. "Oh—"

"There you go," he whispers, not stopping, pressing exactly where I need him to press. "Fucking gorgeous."

Sounds come out of me that I've never made before, hums and incomprehensible words and pants. My grip gets tighter around his neck, his thigh. Pressure builds, the orgasm just out of reach. "Ansel," I moan, drawing out the last syllable.

"God, yes," he grunts. "You're so close. You want to come for me. Be loud, Elodie. Give me your voice. Come on. Come for me, Elodie. Come. Please."

It's the *please* that tips me over the edge. I shatter, my entire body going rigid as I arch up, his fingers still stroking me as I shout and gasp his name. My walls pulse with the intensity, my hips rocking in time to the pleasure coursing through me, literal waves in the water matching the waves of bliss crashing inside me.

"Absolutely beautiful," he says softly. "I want to watch you do that again and again."

My only response—the only thing I can get out—is a low hum. Ansel's fingers slow and ease up, his own body seeming to follow mine as I come down from the orgasm.

Finally, I slump against him, the feel of him rock hard against my back as I release my grip on his neck.

He brings his hand up my belly and chest until he's lightly tipping my chin up and back toward him. He leans down, claiming my mouth in a deep, searching kiss, and eventually I turn and rise, settling myself once again over his thighs. Only this time, there are no clothes between us. No one to find us.

Like then, his arms tighten around me, but this time, I let myself get as close as possible. His dick juts between us, and as we kiss—have mercy, this man can *kiss*—I run my palm down his torso, feeling the hard planes of muscles and the patch of dark hair. When my fingers travel farther, he moves quickly, capturing my hand and pressing it to his chest.

"No need," he mutters against my lips. "This is perfect."

"Your body says differently," I smile, leaning back to admire him.

"I know, but I promise," he answers.

I want to argue, but I shiver, the heat that built inside me having dissipated with the orgasm.

His thick brows knit together. "The water's getting cold. Let's get out."

"No," I whine, not wanting to break the spell. But as I speak, I tremble again.

His jaw clenches. "We're getting out."

I almost giggle. "That's quite a stern face you're giving me right now." I pause. "Wait. How are we—"

"Getting out of the tub?" he asks, a wicked grin forming. "I was wondering when you'd think about that."

I pinch his arm.

"Ow!" He laughs, then pulls me close again. "Did I, or did I not, just make you come?"

Heat singes my cheeks as I look down.

"God, you're adorable when you blush," he murmurs, guiding his finger under my chin to force my eyes back to his. They're a warm brown, kind and gentle with the tiniest glint of teasing in them. "I want to see all of you, Elodie. As far as I'm concerned, your body is flawless. It's everything I want. But I only want to see what you're comfortable showing me."

"It's not me I'm worried about," I say, and I mean it. "It's you." My cheeks flame hotter.

His sweet grin morphs into a full-on smirk. "Explain."

I cover my face.

A soft chuckle escapes him as he works carefully to peel my hands away. "Hurry, before the water gets ice cold." Then he winks. "You afraid to see what's between my legs?"

I pinch him again, going for the fleshy part of his chest right on the inside of his armpit.

"Ow!" He rubs the spot and fakes a scowl. "Okay, okay, I'm getting out. Or do you want to get out first?"

Admittedly, I haven't thought this through. If I get out first, then my lady parts are going to be right in front of his face. But if *he* gets out first, then it's *his* parts that are in *my* face.

And that's the problem, because I think...I think I'd like that. A lot.

Ansel doesn't need to know that I've only had one partner, *and* that it was the man I thought I was going to marry, *and* that I rarely orgasmed with him. He also doesn't need to know that my ex was never a fan of giving or receiving oral. And Ansel most *definitely* doesn't need to know that, right now, all I want to do is throw him on the bed and see how long it takes me to run my lips over every part of his body.

His spectacular, muscular, big-thighed body.

Seriously. God bless rugby.

"Earth to Elodie," Ansel teases. "Who's putting their ass in front of whose face?"

My jaw unhinges. "Oh my God, did you seriously just say that?"

He laughs, the sound burrowing deep into my heart. "I did. Now answer me, love."

"You," I blurt. "No! Wait. Me."

His lips quirk. "Are you sure? I'll cover my eyes if you want me to."

"You can look."

It's as though he's a kid who's just been told he has a pile of presents to open. "Yeah?"

I nod. "You did just make me come, after all," I say with a grin.

"That I did." He wiggles his fingers. "Up you go."

I stand before I can think more about it, turning away from him as shyness punches into me. I hustle out onto the plush mat, then step to grab the towel he laid out and wrap it around me. I don't bother trying to dry myself; my only goal is to cover up.

It's only then that I notice how quiet Ansel's gone.

I turn, not knowing what to expect, and a soft gasp leaves my mouth.

Gone is the sweet man I know. The man who puts everyone before himself. The man who insists on *please* and *thank you*. In its place is a predator. A man with dark, hooded eyes who stares at me as if he's starving, and I am his meal.

Instantly, my core tightens and warms. Because I really, *really* like this look.

Without a word, he stands. Water and bubbles sluice down his body, and I shamelessly take my fill. God, he is *beautiful*. Taut, honed muscles grace nearly every inch of him, his broad shoulders angling down to hips that divot down to an impressive dick that makes my mouth water. His thigh muscles flex and pulse as he steps out of the tub, and I finally see the entirety of the rose tattoo, its deep red hues even darker in the dim light.

When I finally drag my eyes back up to his, Ansel raises an eyebrow. "Like what you see?"

I lick my lips and nod, my mouth dry.

He clocks the move and groans, stalking to me as I stand motionless, not knowing what to do.

When he reaches me, he yanks my towel off. "Don't ever hide yourself around me, Elodie," he growls. Then he hauls me into his arms, his damp body pressed against mine, pulling me to him with such force I'm thrown off balance. "Jump," he commands, then crushes his mouth to mine.

I do as he says, his arms cradling my hips when my legs encircle his waist. He's wet, but I don't care. His dick bounces against the bottom of my ass as I hook my ankles together, and I use the angle to take control of the kiss. It's a tangle of lips and teeth and tongues, hunger and need overtaking us.

He walks us to the bedroom, moving to the bed and breaking the kiss with a gasp. "I need to taste you," he says, his voice dark and husky.

With that, he sits me on the mattress, and I scoot up and over, moving to the center as he watches. The only light is from the candles in the bathroom. As I stare at his darkened form, lightning streaks across the sky outside, giving me brief glimpses of his body. And have mercy, the way this man is looking at me.

"Take whatever you want, Ansel," I whisper.

"Oh, sweetheart," he says, his voice dark and low,

kneeling on the floor and grabbing my ankles, "I plan on it." Then he yanks me down the bed until my butt is at the edge of the mattress. "Watch me," he directs. His tone brooks no dissent, but his touch is gentle. Reverent. The dichotomy is enough to set me on edge, excitement mixing with the unknown.

I rise to my elbows and look down, nearly combusting at what I see in the dimness. His hair, normally brushed back and away from his face, falls onto his forehead in thick, unruly locks. He stares at me through predatory, hooded eyes, and as I watch, he spreads my legs and takes in my center.

"Jesus fucking Christ," he murmurs reverently.

My breathing speeds up as I grip the comforter. "Ansel," I whisper.

His gaze, dark and feral, meets mine and holds as he leans forward, pressing his nose against my mound and inhaling.

"Fuck," I exhale, the sight so unbelievably hot and sexy that I feel the wetness of my arousal.

His eyes flash with satisfaction. I never cuss, but with this version of Ansel? He's going to get all my words. "Is this what it takes, angel?" he asks, still so close, his breath hot against my center. "Because I have not even begun to worship you."

I suck in air, wordless in the face of this man. I'm frozen, unable to even move as I drink him in.

He gives a feral grin as his thumbs spread me wide. "Get ready, Elodie. Eyes on me."

I swallow.

He descends.

I moan at the first touch of his tongue. Hot and wet, he moves it lazily around me, up and down, circling my clit, his hands keeping my legs apart for his attentions. Back and forth he moves, learning the most secret parts of me, listening to my pants and groans, repeating a movement when I hitch a breath.

"Is this good?" he asks, his dark eyes finding mine in the dim light.

"Yes, fuck yes," I breathe. It takes everything I have to keep looking at him. It feels too intimate, too soul baring. Terrifying. But then he latches onto my clit and sucks, and I see stars.

He brings me to the edge quickly. My legs start to quiver, and without a word, he puts my calves on his shoulders. The position locks his face between my thighs, the scruff of his beard scratching deliciously against my sensitive skin. He eases up just enough for me to catch my breath, and as I let out an exhale, he chuckles. "Still good?"

I mumble a response, my head thrown back.

"Eyes, Elodie. Give me those gorgeous eyes. I want to see your face as I taste your orgasm."

Holy mother of God. I pull my head up and look down again in time to watch him swirl his tongue around my clit. "Harder," I gasp.

"Not yet."

"I'm so close," I whine, my hips bucking as I chase the pleasure that's just out of reach.

"Beg."

I have no idea where this dominance is coming from, and I don't care. "Please, Ansel. Please."

He pulls his mouth away and blows on me, making me choke out a near cry. "Not good enough. Beg for me, Elodie."

"Please put your mouth on me. Lick me, let me come,

please, Ansel." On and on I plead, a chant of words as my hips swivel of their own accord.

"Good girl," he praises.

I whimper in return.

"Keep watching." He gives me what I want, driving me closer and closer to climax as his eyes stay on mine.

Pleasure swirls and builds, my thighs shaking with effort, and finally—*finally*—I'm almost there.

He bears down, working me like he's done it for decades, and just as I'm tipping over the edge, he pushes two thick fingers into me.

I shatter, the orgasm ripping through me as I shout his name, my muscles pulsing around his fingers as he takes me through the deepest, most intense orgasm of my life. He doesn't let up, drawing the pleasure out of me until I'm nearly sobbing, out of my mind with what he's done to me.

"Ansel." His name is a prayer, a plea as I finally come down. My entire body tingles with pleasure.

As I watch, he pulls his fingers out of me and puts them into his mouth, sucking and licking them clean. He continues to hold my gaze, his own still dark and possessive. "You taste so good, Elodie. Perfect."

"Kiss me," I whisper. It's all I can think to say.

He shifts my legs off his shoulders, and I sit up. Something vulnerable flashes in his eyes, so quickly that I almost don't see it.

I pull his mouth to mine as he wraps his arms around me, pulling me flush against him so my wet center presses against his hard chest. The kiss is deep, searching. I thread my hands through his hair, and he moans. I do it again, and his torso surges up at the motion.

Realization hits. He's starved for touch—for *this* kind of touch. The kind that wants only to deliver pleasure without anything in return. He's beaten and tackled on the pitch, and given hugs and love at home, sure, but who gives him this? I increase the pressure, using my nails, and he responds with a groan. "Your turn. Tell me what you want," I whisper against his lips.

He doesn't answer.

I pull away, our positions making it so that I'm looking down into his eyes. They're back to soft and gentle, the dominant man of minutes before tucked safely away in place of a man who's so accustomed to giving that I'm not sure he can even articulate his wants. Not when they're about him.

Cradling his face in my palms and stroking his beard with my thumbs, I press a light kiss against his forehead, then each eyelid, before kissing him again. "Tell me," I urge.

A shadow passes over his face, and he gives the subtlest shake of his head. "This is about you."

"No," I push back. "You matter, Ansel. What you want matters."

His expression shutters, but it's still so soft and sweet that I almost don't see it. "Let's get you into something warm, okay?" He presses a quick kiss to my lips before rising and crossing to the dresser.

Something in my heart cracks wide open as he withdraws, turning to grab a pair of sweatpants and a tee from the drawers. His movements are practiced, efficient. It's only after he's handed them over that he turns to his own needs, pulling boxer briefs from a drawer and pulling them on.

"What can I get you? Water? I think I have a spare toothbrush—"

"I don't need a thing, Ansel," I say softly, my chest aching for him.

I dress and let him guide me into bed and under the covers. He climbs in with me, and before he can spoon me, I turn and wrap myself around him, maneuvering him into the little spoon position. He gives a surprised laugh but doesn't stop me. I press my nose to his back, breathing him in and kissing the strong muscles as I flatten my hand against his chest.

His hand comes up to cover mine, threading our fingers together before raising them and kissing my palm. "Thank you," he says quietly.

It's enough. For tonight, it's enough.

Chapter 17
Ansel

Two weeks later

I THINK ABOUT waking up with Elodie in my arms almost every single second. The sleepy morning scent of her, the tiny squeal she made as she stretched and woke up beside me...the way she took care of me the night before. As if she somehow knew what I needed to hear, and actually said it to me, even if I didn't entirely believe it.

Everything changed between us after the date two weeks ago, but to look at us, almost nothing has changed at all. We haven't gotten to go on another date, and we sure as hell haven't tumbled back into bed with each other.

But every morning I look at her and want to pin her against a wall to kiss her senseless. And while I don't get to pin her to a wall, exactly, I do find the time to kiss her, to squeeze her hand, to find some kind of way to let her know I want her. And every night, I look at the guesthouse and want so fucking badly to haul her into my home that my chest burns with it.

But at the same time, the idea of really going down this road with her...I can't make it work. My life doesn't allow it. And when the season actually starts up? Forget it. There's barely any time for Rosalie, let alone someone like Elodie, who deserves one hundred percent of someone's time and attention.

Speaking of the season. I need to make my weekly call to the preschool to see if they have an early opening. You'd think they'd be sick of me by now, and they probably are, but all they do is tell me that they have a slot reserved for her come September. Which is good, because no way Elodie will be interested in staying on as her nanny. I don't blame her; she has her new business to get up and running. But maybe if I'm lucky, I can at least convince her to stay in the guesthouse.

I need Lennox. He's my best friend, and I miss him. He's only five hours ahead, so maybe I'll give him a call on the way home from practice. I don't know that he'll have any sort of earth-shattering advice, but he's the only one I can spill my guts to without worrying about a reaction. Certainly can't call my parents—Dad is hyper-traditional in many ways, and Mom would start planning a wedding the second I uttered any of the thoughts swirling in my head.

Elodie breezes into the kitchen as I'm peeling a tangerine for Rosie, giving me a heart-stopping smile and nearly bringing me to my knees in the process. Her hair is down, tumbling over her shoulders in a wave of curls. "Good morning!"

"G'morning, Elle Belle!" Rosie sing-songs, then she gasps. "Your *hair*!"

Elodie beams. "You like it? I thought we'd see if your hair wanted to do the same."

Rosie's eyes nearly pop out of her head. "You think my hair could do that?" She swings her gaze to me. "Daddy, can my hair do that?"

I hold my hands up in surrender. "I don't know, Rosie

Posie. My styling prowess is limited to detangling spray and pigtail braids."

"And those are *wonderful*," Elodie says. "We're going to try something new today."

I leave the girls to it, grabbing my kit and heading to practice—but not before asking Elodie to help me look at something in the foyer.

She follows, her brows scrunched in question as we exit the kitchen. It's not until we get to the front that I turn and yank her to me, then back her against the door to kiss her. She melts against me, her body instantly giving in as I drag my hands up her T-shirt to cup her breasts, my thumbs scraping against the stiff peaks of her nipples.

"Ansel," she gasps.

I push my leg between her thighs, getting off on the way she grinds against me. "Fuck yes, baby." She's already soaked, whimpering as I kiss her neck. "Good girl for wearing these loose shorts. Can you be quiet?"

A wordless moan that I think means *yes* comes out of her, and I take that as my cue. I shove my hand down the elastic waistband of her shorts and into her panties, grunting softly as my fingers slip between her wet folds.

She chokes back a noise, her hazel eyes going wide as I push into her.

"Shh," I whisper, greedily drinking in the pleasure written all over her face. I press my thumb against her clit as I pump into her. So fucking responsive. I'll never get over it. "Swivel those hips, baby. You're almost there already."

"Fffuuckkk," she whimpers, her hands clamping onto my biceps. "Ansel, fuck, ohmygod—"

Her walls contract as she comes, her hips jerking as the orgasm takes over. Her eyes roll back as she lets her head fall against the door, the soft thud the only sound in the foyer. I keep moving my fingers, pulling her through the climax until she goes limp against the door, her hands falling away from my arms.

"Look at me," I command softly, pulling my hand out of her shorts.

She straightens and meets my eyes, her creamy skin flushed a beautiful pink from the orgasm.

I bring my fingers to my mouth, licking her arousal off and nearly losing my mind at how good she tastes. Before I can finish, she pulls my hand away, turning it and sucking those same fingers into her mouth.

My cock springs to attention, my jaw clenched as I fight to stay upright even as her hot, wet tongue circles my fingers. "Holy fuck," I whisper, my attention rapt on her lips even as her eyes stay on me. I might come in my shorts. *That's* how good this feels.

Wordlessly, her free hand presses against my cock, and I curse again. She sucks harder, and there is no stopping her as she slides her hand into my shorts and wraps around me. I press my palm against the door above her head, getting dizzy from the dual sensations. "Elle—"

She raises an eyebrow and pumps me, her hand and mouth beginning to move in sync as she wipes her thumb across the tip of my cock. I'm coiled tight, about to explode, and even though I know I shouldn't let this happen—it was supposed to be about her—I can't find it in me to make her stop. Her fucking *mouth*, Jesus Christ.

She hums against my fingers, her tongue sliding between them as she grips my cock. And I explode, climaxing so hard that I see stars. I grunt as I come, needing so fucking badly to roar and being utterly unable to do so, and try to stay upright through the pleasure.

As I finish, panting so hard it feels like I've just run a set of stadiums, she pulls my fingers out of her mouth with a pop. "Good boy," she purrs, her eyes alight with mischief.

"Oh," I puff out, unable to stop the grin that spreads across my face, "you are in so much trouble for that."

She winks even as another pretty blush stains her cheeks. "Seems I'm not the one who needs cleaning up."

I narrow my eyes playfully at her. "I'm getting you back for this."

She shrugs. "Might need to change before you head to practice."

Ten minutes later, my head is blissfully empty as I weave through the interstate traffic. Maybe I should start every day with an orgasm delivered by a hot woman named Elodie in my foyer.

My phone rings. I curse. It's my lawyer. Taking a deep breath and hoping like hell I can keep this blissful mood going, I answer her call with the car's system.

"Jennifer." I don't bother with pleasantries, but I don't feel bad. I assume she's used to it.

"I want you to remember that we have a court order that gives you full custody," she starts.

Well, there goes my mood. "Which we've had pretty much from the very beginning," I remind her. "What's that got to do with anything?"

"We've tracked her down," she replies.

"And?"

"And she's living in Atlanta."

My knuckles blanch on the steering wheel as I focus on not ramming into the car in front of me. "What did you just say?" I growl.

"She's in Atlanta. And before you ask, there's nothing I can do in terms of keeping her away from Rosalie, Ansel. She's not done anything."

"That's the fucking *point*," I yell.

Jennifer stays silent.

On a deep inhale, I try again. "I apologize. But are you sure?"

"I am," she confirms. "Have you heard anything else from her?"

"No."

"Looks like she's new to the area. She's been pretty itinerant, and that works in our favor."

I nearly freeze with rage. "What are you implying, Jennifer?"

"I'm implying that you should prepare yourself—and Rosalie—for the worst."

"She's five." I have to force my eyes to focus on what's in front of me. I'm on a seven-lane stretch of interstate. I should not have answered this call.

Jennifer continues, her voice clipped, "It doesn't matter how young she is, Ansel. She needs to be prepared if a judge determines that her mother has a right to see her. Or more."

This can't be happening. This entire conversation is a joke. It has to be. "That woman has no right to be called her mother. None."

"Should I refer to her as the dragon lady instead, Ansel?" Her sarcasm comes through easily.

I ignore that. "Do you really think a judge would agree to that?"

She sighs. "Hard to tell. But seriously, if you haven't talked with Rosalie—"

"That's my business," I snap, my nerves frayed.

"It is," Jennifer concedes.

"Anything else?"

"No. There's nothing more for us to do until or unless

she makes a move."

"Okay. Thanks," I bite out.

It's only after she ends the call that I yell, over and over in the safety of my Land Rover, until I'm nearly hoarse. It's my fucking luck that I'd go from one of the best mornings of my life to this.

I screech into the parking lot and stomp into the building. After tossing my kit into the locker, I stalk to the weight room, desperately wishing we were running drills on the pitch instead. As usual, the forwards are the ones with the heavier weights, and the backs are practically playing patty-cake with how much lighter theirs are. My role as a fly-half would typically mean I'm lifting lighter weights with the backs, but I've found I perform better if I'm a bit bulkier. Not as bulky as some of our guys, but just a little.

Today, however, I'm going to pretend that I'm one of our locks, so I throw as much weight on as I possibly can. I need to get out of my fucking head. It's not until I've loaded well over my usual weight for hip thrusts that Carter saunters over.

"You trying to break something, Captain?" he teases.

"Just that pretty face of yours if you keep gabbing," I toss back, then grunt as I thrust up.

"Don't be jealous, man, it doesn't suit you." He winks and adjusts the machine next to mine, then settles in. "Do we need to talk about it?"

"No," I growl.

He raises his hands. "Okay, okay, just checking."

The only person I'd talk to about all of this isn't even in the damn country. Carter may be a great teammate on the field, but off? He's not even remotely someone I'd trust with this kind of conversation. He's young and still enjoying all the perks of being a rugger. And good for him—no judgment here.

I hit station after station, grunting and growling my way through, pushing myself to the brink every time. When Coach walks in and tells us we're running drills to give the social media team some content, I couldn't be happier. I need exhaustion. I need to not think. Because if I think, bad things will happen.

An hour later, Coach has run us into the ground. Stadiums, suicide runs, passing drills, lunges up and back, and a ton of other exercises. I'm dripping with sweat and my legs are one drill away from simply detaching from me, but I still can't shake my foul mood.

"The fuck is wrong with you, running down the field like you're going to kill someone?" A familiar Scottish burr growls behind me.

I turn, disbelief at the redheaded man standing in front of me. But even though the tiniest bit of weight lifts at the sight of this asshole, it's not relief I feel. Not yet. "You," I say.

"Aye. Me," he says, then opens his arms.

I rush him.

A feral grin splits his face as he squats, ready to take me.

I tackle him, but the fucker doesn't go down. He never does. Could I try harder? Probably. Would one of us get hurt? Definitely.

He grips my shirt and swings me off him, and I yell in frustration.

"Ah, yer a feisty little twat when Daddy's not around to keep you in check, aren't ya?" he teases.

"Fuck. *You*," I grunt, leaping at his waist, wrapping my arms around him in another futile effort.

He laughs. This asshole just *laughs*. "I missed you, too, Ans." He tosses me off again.

I run at him a third time, juking him and managing to wrap my arms around his waist. He steps back with my weight, letting me feel like I've actually done something before removing my hands and spreading them up and above my head. Without any effort whatsoever, he tucks both my wrists into one meaty palm before pointing a finger at me. "Now say yer sorry and I won't tickle your pits."

I spit on the ground. "No."

"Seriously, what the fuck?" he asks, still holding my wrists above me. While I continue struggling to get free, mind you. Anytime I think I'm strong, all I have to do is go up against Lennox and I'm put right back in my place.

He squeezes my wrists, my bones twisting painfully in his grip, and I fold. "Fine! Fine. I'm sorry," I growl. "Let me go."

His eyes narrow. "Are you going to behave?"

"Yes," I promise. Immediately, relief hits as he lets me go. I rub one wrist and the next, scowling at his cheery face.

Something in my expression must finally hit him, though, because his smile drops. "Ans?"

I sigh. "It's Lauren. She's here." My voice hitches on the last word, nearly turning into a sob.

"Fuck." His face darkens. "Tell me everything."

Chapter 18
Elodie

LISTEN. I AM a patient woman. I am.

But when a man makes me orgasm *twice* in one night and then leaves me high and dry for the next two weeks, only to press me against a door and make me come in under a minute? Sure, I paid him back, but this is getting ridiculous.

I walk into the house each morning and he's in there, showing off those thighs and wearing those glasses and finding every reason to touch me when Rosalie isn't looking. And he keeps making me breakfast before heading to practice, but insists I spend the nights working on getting my business off the ground?

I am hanging by a thread.

A *thread*. Lord help me.

I don't know how much more I can take. Seriously. I might jump the man and climb him like a tree if something doesn't happen soon.

Something's going on with Ansel, too. He won't talk about it, but I can see the tension bracketing his eyes. The smudges of purple beneath them. I suspect it's got some-thing to do with the phone call he got that night. I've asked him if everything's okay, but his answer is always the same: *Nothing for you to worry about.*

Which is, of course, horse hooey.

But I can't do anything about it right now. It's a beauti-ful, hot, summer Saturday morning, and I'm getting ready to meet Kari and Allyson to talk about Allyson's honeymoon. I could almost pinch myself with excitement—that, or throw up. It's one or the other.

As I walk out of my house, Ansel and Rosie are in the backyard, Rosie paddling in the pool while Ansel sprawls on one of the lounge chairs, frowning at something on his phone. He finally looks up after Rosie and I exchange our hellos, and as always, I have to brace myself at how hot he is.

He's clad only in short swim trunks, his tanned skin on full display for me to ogle. And I do, taking full advantage of the moment to let my eyes travel up his legs to feast on those thick thighs and compact stomach and broad chest. Because it's morning, or perhaps because he knows what it does to me, he's wearing his wire-rimmed glasses, too, so when I finally meet those deep brown eyes of his, they're twinkling with amusement.

"Heading to meet your first client?" he asks.

I lick my lips, not missing how his gaze dips to watch the movement, and adjust the tote on my shoulder. "I am." Huffing a laugh, I admit, "I was actually worried that these pants wouldn't fit. Haven't worn them since leaving the day job." I wanted to dress professional, but I'm already regret-ting the structured slacks and silk top.

"Those curves are perfection, Elodie," he says, his expression ravenous.

Heat blooms on my cheeks and neck at the compliment, and I shift uncomfortably, unsure how perfect they are if he isn't going to do anything with them. But I don't respond. Instead, I toss him a flirty, "Wish me luck," then leave without a backward glance.

The coffee shop Kari picked is, naturally, perfect. Located in a bustling part of Atlanta that's closest to Allyson, it's filled to the brim with every type of person the city has to offer. I absolutely love it. I also love that they allow a small number of tables on the balcony to be reserved, so I head up to the one I snagged last week online and dump my bag, then go back to order a drink and some pastries for us to share.

I've just gotten set up when Kari and Allyson walk in, laughing at something one of them has said. Allyson is tall and graceful; her ebony skin beautifully complemented by the Kelly-green linen skirt and top she wears. She's draped in gold: bangles, necklaces, and big hoops that dangle almost to her shoulders, and her hair is in long box braids that swing down her back. When they make it up the stairs with their coffees and she leans in for a hug, I catch a woodsy, almost masculine scent that works so perfectly with her that I'm instantly in love. No wonder the team's burly Samoan was brought to his knees by this woman.

Her glossy lips part in a wide smile as she sits. "It's so good to meet you. Kari has blown you up to me, so I'm fully prepared for you to deliver me a miracle."

I laugh. "I don't know about that."

"*I* do," Kari says, releasing me from the hug she'd pulled me into and taking a seat.

Allyson beams. "If Kari tells me you're good, then it's settled: you're good."

"She's in public relations—it's her job to make people look good," I protest, but it's halfhearted. Inwardly, I'm blooming with love for my friend. Clearing my throat before I do something embarrassing like get choked up, I open up my iPad and pull up my latest organizational app. "So," I say, grabbing my Apple pen and doing my best to look like I know what I'm doing, "let's get started. Maybe you can tell me a little about your vision, and then I can offer some ideas."

Allyson clasps her hands together and wiggles her shoulders, practically squealing in excitement. "Does this mean you'll do it?"

I blink, confused. "I thought this was more like an interview." Then I glance at Kari. "You *did* tell her that she's my very first potential client, right?"

Kari has the decency to at least appear a bit chastened. "I mean..."

Allyson's bangles slide down her arm as she holds a hand up. "Wait. Wait, wait, wait."

I hold my breath.

She continues, "Are you saying that I get to be your very first client?"

Again, I blink as her words settle around me. *Get* to be. *Very first client.* And I realize the gift she's giving me, this belief. This unspoken generosity of trust and faith that I'll do exactly as she's hoping for and then some. It's enough to remind me that I *do* have something to offer. That it doesn't matter that I've not done this for anyone, because I've still got the talent and the knowledge to make it happen. The smile on my face is huge as I say, "Yes. Yes, you do."

She winks knowingly. "Atta girl."

Kari reaches for my free hand and squeezes it.

"You're looking for an adventure honeymoon, right? You want it hot or cold?"

Allyson takes a sip of her coffee, some kind of whipped ice confection with cream on top, and grins. "Cold. My sweet man wants cold, so we'll give him cold. Besides," she says, her grin growing wicked, "there's always something we can do to warm up."

"Hell yes, there is." Kari winks and laughs.

And just like that, I know I've made a new friend. I tap open the folder of ideas for discussion and launch in.

KARI and I go thrifting after the meeting, so it's nearly dinner time before I roll up to Ansel's house and make my way out of the house. I inhale deeply as I walk through the gate, catching the scent of grilled hamburgers as I close the latch behind me.

"Elle Belle!" Rosalie whips around the corner and barrels into me. "I missed you!"

I smile into her hazel eyes, trying and failing for the hundredth time not to think how remarkably similar they are to my own. Between the eyes and unruly hair, the resemblance between us is sometimes a little uncanny. I still don't know anything about her mother; only that she's not in the picture. But I don't know why, nor do I know how much of this sweet girl's life she's missed. Every time I want to ask, something tells me to hold off. That Ansel will tell me when he's ready.

"I missed you, too, Rosie bug," I tell her, then scoop her into my arms as she jumps up, monkeying onto me.

She peeks into the tote on my other arm. "What'd you get? Anything for me?"

I chuckle as I walk us around the corner of the house and toward the outside kitchen, where Ansel stands over the grill. "Nope, nothing for you," I say. "Just a pretty shirt that I found at the thrift store."

"Can I go to the thrift store with you?" she wheedles. "I bet *I* could find pretty shirts for me, too."

"It's a date," I confirm, bopping her on the nose. "We'll go next week."

"Yay!" She wiggles down and runs to Ansel. "Daddy, Elle Belle is taking me shopping next week!"

Ansel turns, tongs in hand, and I snort out a laugh. He sports a pink frilly apron, and between it and the tank top and shorter shorts he's got on, it almost looks as if that's the *only* thing he's wearing from the front. He looks down, then back up, and smirks. "The guys thought it'd be funny to prank me the last time I had them over for a cookout. Took my aprons and left me only with this one."

"And you haven't gotten them back?" I prompt, giggling at him.

He shrugs, a tinge of pink staining the skin above his beard. "It's...kind of comfortable. And it has better pockets!"

I can't do anything except shake my head and grin.

He flips the burgers, then turns his attention back to me. "How did it go?"

"I got it!" I say, cheesing so hard my cheeks might actually cramp up. "Ansel, she is *so cool*, and her ideas are amazing, and we just vibed, and Kari was all 'I knew it' and smug about it, but Allyson—that's her name, Allyson—she's the chillest person, and does Jake have any clue how lucky he is to have her? Have you *seen* her? She is gorgeous!" I clamp my mouth shut, because I have babbled beyond all babbling.

"Sorry," I say, waving my hand dismissively as I see how broadly he's smiling. "I know I'm being silly. It's just—"

"No way." Ansel puts the tongs down and closes the distance between us. Warm hands grasp mine as he continues, "This is great, Elodie. It's amazing. You're glowing, and I'm so damn proud of you." He stops. "Now *I'm* the one being sorry—is it weird that I'm proud of you? It's weird, isn't it?"

I didn't think it was possible, but I smile even bigger as butterflies erupt in my chest. "You're proud of me?"

He squeezes my hands, then lets go and grabs my arms, looking at me with the sternest expression I think I've ever seen. "Elodie. I am beyond proud of you. You've created something out of thin air. You're chasing your passion. Your dream. Of course, I'm proud of you. I have no right to—*oof*." He grunts out a breath as I crash into him, squeezing him hard.

His arms wrap around me, their warmth seeping deep into my skin as I breathe him in.

"Group hug!" Rosie shouts, running over and wrapping her tiny arms around us.

The whole thing makes me nearly cry. I shouldn't be so emotional about it, but I never got these kinds of moments growing up. The only time my mother was even close to being proud of me was when I won a regional pageant—and even then, all she gave me was a crisp nod and the barest of smiles. This is the woman who still doesn't know I lost my job.

How is it that I've only known Ansel for two short months? It feels like he and Rosalie have been a part of my life forever. "Thank you," I whisper against his chest.

"You did it all on your own, Elle. I'm just the lucky guy who gets to watch you succeed." He kisses the top of my head and steps away with a wry grin. "Burgers," he says with a nod to the grill. "Join us? Rosie here insisted I ask."

"Cleocatra, too!" Rosie pipes up.

I laugh and wipe the rogue tear from my eye. "Sounds delicious."

Chapter 19
Ansel

I CAN'T MAKE myself tell Rosie no when she asks if Elodie and the cat can stay to watch a movie after dinner. I can't make myself say no when she demands that Elodie be the one to take her through her nighttime routine before the movie. And I sure as hell can't say no when Rosie climbs onto me, fresh from the bath with twin French braids going down her back, and declares that she wants to be the middle of a Daddy and Elle Belle sandwich.

We watch the entirety of *Brave*, even though Rosie falls asleep an hour in, her head in my lap and her feet in Elodie's. As the credits roll, I glance over. Elodie smiles at me, her expression soft. She's pulled her hair down, the unbound curls falling wild around her face and down her shoulders. She looks absolutely perfect here. Like she belongs. Like this is where we're all supposed to be.

"Stay," I say. It's not a question, not exactly.

She meets my gaze, and I see the question in her hazel eyes, the hesitation and wondering. I know I've put it there with the way I've acted. But she nods anyway, biting her lower lip and wringing her hands as I stand with Rosie in my arms.

I don't realize she's followed me upstairs until she's leaning against the door while I put my daughter to bed, tucking the comforter around her as she snuggles deeper in.

I shut the door behind me, and we stand in the darkened hallway. And as she looks up at me, one hand tucked into the back pocket of her lounge shorts, I feel myself moving closer and closer to that edge. The one where, if I fall off, there's no going back.

I don't care about falling.

Because I think if I do fall, she'll be there to catch me.

"Should we go back downstairs?" she whispers.

Absolutely not.

I reach for her hand, and she meets me halfway. I turn, leading her to my room at the end of the hall and pulling her in, shutting the door behind us. The full moon streams through partially open blinds as I face her, bathing her in a pale, ethereal light as she blinks up at me, her sweatshirt falling off one creamy shoulder. She's the picture of innocence, and twin desires to protect her and debauch her war within me.

I'll do both.

"One word from you and I stop," I tell her, my voice already hoarse as I step closer.

"I don't want you to stop," she answers.

I stop in front of her, my hands fisting. "Are you sure?"

Swallowing, she nods. "Yes."

It's all I need to hear.

I tug her to me, cradling her face and feeling the way she arches into me as I claim her lips. She submits readily, and I plunge my tongue into her mouth, tasting her, feasting on her. She lets out a soft groan as her hands move beneath my shirt, and I break the kiss long enough to pull it off.

Her eyes trail over my chest, and I don't think I'll ever get over the look of wonder she has when she looks at me. As though she's the lucky one.

She's not. I'm the miserable bastard who didn't even know he was living half a life until she crashed into it.

"I want you, Ansel."

I stare. The way she says it, as though she isn't sure what my reaction will be, but she's brave enough to do it anyway, thaws something inside me.

"Good," I answer. "Because you're getting me." I take her sweatshirt off, followed by the lacy confection surrounding her breasts. Next, I kneel and pull off her shorts and panties, leaving her naked before me. I place a kiss just below her belly before standing back up, then scooping her into my arms. She lets out a surprised gasp as I walk her to the bed.

"I'm not too heavy?" she asks.

"Never," I promise her with a smile. "You're perfect."

After laying her down on the bed, I finish undressing myself, barely able to see her eyes in the dark but knowing they're trailing over my body the same way my eyes are feasting on hers. I've memorized every curve of her pale form, but I want more. I'll always want more.

I crawl onto the mattress and lower myself down, settling into the cradle of her legs and feeling the damp heat of her. It takes every ounce of willpower I have not to push into her, to claim her as mine and damn the consequences.

She's so fucking soft, so responsive to every touch, writhing and moaning and uttering tiny words of nonsense as I worship her, kissing and nipping and licking her neck and chest. Then I go lower, taking one of those glorious breasts in my hand and sucking on her nipple.

"Fuck," she whispers, sliding a hand against the back of my head to hold me in place.

I smile against her skin, not stopping. I love making her curse; it's the only time she does it, and the hit of dopamine it sends through me is like nothing else. After giving her other breast the same amount of love and attention, bringing the peak into my mouth and sucking until she hisses and bucks beneath me, I finally move down her body.

"Want me to make you come again, sweetheart?" I ask, burying my face in her plush stomach and relishing the feel of her nails against my scalp.

"God, yes," she answers.

I lift back up and kiss her, shifting to lie beside her before moving a hand between her legs. She arches into my touch, her body begging for what she's not yet saying out loud. "You've got to be quiet, Elodie. Can you do that for me?"

"Pretty sure I've proven that," she whispers, the bit of light seeping in from the blinds highlighting the naughty smirk on her lips. "Or have you forgotten?"

Fair point. "What if I do this?" I slide my middle finger around her clit.

She moans quietly, closing her eyes at the touch.

"Mm, not bad," I praise, still swirling my finger around that bundle of nerves. "But you know I want those beautiful eyes on me."

Her eyes pop open.

"Time for another test."

She bites her lip, and I hold back a groan. "What happens if I touch you like this?" I push my finger into her, feeling the wet heat of her body wrap around it.

She inhales sharply, her hands clutching at me as her hips rise. "Oh, God," she whispers.

I push a second finger in, pumping slowly, before using my thumb to find her clit again. She whimpers, and I swallow down her noises with a kiss. Her legs fall open as her breaths come faster, her inner muscles already starting to tighten around my fingers.

"Ansel." My name comes out in a whimper.

"You're doing so well," I tell her. "Now, grab that pillow and scream into it if you need. But otherwise, I want your eyes. Do you understand?" I push my fingers farther into her.

"Yes, please yes," she chants.

I pull my fingers out and slide down, needing to taste her more than I need to fucking breathe. When my mouth finally meets her pussy, we both groan as I take my time with her. Tasting her arousal and letting it coat my tongue before focusing on a spot just below her clit as I push my fingers back into her. She responds just like she did the last time, the pressure of my tongue sending her closer and closer.

It takes no time. I wrap my lips around her clit and look up to make sure she's watching, and she is. Her orgasm is close, too. "Good girl," I praise again, pressing as deep into her as I can. "Now come for me."

She bucks up as I bend my head to her again, opening her mouth in a silent scream as her walls throb against my fingers, her whole body pulsing in rhythm to her climax. She's so fucking gorgeous, so unbelievably sexy as she shudders above me, her eyes wide and glassy.

She inhales, then looses a breathy, drawn-out curse as she lets herself fall back onto the bed. "My God, Ansel."

I crawl up her body, kissing her softly rounded belly,

licking the underside of her breasts, and circling each nipple into a taut peak before sucking it, one hand exploring her curves as I go. When I get to her mouth, she opens wide for me, and I take her, needing every bit of her that I can have.

She wraps her arms and legs around me, and before I know what's happening, she's rolling us, settling on top of me, and grinning in the dim light.

"My turn."

Chapter 20
Elodie

HIS EYES WIDEN to an almost comical size at my words, then his eyebrows slam down. "Elle—"

I cover his mouth with my hand. "Ansel."

He relents, his body relaxing beneath me. God, his *body*. But I'll get to it. I remind myself to be brave, then say, "I've been working very hard on things. On my business."

He nods against my palm.

"On learning to stop being so nice."

A brow rises, hard to see but discernible, nonetheless.

I giggle. "Believe it or not, I've really been improving."

"Bullshit," he mutters, his lips tickling my palm.

I swivel my hips on him, and he groans. "*And* I have been working on being more assertive. This is me being assertive." I take a deep breath, still addled from the insane orgasm he just delivered, and hope my voice doesn't shake when I say the next part. "Right now, what I want—what I *need*—is to give you a blowjob."

His eyes twinkle, his lips curving into a smile behind my

hand before I pull it away for him to speak. "I don't think I've heard it called a blowjob since I was in high school."

Heat flames my cheeks. "What else would you call it, then?"

He reaches a hand up to caress my face, his grin going positively naughty. "Promise me you'll say the words once I tell you."

I agree with a hesitant jerk of my chin. "Okay."

His gaze drops to my clasped hands. "So innocent," he murmurs, then focuses back on me, his eyes hooded with lust. "The words you're looking for, my sweet Elodie, are these: You want to suck my cock."

As my eyes widen, he repeats himself. "Suck. My. Cock."

My core heats at the dirty words, wetness coating between my legs.

"Say it, Elodie," he demands softly. "Tell me you want to suck my cock."

I swivel against him again, needing relief, before murmuring, "I want to suck your cock."

"No whispers, sweetheart." His hands dig into my hips. "Say it out loud."

"I want to suck your cock," I repeat.

His eyes roll back in his head as he groans. "Perfect, Elodie. Fuck me, you are so perfect. Say it again."

Emboldened, I rise onto my knees and bend over, bracketing his head with my hands. I lean down so close our lips almost touch, then let my lips graze the side of his mouth and cheek before whispering in his ear, "I'm going to suck your cock now, Ansel."

He groans. "Good girl. Yes, please," he says, his voice hoarse.

Pleased with myself, I tour down his body, taking just as

much time on him as he did with me. I explore the hard planes of his chest, the light covering of hair that starts out broad and narrows to guide me down to the place I most want to be. His fingers stroke up and down my arms, halting as I find those incredible divots on the front of his hips, honed and sculpted by years of hard work and training.

I lick them, delighting in the shiver he can't hold back, listening to the deep rumble of his voice as he groans. But I can't *see* anything, and I'm desperate to. I want to look at this beautiful body at my mercy. I rise up and crawl to the top of the bed.

"What are you doing?" he asks.

Angling over him, my breasts dangling over his prone form, I find the bedside lamp and click it on. Its light is dimmer than most, but it's more than enough for me to understand the way he looks at me: hungry.

He captures me by the waist, sucking on my breast and tracing the curves of my body. And it feels good, *so* good, but I won't be stopped.

His skin practically glows in the ambience, tan and sculpted. Even lying down, his muscles are defined, twitching and flattening as he moves. When I meet his eyes, his expression is downright tortured, and I laugh.

"I told you it's my turn," I remind him. "Relax and enjoy it."

With that, I slide back down, purposefully ignoring his impressive cock in favor of finally—dear God, *finally*—getting my mouth on his thighs. His thick, strong, gorgeous thighs. I press my lips to the left one, skimming my teeth over it as he hisses an inhale.

"Elle, what are you—"

Then I bite.

"Fuck," he grunts, nearly coming off the bed in surprise.

I drag a hand up his stomach, moaning at the feel of muscles bunching beneath my palm. "Be still." I don't recognize my voice, raw and raspy.

He relaxes, and I return to my own little feast. If I could wrap myself up in these thighs, I would. *That's* how much I love them. I savor them, kissing and nipping at one, then the other, while Ansel's hands clench and unclench beside me. When he's good and bothered, I readjust myself between his legs, pulling my hair to one side and leaning down to where his penis lies.

Cock, I remind myself with a smirk.

I look up to meet his eyes, and they blaze with desire, the brown irises disappearing into the blown darkness of his pupils. "You ready for me to suck your cock, Ansel?"

His breath hitches as he nods, and it occurs to me that even though I'm the more inexperienced of us, *he's* the nervous one. "Yes," he manages.

I quirk a smile. "Yes, what?"

He huffs a laugh, and it sends butterflies through me. "Yes, please, Elodie. Please take that gorgeous mouth and put it around my cock."

So I do. Without preamble, without so much as an opening lick, I simply take him into my mouth like a lollipop, pulling him as deep as I can.

The sound he makes—feral, undone, grateful—cracks me wide open.

Gentle hands wrap my hair to the side as he breathes out a curse, his eyes locked onto my eyes, my mouth. "Elodie."

I hum, licking him up and down, paying attention to every noise he makes. I can count on one hand the number of times I've done this, and it's already a million times better than ever before. It's not that I've turned into some blowjob goddess—or cock-sucking champion, perhaps?—but it's the first time I've *wanted* to do it.

Ansel murmurs words of praise above me, and right when I'm hitting my stride, he pulls me up to him, crushing me down on top of him and flipping us in one smooth motion. Way better than my own moves, but to be fair, he *is* a lot bigger than me.

"Tell me I can be inside you," he says, his eyes searching mine. "Tell me you want all of this."

Is he kidding? "I want all of this. All of you." I pause. "I want your cock inside me."

"Thank fuck," he breathes, a relieved smile on his face.

I giggle. "Did you think I'd say no?"

"I didn't want to assume," he admits. "Don't move." He leans over to the bedside table and pulls out a condom, then gives me a bashful look. "These are—um." He looks away, seeming to search for the words. "I've never done this. Here, I mean. No one's been here. It's, ah, it's been a long time."

"Ansel." My voice is soft as I beckon him. "It doesn't matter." I've almost got whiplash, moving between the dominating man who demands I orgasm one moment and the sweet guy who confesses it's been a long time since he's had sex the next.

But my words must settle things, because he opens the foil and rolls the condom on. He resettles between my legs, the warmth of him seeping into me. And when his eyes hold mine as one strong hand grips the back of my thigh, guiding it up so my foot is on the mattress and opening me wide for him, I hold my breath.

"You're so beautiful, Elodie," he says, notching himself against me.

I exhale.

On my next inhale, shaky and overcome, he pushes in.

We moan together, his low and guttural, mine nearly matching it, and my body reacts instantly, clenching him tight.

"Fuck, Elle, *baby*," he chokes.

"I—" It's all I can say as he withdraws and thrusts again, getting deeper.

"You can take it," he whispers, his voice a caress against my ear. "Take me deep, Elodie. Let me in. Give me heaven."

His words turn me molten, my core softening and opening.

"There's my good girl," he says, pulling out and pausing. His eyes search mine. "Are you ready for me, love?"

My answer is to arch up and nip at his bottom lip. Grabbing onto the sliver of bravery still inside me, I hold his gaze. "Fuck me, Ansel."

He growls and slams home, both of us crying out as he bottoms out. I'm so full, fuller than I've ever been. My eyes roll back in my head as he does it again and again.

"So good," I breathe, dimly remembering that I need to be quiet. "You feel so good. My God, Ansel. My God."

My words unleash him even more, as he loses himself inside me. His eyes are wild, dark with lust and wonder and pleasure. He hikes my leg up higher, the angle allowing him to go even deeper, hitting a part of me that I didn't know was possible.

"Fuck me, Elodie," he grunts. "You are heaven. So hot. So fucking *tight* against my cock. Tell me you like it."

My throat tightens.

He slams into me again, and I moan in ecstasy. "Tell me."

"God*damn*, I like it, Ansel. I love your cock. Love the way you make me feel. Love—"

He cuts me off with a bruising kiss and practically bends me in half. It's harsh, brutal...and absolutely exactly what I asked for. There's nothing sweet or gentle about him anymore. He's fucking me, hard and deep, his hips swirling up and back, and I start to lose my ever-loving mind.

"Ansssssel," I moan. "Fuck, I'm—I'm—" I break off with another moan against his mouth.

"Be quiet, Elle," he warns.

But it's impossible, because even as the words leave his mouth, he increases the pace, slamming into me so hard that the headboard hits the wall. He moves us down just enough to keep it from happening again, then slams home once more. Faster and faster he pistons into me, and when my orgasm begins to swirl into existence, my eyelids flutter shut.

"No," he commands, his words soft but urgent. "No. Together. Look at me."

And as I force my eyes open, his own are right there, studying me even as his face contorts with his own impending climax. I grip his sweat-slicked back, my nails scraping down the muscles as I shatter with a low groan.

"Fuck," he hisses, slamming one final time into me and stilling as he comes. He's glorious. Every piece of him flits across his face before he leans his forehead to mine, breathing hard.

We stay there, gripping each other tightly, breathing shared air as we settle back into our bodies. After a few moments, he lets go of my leg and guides it lower, and I wrap my arms tight around him, pulling his weight to rest on top of me.

"I'm too heavy," he protests, trying to rise almost immediately.

"No," I say, tightening my grip. "Stay here. Stay inside me. I want to feel you."

Kissing me tenderly, he relents, groaning as I reach to scratch my fingers through his hair. We remain like that for a long while, kissing, touching, caressing. Staring at each other. Memorizing everything. Finally, he kisses my forehead, then rolls out of the bed to pad to the en-suite bathroom and dispose of the condom.

He's back instantly, pulling the covers around us before gathering me into his arms, nuzzling at my neck and ear, his hands roaming my body in long strokes.

"Careful," I murmur, "or I'll want to do that all over again."

He releases a laugh. "You act like that's a bad thing."

"I can't stay," I say, reality slithering back into me. Remembering that a precious little girl is just down the hall.

"Maybe not," he admits, "but that doesn't mean you have to leave yet."

I rise onto my elbow and look at him. "No?"

"No." He smiles. Then he turns us and lowers his head to my body once more.

Chapter 21
Elodie

MY BODY IS deliciously sore as I shower a few days later, feeling the twinge in my back as I bend to shave my legs. I haven't been able to wipe the smile off my face since that first night. We got almost no sleep, tangling up with each other time and again, dozing only to wake ravenous for the other's skin. It was nearly dawn when we finally parted, Ansel walking me to the kitchen door and closing it softly behind me as I padded around the pool to the guesthouse.

We've been together every night since. I have never felt like this. Never thirsted for someone so thoroughly. It wasn't even close to this with my ex, this kind of all-consuming desire that won't stop. And it's not just physical—though, my Lord, that man is heaven-sent—but it's more. Like I'd do just about anything to protect him, his heart, his family. It doesn't make sense, the way I'm so filled up with emotion. How could a few days of him have me so twisted up?

Because it's been more than a few days. Because I've been falling for him from the moment I saw him walk into that room at the Granite headquarters. Because he and his daughter are the very thing I never knew I was looking for.

Is this what it feels like to be cherished for who you truly are, and not what you can or can't win? To be seen for me, not what my body can or can't do?

I know there's still a lot we both have to learn about each other, but even still. Whatever this is, I like it.

After my shower, I get dressed and I head over. Ansel's in the kitchen like always, his wire-rimmed glasses sliding down his nose as he concentrates on the French braid he's weaving down Rosalie's back. I taught him the new braid and he's been working on perfecting it every day since, much to Rosie's delight.

Father and daughter look up simultaneously as I enter, both of them smiling broadly. Their happiness mirrors my own as my stomach clenches, emotions threatening to drown me. I blink back a sudden rush of tears. I am *all* up in my feels this morning.

"Who wants breakfast?" I ask, having finally bullied Ansel into taking my help in the mornings. As much as I love his desire to take care of, well, everyone, I'm also determined to make the man accept help.

"Me!" Rosalie chirps. "Can I have toasty eggs?"

"Yes, ma'am!" I answer, giving her a salute and turning to gather the supplies. When I look back at Ansel, I catch him eyeing my butt and I stick my tongue out at him. With a silent laugh, I ask, "Want a smoothie?"

He smiles softly. "I've already had it. Thank you." He finishes with Rosalie's braid, and she hops down, darting out of the kitchen to do who knows what.

Ansel takes the opportunity to slide up behind me, running his hands down my waist before gripping my hips and pressing against my bottom. There's no mistaking his hardness. "You're killing me in that outfit," he growls, leaning to scrape his teeth against my neck.

I shiver, barely managing to set the eggs and shredded cheddar cheese on the counter before he's turning me around and kissing me deeply. I press against him, pliant and willing to take anything he wants to give me. His hands slide up to my breasts, his thumbs circling my nipples through the body-skimming halter dress I'm in. I'd put it on because it was comfortable, not thinking a thing about it. But now, my core throbbing with want as Ansel leans into me, the countertop digging into my back as he slides a hand beneath the fabric, I'm applauding my fantastic choice.

He slides the silk of my panties to the side, and I bite my lower lip as he dips a finger into me.

"Fuck," I whisper.

"Damn, woman," he rasps. "You gonna let me make you come right here, Elodie?"

I grind against his hand, my breath hitching.

"Daddy!"

We fly apart, Ansel angling his body to cover me as I shove my dress into place, my cheeks flaming. "Hey, Rosie bug!"

She waves a half-finished drawing at him. "I found it! I'll finish it for you today, okay?"

"Sounds amazing," he says, reaching back to squeeze my leg before moving to the sink to wash his hands.

The transformation is so thorough that I can't help but be impressed. He picks Rosie up as she flings herself at him, throwing a wink at me over her head.

I swoon.

LATER, after Rosie takes a surprising but welcome nap, we decide to go to the library. She returns the stack of books we'd borrowed a couple of weeks ago, and grabs my hand to lead me through the stacks for a fresh batch. Her hand fits perfectly in mine, soft and warm, and I squeeze it.

She looks up at me, hazel eyes crinkling. "I love you, Elle Belle."

The words slam into me, catching me so thoroughly off-guard that I nearly stumble. "I love you, too, Rosie Bug." I mean it, too. The love I have for this little girl surges through me something fierce.

She grins. "Of course you do."

I giggle. "Okay, missy. Let's pick some books."

We're stopped at a red light on our way home when the back of my neck tingles with awareness. I look at Rosie through the rearview mirror, but she's buckled in her booster seat and flipping happily through one of the new books. Then I notice the car behind us, realizing it's been following us since we left the library's parking lot, and—my brow furrows. Does he have a *camera*?

Adrenaline floods my system, and I punch the gas when the light turns green. The car keeps up, even as I take a turn away from the house. It stays with us, turn after turn, and I know, deep in my bones, that the driver is following us.

I make the decision on instinct. Forcing my voice to remain calm, I say, "Let's go see Daddy, sound good?"

"Yay!" she answers, her little face lighting up in the rearview mirror.

I weave through a few streets before getting to the interstate, the man in the car still following me. But I've picked this entrance on purpose, knowing it forces cars to stop one after the other before entering the merge lane, and I floor it. I weave into the congestion, driving my Honda as fast as I safely can, praying I'll lose the other car in the heavy Atlanta traffic.

It works, but I don't slow down. My hands shake as I pull into the Granite's headquarters, and it takes all my strength to act like everything is fine as she grips onto my hand again, skipping into the entrance.

"Let's go see Kari first, yeah? Daddy's probably working very hard right now."

She nods, and we take the elevator to the top floor.

Kari's bright smile falters when she sees my face, but she recovers quickly. "What a surprise!" she exclaims, rising and walking around her desk to give Rosie a big hug. Rising, she pulls me into an embrace. "You okay?" she murmurs.

"We were followed, and I didn't know what to do," I mutter back.

She stiffens, then leans back to study me. "He's pretty famous, Elodie," she says, her voice low.

My gut clenches. "But we weren't with him," I point out. "It was me and his daughter. In *my* car."

Her eyes widen, and she nods. "Okay. You're right. I think the team might be finishing up, but let me check the news? See if something's going on that would have warranted it?"

I shake my head. "This wasn't sports paparazzi, Kari. I know it wasn't."

After studying me for a moment, she relents. "Okay. If it wasn't a pap, then..."

"Then who was it? And why?" Dread courses through me.

Kari raises an eyebrow. When I still don't speak, she seems to make a decision. "How about you two go raid the snack room while I see if I can find your dad, Rosalie?"

She nods happily at Kari, then looks up at me while hooking a thumb over her shoulder. "Come on, Elle Belle. I know my way around," she says proudly.

Defeated, yet not really able to articulate why, I let Rosie lead me out while Kari heads down the stairs two at a time.

They must have been showering, because when Ansel walks in, his hair is wet and his heather-gray Granite shirt is clinging to him in wet splotches. He eats up the distance, going straight to where Rosie sits, separating Skittles into little piles by color. Lennox is right behind him, followed by Kari.

"Hi, Daddy!" Rosalie says, her feet swinging on the chair. "Want the orange ones?"

"Of course I do," he answers, holding his palm out as he kneels beside her. She drops the candy into his hand, counting each piece as she goes, while he looks over every inch of her, seeking out any potential harm. It's only when she's finished counting ten candies into his waiting hand that he's satisfied she's safe. "Thank you, Rosie," he says, rising and planting a kiss on the top of her head while pocketing the Skittles.

Then he turns to me. And I don't know what it is that he sees in my expression, but anguish passes over his own before he schools it away. Stepping toward me, he asks, "Are you okay?"

The question makes my throat tight with emotion. Emotion over the way his first concern was his daughter, and then for me. Not a demand to know what happened. Not a reprimand for coming here. Nothing but genuine concern.

And it shouldn't, but his reaction nearly undoes me. Tears spring to my eyes.

Ansel comes closer, murmuring, "Shh, it's okay. You're okay." He brings his hands to my face, thumbing away the tears as they spill. When I can't stop crying, he pulls me into his arms and holds me there, gently rocking us while I take a moment to fall apart.

But I can't wallow, especially when I can't even explain what just happened. I sniff and make myself step back, aware that Rosalie doesn't need to see us and wonder what's going on. Wiping my face and taking a deep breath, I blow it out and meet Ansel's eyes as Kari and Lennox hover in my periphery.

"We were followed," I start.

"I *know*." Ansel's voice is low and angry.

"Easy, man," Lennox cuts in, putting a hand on Ansel's arm.

The touch seems to relax him, and he exhales roughly. "Sorry."

I dive in, giving them the story quickly. There isn't much to tell, it turns out, but even though I have only the barest idea of what the man looked like, I tell them the make and model of the car.

Meanwhile, Ansel's gone from mad to nearly apoplectic, coiled and ready to spring. "And you lost him on the interstate?" he asks for the third time.

I nod, giving him a tentative smile. "Guess that training my dad made me take when I was a teenager finally came in handy."

Lennox raises a questioning brow.

"Defensive driving class taught by ex-police officers," I explain. "Learned all kinds of things."

"Your dad's a cop?" Ansel asks.

"Retired," I answer.

"Should we call him? See if he can help somehow?"

"No." The answer is flying out of my mouth before he even finishes the question. While my father might be the tiniest bit useful here, he'd fold the instant my mother voiced any kind of opinion. "He can't help."

"Are you sure?" Ansel asks.

"She's sure," Kari answers for me, her voice steely.

I let out the breath I didn't know I was holding, immensely grateful for my best friend. "I just don't understand why anyone would want to follow us," I muse.

"I do," Ansel states flatly.

My eyes fly to his, but he's grabbing his phone and stalking out of the room.

"Give the man a few minutes, yeah?" Lennox says softly. "It's complicated."

I cross my arms over my chest. "Do you know something?"

He grips his neck and grimaces, clearly uncomfortable. "It's...not my story to tell."

Kari crosses her arms. "Seriously, Lennox? My best friend was *terrified* when she got here. Not to mention the safety of that little girl. And you're going to hide behind a stupid statement like that?"

Pain flashes across Lennox's face before he schools it away. "I said what I said."

"Pathetic." Kari practically spits the word.

I look between the two of them. There's definitely something deeper between them going on here, but no way Kari will tell me right now.

Ansel reappears, beelining for me. "Ready? I'll take her home."

I gape at him. "Are you—What's going on?"

"Later," he says. Then he turns to his daughter and crouches down, scooping her into his arms and letting her pop a candy into his mouth as they go.

I force a smile at Rosalie as she waves at me behind Ansel's back. "See you at the house!"

Tamping down the irritation that threatens to overtake me, I turn. "Lennox," I start.

He holds his hands up, remorse all over his ruddy face. "I'm sorry, Elodie. But I can't. Whatever Ansel has or hasn't told you, he's done it for a reason. I'm not going to override that."

"Fucking coward," Kari bites out. "Like always."

Lennox clenches his jaw, but keeps his eyes on me, not backing down.

Sighing, I grab my keys. "It's okay, Lennox. I understand." Even though I don't. Not really.

To Kari, I say, "I'll call you."

Ansel and Rosalie are gone by the time I make my slow way to my CR-V. Who was that? Better yet, why?

I tuck myself into the driver's seat and breathe, my hands flexing on the wheel after I start the engine. *Ansel's focus is on his daughter. Not me. He's not mad at me.* And even though I repeat the words over and over as I weave into traffic, it's hard to get past the fact that there's something he's keeping from me.

Chapter 22
Ansel

I T TAKES HOURS before I'm calm enough to think rationally. It's only after I've put Rosie to bed that I manage to float out of my rage-induced haze and fully comprehend that Elodie's been here the whole time. Quietly watching me, helping with dinner, and then stepping into the kitchen without a word so I could take Rosie through her nighttime routine.

Shit.

I need to apologize. To maybe—maybe try explaining the situation. Letting her in that much more.

The thought makes my heartbeat hitch. Could I do it? Lay it all on the table?

What if it's too much? What if me and Rosie aren't worth it?

No. The answer clangs through me, clear as a bell. She wouldn't think that. I can trust her. I *do* trust her. I hustle down the stairs, already sorting out the words to use. But when I round the banister, she's gone.

For a moment, I consider calling her back over.

Handing over this final piece of me and Rosie, and hoping like hell she wants to take it.

I blow out a breath. Maybe this is for the best. This—*we*—aren't her problem. I can handle it, the same way I've handled everything for Rosalie from the moment Lauren abandoned her on my doorstep. I've built my entire life around my little girl, fought for the success and safety we have, and the thought of someone—of Lauren, especially—waltzing back in here and taking her from me?

No.

Absolutely the fuck not.

My hands shake as I pace the living room. No, this entire thing is volatile and terrible and nothing that Elodie needs to be concerned with. It's my problem. I'll deal with it.

I barely get any sleep, and when I do, it's filled with nightmares about Rosie being dragged out of the house. When I feel a tiny hand on my cheek, I jerk upright.

Rosie's grinning at me, her sweet face so innocent that it makes me physically hurt. "Hi, Daddy."

I scrub a hand down my face and try to wake up. "Hi, Rosie girl."

She tilts her head, curls falling into her face with the movement. "I'm hungry. Elle Belle said I should come wake you up while she makes me breakfast."

Bleary-eyed, I look at the clock. "Guess I overslept, huh?"

Rosie nods seriously.

I need to pull it together. I widen my eyes and snarl, "Doesn't mean I can't still tickle you to pieces!" Then I snatch her giggling body up and into my arms. But I don't tickle her. I just hold her.

Rosie's finished breakfast by the time I make it downstairs, but Elodie is in the kitchen.

"Good morning."

She turns, and the sight of her takes my breath away. Sunlight frames her face as she smiles tentatively at me. "Rough night?"

I'm a fool. I should have told her everything last night. My shoulders slump. "I'm sorry."

"It's okay." She waves my apology away with a smile that I know isn't genuine. "You don't owe me anything."

The cavalier way she says it punches my chest in. As if Nice Elodie is here, and not the woman who I've started feeling things for that I probably shouldn't. I cross the room and pull her hands into mine. "It's not okay. I need to explain—"

My phone rings, reminding me that I'm going to be late.

Elodie squeezes my hands before releasing them and shooing me away. "Answer it. Go. We'll talk later."

When I pull the phone out of my pocket, I see my lawyer's name on the screen. I exhale in frustration and bite back a curse. "I need to take this. I'm—"

"Go," she insists, that fake smile still plastered on her face.

I don't want to. I want to pull her into my arms and bury my nose in her neck. Tell her everything. But now's not the time. "Tonight," I promise her.

When the smile doesn't leave, I sigh and nod, picking up my kit and snagging the keys off the entryway table. "Jennifer." My voice is clipped as I pull the front door shut, making certain to lock it.

Practice is fucking brutal. Coach is running us like the preseason opener is next week instead of in January.

"Miles!" he barks, waving me over to the sidelines. The

man doesn't so much as break a sweat out here, looking cool as a cucumber in the late August heat. I swear he's not human.

I jog over to him, increasing my pace when his usual scowl deepens even further.

"What is that shit?"

"What is what shit?"

He gestures with his notebook. "You're practically skipping out there. You get paid to *run*, Miles. To grab the ball and run. Or kick and run. Or pass and run. Or tackle and then *run*. Whatever the fuck is going on, solve it."

I blanch, not used to being on the receiving end of this kind of dressing-down. "Coach, I'm sorry."

"I don't want your apologies," he retorts. "I want you working. Being an example. You seem to have forgotten that you're the captain. I'd like to remind you that we're out here, in the middle of fucking August, in Georgia, because of you." He jabs his finger in my chest for emphasis. "Get your shit together and do your job."

I jerk my chin down. "Understood."

I join the rest of the team where they're taking a water break, shaking my head at Lennox as he gives me a questioning look. He knows how intense Coach is, so he simply nods in understanding and holds a cup of water up for me.

"Time to decide which of the new kids we're keeping?" he asks as I take the water and down it.

"Probably, but that's not what he wanted," I answer. I need to remember to start delegating. We named captains for the forwards and backs for this exact purpose, so I call over to our co-captains. Woods, our hooker co-captain for the forwards, and Carter, our wing and co-captain for the backs.

Woods hustles over, and Carter, the cocky fucker, practically sashays to where we stand. "Look at that, Woods," Carter says with a nudge to the other captain. "Ol' Cap here finally decided to remember we existed."

I roll my eyes. "Maybe I've been waiting for the two of you to come up with some ideas. You know—actually *lead* instead of waiting to be told?"

Woods appears to consider it, but Carter sucks his teeth, knowing full well that I'm bullshitting. "Nah," he says. "You forgot."

"I've been studying game tape from this past season," Woods offers. "I've got some specific plays in mind that we need to do better. Hone our ball-passing skills and see which of the potential new players can keep up."

I gesture at Woods as I look at Carter. "See? No mouthing off. Just ready to work. Take a page from Woods."

"I just need the forwards to do their job so that I and the rest of the backs can score the tries," he says with a shrug. "It's that simple."

Woods turns a raised brow at me. "Exactly *why* did you pick him as captain again?"

Lennox laughs. "Because he's our second-best scorer next to Ansel here. He's a peacock and an idiot, but he's talented as hell."

"Aw, you got a crush on me?" Carter coos to Lennox, who scowls at him.

"I regret coming back early," Lennox says dryly.

"Miles!" Coach barks. When I turn, he makes a *let's get on with it* gesture.

Sighing, I get us all back out on the pitch.

Mom calls on my way home. I punch the speaker to take it while I drive and answer with, "Everything okay?"

"Can't I call my only child to see how he's doing without causing alarm?" she responds.

"No," I state flatly.

She laughs. "Everything is fine. Thought you'd want an update on your father."

My grip on the steering wheel loosens. "How is the old man?"

"Furious if he heard you call him that—despite falling off a ladder and needing the surgery that kept us from keeping that sweet grandbaby of ours," she *tsks*.

"It's...all worked out," I say, eyeing the cars in my rearview mirror far more closely than usual.

"Oh?" Her voice rises with interest. "How, exactly, have they worked out?"

I can practically see the heart eyes she's probably making. "Ease up, Mom." Even though I, too, have heart eyes at this point. But I shake the thought off, knowing it's too soon.

"Fine, fine," she relents. "Your father is being an old coot, and I told him I'd call you and tell on him."

I laugh, grateful that she's shifted back to the original topic of conversation. "What's he done this time? You know I told you to call me if you need me."

"Ansel, you're four hours away—" she starts.

"I'd be a lot closer if you'd move here and let me take care of you."

"First of all, young man, we don't need *taking care of*. And secondly, we planned to move here for our retirement. You knew that. And finally," she says, her voice softening, "we really, truly don't need you worrying about us. You have too much on your plate as it is."

"I'm your only son," I remind her. "It's my job to worry about you."

She chuckles. "No, Ansel, it's not. And the day I manage to convince you of that may well be the happiest day of my life. Well," she hedges, "second to giving me a daughter-in-law."

I groan. "I'm ignoring that."

We talk all the way home, and it almost works: a sense of calm has nearly settled over me.

Until I get out of my Land Rover and see a woman exiting a car parked across the street. She's in jeans and some kind of strapless shirt, and looks exactly the same as the night we slept together.

Lauren's here.

Chapter 23
Ansel

I'M SLAMMING THE door and crossing the street before I even register what I'm doing.

"What the *fuck* are you doing here?" I demand, coming to a halt far too close to her.

"Careful, Ansel," she warns with an arch of a perfectly groomed eyebrow. "You never know who might be watching."

"Exactly what do you mean by that?" I growl.

She shrinks away from me for the briefest of seconds before straightening to her full height and staring cooly at me. "I want to see my daughter," she says, crossing her arms and looking me up and down as if I'm trash. Nothing is out of place on her. Hair, nails, the whole thing. Looking at her now, the effort at perfection makes my lip curl.

"*My* daughter," I correct her with a snarl. "She is *my* daughter. You lost the right to call her anything the moment you left her on my doorstep."

"She is mine as much as she is yours," Lauren shoots back.

"Wrong." I cross my arms. "You need to leave. Leave and never come back. We don't need you here."

"And why's that? Because you've got your fancy captain title and you're making big money with all your sponsorship deals? Because trust me, I'm well aware of them. Oh, wait." She pretends as if something has just occurred to her. "It's because you're fucking the nanny."

A wave of anger flashes through me and I see red, but I keep my clenched fists at my side. I'd never hit a woman, *ever,* but Lauren is pushing every button I have. "Say one more word about her," I seethe, "and you will regret it for the rest of your life."

Lauren has the sense to take half a step back, but she's not done. "I have tried to be nice. To do this the right way. But I want to see her."

"No."

Her eyes flash. "Do you really think you can just tell me no and have that be the end of it?"

"I do. Because what you've been doing—the way you've terrorized them—is not okay."

"*Terrorized?*"

I scoff. "So you weren't the one who had them followed yesterday? How many other times have you had someone follow *my child*, Lauren? That's not something a mother does."

"I needed information," she spits back. "And it's not like you were giving it to me."

"How many times?" I demand.

Her eyes slide away from mine.

Christ. My stomach roils. "Is it about money?" I ask.

"No!" she protests, but I see the lie on her face.

"That's it, isn't it?" I really am going to be sick. Deep, deep down, I had hoped that Lauren would come back around with a real desire to see her daughter. But whatever this is, it's not it. Random text messages, hiring who knows what kind of people to follow my daughter, and now showing up here? If I didn't have the profile I had, the chances of taking my anger out on her car would be sky high.

I press forward. "You always were an opportunist, Lauren. You've clearly seen the news. How the league is getting more attention. How we're pulling in bigger crowds. The sponsorships that the team has." I refuse to confirm her suspicions that *I'm* picking up better sponsorship deals.

She doesn't say anything.

And it's her silence that damns her.

But it damns me, too, because I ask, "How much will it cost to make you go away?"

Regret fills her eyes, but I don't believe it for a second. "I made a mistake. I just want—"

"Stop." I look her up and down. "You absolutely made a mistake. Several, in fact. The first was never telling me you got pregnant. The second was dropping her at my front door with nothing but a fucking *note*, like she's some shameful secret instead of the most precious being in the world. And the third? The third was coming back here. I barely know you, but I know enough to see that nothing about you has changed. It's obvious. That sweet girl cramped your style from the second you got pregnant with her, and you clearly regretted it, but me? She's the best thing that ever happened to me." I step closer, not caring how intimidating I might look. "And I'll be damned if I let you come around and pretend to want to see her, when all you want is money. Name your price, Lauren. How much?"

She shakes her head, expression cold. "Fuck you, Ansel."

"Oh, see, but you already did, sweetheart. And look where that got you." The words are so vicious that I don't recognize myself right now.

"This isn't over," she says, her voice shaking.

"You can expect a restraining order tomorrow." My words are flat, unfeeling. "I don't want you anywhere close to her."

"Try it and see how fast I go to the media," she says.

I don't answer, afraid that if another word comes out of my mouth, I'll end up in jail. And that will *definitely* be in the news. I don't want my life any more public than it already is.

She gets back in the car—a sleek black Mercedes two-seater, something that Rosalie couldn't fit in—and starts the engine.

I step back just in time, moving away as she revs into the street. I snap a picture of the license plate, then stand there, lost in my fury in the middle of the road. It's only when Sharon's Mini Cooper turns onto the street that I shake myself out of it and move back to my driveway.

Sharon pulls into her driveway and gets out, setting her mini daschund Dolly onto the ground. She bolts over to me, undoubtedly looking around for Rosie. "Sorry," Sharon says with a smile, her large sunglasses covering most of her face. "You know how Dolly is. She's been missing her favorite five-year-old." Then she gets a good look at me and frowns. "What's going on?"

I shake my head, unable to put it into words.

"Is Rosalie okay?" She crosses into my yard, noting the still-running Land Rover. "Your parents?"

I gesture vaguely at the street. "She was just here."

"Who?" Sharon looks around.

"Rosie's birth mother." It comes out as a growl.

Sharon stiffens. She's a second grandmother to Rosie and has seen us through more than even my own mom thanks to her proximity. "Did Rosie see her?"

I shake my head, my entire body shaking with adrenaline. "I can't—I need—"

She immediately understands. "Go," she says. "I can take care of them. It'll be a play date for Rosie and Dolly."

"I can't go inside." I'd either burst into tears or I'd punch holes in the walls. Either is possible right now. I can't let Rosie see me like this. Elodie, either. This is exactly the kind of mess she doesn't need be involved in.

Sharon nods. "It's okay."

"Thank you." With that, I climb back into my car and reverse out of the driveway.

Chapter 24
Elodie

I DIDN'T KNOW what to think when Sharon came over last night and declared it "girls' night for Rosalie and Dolly," but it was clear enough that she'd come at Ansel's request, and that I was free the rest of the evening. The good part was that Rosie was beyond thrilled. The bad part was that I'd really been hoping to talk to Ansel.

So I texted him.

> Hey—everything okay? Sharon came over, and she and Rosie have plans for the rest of the night.

ANSEL

> Thank you. Lots on my mind, and I just needed some time to myself. I know I owe you an explanation.

I swallowed down the lump of emotion that threatened. For whatever reason, Ansel's particular brand of honesty and earnestness really got to me. In a good way. Even though I was getting more and more frustrated at not knowing what was going on.

It's okay

ANSEL

No, it's still not okay.

Well, he wasn't wrong. Since it was obvious he wasn't in the mood to talk—he wouldn't have taken off if he actually felt like discussing whatever was bothering him—I didn't respond.

Instead, I blackened my screen and turned back to planning Allyson and Jake's honeymoon. I had plans on plans on plans for them to choose from. Who knew that after eight years of working in corporate, I'd find my calling as a honeymoon planner? I ended up falling asleep with the light on, and this morning I woke up to Cleocatra attempting to shred the spreadsheets I'd printed out at Ansel's the other day.

Clearly, my cat has no issues with giving me her thoughts on the formatting I spent way too long on. And honestly? Valid. No one will ever see those spreadsheets but me.

After feeding her, cleaning the litter box, and taking a shower, I finally let myself think about the past couple of days. *Really* think. Rosalie and I were followed and photographed, and Ansel hasn't given me any sort of explanation. In fact, he's done the very opposite and avoided the heck out of me. This, from the man who'd practically glued himself to my side over the past weeks whenever Rosie was out of sight. And who'd cherished me with his body and mouth night after night after putting her to bed.

And last night, instead of coming home and finally telling me what in the world was going on, he just...bolted? And sent the neighbor over?

I think I might be mad.

No, I *know* I am.

I blink, spitting my toothpaste into the sink and rinsing. As I grab the mouthwash and tip back a capful, I try to decide if it's weird to be proud of myself for getting mad. After all, New Elodie is trying very hard not to be so nice all the time. Look where it got me. So yeah. I'm mad.

"I'm mad," I say to my reflection.

It sounds ridiculous coming out of my mouth.

"I'm *mad*," I repeat.

Then I giggle. Because only I would try saying *I'm mad* as some kind of affirmation. Still, the feeling of anger...it's kind of nice. Nice in that I actually *feel* it.

Happy with myself, I finish getting ready and take myself over to the main house.

I find Ansel and Rosie exactly where I expect them to be: Rosie swinging her legs from her perch on the stool at the kitchen island, and Ansel frowning as he wrangles with her hair.

And even though I'm angry, I smile at them both.

"Will you give me fishbone braids, Elle Belle?" Rosie asks.

Ansel's mouth tips into a crooked grin. "I did an image search for them, but I got confused."

"Clearly," I say, looking at the mess he's created and grabbing the spray bottle to soak her curls. Leaning down to Rosalie, I tell her, "We can do it, but with your hair being so curly, it's going to take some time."

"Okay," she says, going back to her coloring book. "I'm hungry."

"Cereal okay this morning?" Ansel asks. "I need to leave a little early."

At that, my anger increases to a simmer.

"Okay," Rosie chirps again.

"Elodie?"

I glance up, raising an eyebrow in silent inquiry.

"Can we—?" He gestures to the front.

"I'll be right back," I tell Rosie, then walk out of the kitchen.

"Is everything okay?" Ansel asks when he joins me, his duffel already hanging on his shoulder.

"You tell me." The words come out shaky as I cross my arms. My heart races.

His brow furrows, then clears as realization dawns. "You're angry."

"Yes!" I exclaim, torn between excitement that he understood and also, you know, being *mad*.

"You're angry...with *me*," he continues, a flash of hurt crossing his expression.

"Yes," I confirm again.

His shoulders slump. "I'm sorry, Elodie."

"You should be," I say, trying hard to lean into the anger, even though I really want to drop it. "Because I thought we had something." My words dip, getting softer at the end. "Whatever we have, it's early, I know, but—"

He closes the distance and cups my face, staring down at me with such intensity that my breath catches. "No. It may be early, but that doesn't change what this is."

My heart squeezes, anger totally dropping in the wake of him. "You feel it, too?"

He nods, then presses his lips to mine. It's a soft kiss, sweet and gentle, full of promises. I wrap my arms around him, pulling him close and kissing him back with just as much emotion as he's giving me.

With a groan, he releases me. His eyes search mine. "I'll tell you everything tonight."

I fist his T-shirt. "Promise?"

His lips quirk up. "If I don't, will you get mad again?"

I smile back at the teasing. "Maybe."

He kisses me again. "I like you mad. It looks good on you." He lets me go and opens the door, then glances back. "Tonight. I promise."

Then he's gone, and I make my way back to the kitchen to start my day with Rosalie.

A few hours later, there's a knock at the door. Frowning, I look to where Rosie sits on the floor, working on a puzzle. "I'll be right back."

I look through the peephole. A small-statured blonde woman stands on the other side, slim and beautiful. Wishing I could see if there was anyone else on the street with her, I let out a sigh and open the door.

The woman smiles, but it doesn't quite reach her blue eyes. "Hi, is this the Miles residence?"

I nod. "Can I help you?"

"Elle Belle!" Rosie darts up behind me, clasping her tiny arms around my thigh and peeking to the side of my hip. "Who is it?"

Immediately, the woman's attention fixes on Rosalie.

And I know.

I know it with the certainty of gravity.

This is Rosie's mother.

"I'm Lauren," the woman says, kneeling to get a better look at her daughter. "What's your name?"

"Rosalie," she says shyly.

The woman's smile grows, but there's something oily about it. "It's nice to meet you, Rosalie," she coos. "I knew—"

"Why don't you go back to your puzzle, Rosie," I say, cutting off whatever Lauren was about to say.

Rosie looks up at me, blinking those innocent hazel eyes

before saying, "Okay!" She turns to run away, then pivots back to look at Lauren. "Nice to meet you!" Then she darts down the hall, her socked feet making no noise as she goes.

Lauren's attention slides to me, the smile falling off her face.

I look her up and down. "You should leave."

Her eyes narrow. "You aren't going to invite me in?"

I bark out a laugh. "You're kidding, right?"

She tilts her head, studying me. A snake about to strike. "Tell me something," she says. "When he fucks you, does he do that thing with his hips? You know the one," she purrs.

My jaw drops as heat rushes to my face. Did she really just say that? "I—" I start, but nothing comes amid the rushing of static in my head. "Leave."

I slam the door in her face, my heart pounding furiously. Behind it, all I hear is the sound of her laughter as she walks away.

Chapter 25
Ansel

I'M SORE AS hell, my muscles already barking from the intense drills and weights we went through today as I walk into the house.

"Daddy!" Rosalie throws herself into my arms even while I clock Elodie's expression as she rises from the couch. It's thunderous.

Part of me thrills to see it. *There's my angry girl.* But another part of me wants to shrink back and leave, because I'm positive that the dark fury on her face is one hundred percent my doing.

"Hi, sweetie," I tell Rosalie, giving her my full attention. "How was your day?"

"Good!" She wiggles in my arms. "I finished my puzzle, and we colored, and Elle Belle made me a butterfly grilled cheese sandwich."

"Sounds delicious," I say with a smile.

"And we had a lady visit," she continues, then twists to look at Elodie. "What was her name? Lauren?"

I stiffen, sliding my eyes to Elodie's.

Elodie raises a brow at me before saying, "Yes. Lauren."

Rage courses through me, followed immediately by fear. *I will tear that woman apart, limb by limb.* "And what did this Lauren want?"

Rosie shrugs, then wiggles down. "Dunno. Elle Belle told me to leave."

Lauren saw her. My thoughts spin, fury beginning to color my vision.

"Rosie bug, do you mind watching the movie by yourself while your dad and I get dinner ready?" Elodie asks, then tips her head to the kitchen.

I follow her. The second we're out of earshot, I start, "Elodie—"

She whirls, her finger pointing accusingly at me. "What the fuck was that woman doing here, Ansel?"

I blink, stunned. "I—"

"And how *dare* you leave me unprepared," she hisses. "I haven't asked about Rosie's mom because it was obvious you weren't ready to tell me. A choice that I stupidly respected. And clearly, that was the wrong thing to do, because but what happened today? Unacceptable."

"I know." Regret slams into me, shooting ice through my veins. *God, I am such an idiot. I should have gone after her last night. I should have told her a month ago.* I reach for her. "I'm so sorry. I should have told you ages ago."

"No shit!" she counters, moving from my touch. "Was *she* the one behind us being followed?"

I hesitate.

"Oh my God," she breathes. "This is all tied together. How could you leave me in the dark, Ansel?" Tears spring to her eyes, and she blinks them away.

I step toward her, and she backs up. "No. These are angry tears, not sad ones."

"I know." I study her body language as we move across

the kitchen, her going backward as I follow, until we come to a stop. She's pinned against the counter, caged between my arms, her chest heaving as she glares at me. I take her in, marveling at those gorgeous hazel irises that are so much like my daughter's. Take in the wild mass of brown curls that are so quintessentially Elodie that I can't imagine her any other way. Curls that give her the ability to tame Rosie's hair without a second thought. She's furious, but clarity slams into me about *why*. Still, I need to confirm it. "You're not angry at *me*, are you?"

She sucks in a breath, her whole body trembling, as she gives a shake of her head.

"You're angry because my not telling you made you feel like you couldn't protect Rosie."

A single tear slides down her cheek as the sweatshirt she wears slips down one shoulder. She lifts her chin and glares at me. "Don't you *ever* put me in that position again. Do you understand me?"

Desire, white-hot and unrelenting, surges through my body. I need her. Right now. I don't bother parsing it. Instead, I grip her hand and yank her to come with me.

"Ansel!" she hisses, still mad.

It only turns me on even more. I grip her hand harder, looking back to press a finger to my lips as we ascend the stairs.

Her eyes flash, but there's a spark of anticipation in them.

Up the stairs, down the hall, into my room, the door snicking softly into place behind us. The click of the lock. Her legs, freckled and thick and clad in loose lounge shorts. The line of bare stomach with each breath she takes.

"Take off your clothes," I demand roughly. My need for her is all-consuming, and it's taking everything in me not to throw her to the bed and have my way with her. To claim her and beg her forgiveness and lay my life in her hands in one fell swoop.

"Not until—"

"Take. Off. Your. Clothes."

She blinks. Swallows.

I clench my fists, and my next words come out with a growl. "Let me be clear. What you did—what you said down there—you've ruined me. You've cut me off at the knees, and I will never recover. Ever. So I need you naked. Immediately. And if you don't make it happen in the next two seconds, then I'm going to do it for you."

She hesitates for another second, and I start toward her.

It's enough to convince her. Eyes wide, she launches into action, pulling her clothes off at the same rate as I'm undressing, and then I'm on her.

Skin to skin, mouth to mouth. Teeth and tongues clash as I grip her hips so tight they'll bruise. She scrapes her nails down my back, and it hurts. It hurts so fucking good.

Ripping my mouth from hers, I push her to the bed and crawl on after her, throwing her legs apart and diving between them. She's already soaked, and I groan as her taste hits my tongue.

A low moan issues from her, and I nearly come right then. "Ansel," she groans. "Fuck. Now. I need you now."

I pull away from her delicious pussy and move to get the condom.

"No," she demands. "Bare. Fuck me bare."

I freeze.

She pins me with her eyes. "I'm on the pill. I know we're both clean. I can't have kids anyway. Now *fuck* me, Ansel. Fuck me until—"

I don't let her finish. I jerk her into position below me

and claim her mouth, pushing my tongue into her mouth as I slide my cock into her pussy.

We both groan, and I pull back and thrust in again. And again. And again. I'm nearly out of my mind with how good she feels. Hot and slick and...fuck. I can't think. Can't process anything except her. The smell of her skin, the scrape of her nails, the way she's writhing beneath me.

"God, yes," she chants as I thrust. "Right there. Please. Right there. More. Deeper. Fuck," she whimpers on an inhale. Her eyes are wide, irises blown as I pound into her, giving her what we both need, letting my actions tell her everything I haven't let myself utter.

I need you. I can't lose you. You're perfect. Stay with me. Be mine. Always.

We stare at each other, breathing hard, sweat beading. I want to cry. I want to roar. I want fucking everything, and it's all too much. Her walls tighten around me as she gasps my name, and in seconds, she detonates, her teeth digging into my shoulder and nails into my ass as I go harder, deeper, more, *more*, until I find my own release. I barely repress the shout, groaning into her neck as I give one final thrust, feeling my cock jerk inside her still-clenching walls.

"Elodie," I groan softly. "Elodie, Elodie, Elodie."

She hums in response, digging her nails into my sweaty scalp before trailing them down my back. "That was..."

"That was," I agree, kissing her neck and making my way to her mouth. I take it deeply, relishing the kiss as I thrust one last time into her. Finally, I pull out and roll to the side, trying to catch my breath.

A quiet giggle emerges from Elodie. "Did you really just do that?"

I turn my head to smile at her, sated. "Which part?"

Her eyes glitter. "Get turned on because I was mad about Lauren?"

I rise on my elbow, tracing a finger over and around one breast, then the other. Finally, I meet her eyes. "Yes." I huff a laugh. "I know it doesn't make any sense, but...yeah."

Gentling her expression, she says, "Good." Then she leans up to kiss me. "Come on." She sits up, then pauses, bending to kiss my tattoo. "Love these things," she murmurs, gripping my thighs as she kisses it.

I watch as she rises from the bed, her ass wiggling deliciously as she walks to the en-suite bathroom and shuts the door.

I take my turn next, and when I emerge, Elodie is already dressed, her hand on the doorknob.

"Where do you think you're going?" I ask.

"Dinner won't make itself," she answers, opening the door as I grab my underwear and shorts from the floor. "But this changes nothing. You owe me a very, *very* thorough story."

I nod. "I do. After Rosie goes to bed. And Elle?"

She turns back from where she'd already started to leave.

"What you said back there." I jerk my head to the bed behind me. "We're going to talk about that, too."

She lets out a long exhale. "You first. But, yeah. Deal."

I love her. It hits me like a damn freight train. I love her. Fuck me. I love her.

Smiling, I finish dressing and hustle downstairs.

Chapter 26
Elodie

I GRAB THE Irish liqueur and make each of us a drink before joining Ansel on the outside patio. The night is far from quiet, crickets and frogs and cicadas all making their usual noises. It's muggy, too, and the overhead fan serves only to move the humid air around.

Ansel straightens from where he'd been turning on the candles, his attention finding the drinks. He grins. "Smart woman."

I hand him one of the glasses. He takes it, clinking it against mine before bringing it to his lips. We drink, then take a seat.

"Tell me," I say without preamble.

He gives a reluctant smile. "Just diving right in, are we?"

I give him a look. "Yes. We are."

He sighs and runs a hand over his face, scratching at his beard. "There's not much to tell. Once I got out of college, I was never one to, um, indulge in the opportunities that being a rugby player presented."

"Opportunities like rugger huggers?"

He winces. "Yes. I hate the term, but...yes." After a beat, he continues, "But there was one night. We'd won our first game—not just of the season, but the first game as an official team in the league—and one of the guys, Jake, had made the winning try. It was the first try he'd made on the team, and there's a tradition." He breaks off, smiling sheepishly. "I'm not sure you want to hear this."

"Jake, the giant Samoan who's marrying Allyson? Jake, the man whose honeymoon I'm planning?"

He nods. "The one and the same."

"Oh, I want to hear all of it," I assure him with a smile. "Spill it."

With a grin, he tells me, "Any time a player on the team scores their first try in a game, they have to take their clothes off at the bar, and we throw beer on them."

I let out a shocked laugh. "What?"

His cheeks tinge pink in the candlelight. "It's tradition. I don't make the rules. They have to get naked and run a lap around the bar. And we're all waiting, usually with pitchers of beer, to splash on them as they go."

Still smiling, I ask, "And what about the poor patrons who aren't rugby players?"

He shrugs. "They...get wet? Enjoy the show?"

I laugh. "Poor Jake."

"Poor *Jake*?" Ansel says, pretending to be shocked. "I'll have you know that I was the first one to have to do it on that team."

I leer at him. "Bet that was a fabulous sight to behold."

"Shut up," he laughs.

"Wait—is this still a thing? This tradition?"

He shakes his head. "Sort of, but we don't do it in public bars anymore."

"That whole famous, pro athlete thing?" I tease.

"Something like that," he grins. Then he grows serious again. "So, that night, Jake has to do the thing. And there's the usual batch of women hanging out at the bar with us, hoping to get lucky." He exhales. "Lauren was one of them."

I stay quiet.

"And...I don't know. I drank more than I should have. We were all having a great time, and I thought, why not? Just once, right? I'd not seen her around, so I thought maybe she wasn't one of the—"

"Rugger huggers?" I offer.

His mouth twists. "Yeah. We went to her place. I wore a condom. I swear I did. And when it was over, I called an Uber and went home."

"Just like that?"

"Just like that," he confirms. "She walked me to the door, and I left, and...yeah. That was that." He swallows. "And then a year later, everything changed."

My stomach sinks.

He reaches for his drink, downing it in one swallow. "The Granite were rising stars. We weren't Atlanta royalty like the Braves or Falcons, but we were starting to be recognized. I got my first sponsorship deal. The Granite leadership knew what they had with me, and they offered me a stupidly generous deal if I locked in a ten-year contract. Which is unheard of. Especially in a league that was still trying to break through and find its fans."

He looks so pained that I reach over and put my hand on his knee.

"I was riding high, Elodie. For the first time in my life, it felt like everything was locking into place. My parents had just retired, I'd bought this amazing house, and I had friends, *real* friends, for the first time in my life." He looks down. "I was so fucking happy. Invincible." Guilt laces his every word.

"As you should have been," I insist. "You deserve to be happy, Ansel."

He shakes his head.

"*Yes.*" But it's clear he doesn't believe me.

"One morning, I get up like always. And I do what I always do, go about my routine without a care in the world. Until I hear a knock at my door."

I wait, letting him get the words out.

"I answer, and Sharon's there. At her feet is a tiny little baby in a car carrier. And Sharon's looking at me, and I'm looking at her, until she finally asks me why there's a baby on my doorstep." He pauses. "It was eleven in the morning. And I—I still don't know how long she was even out there." His voice cracks on the last words as he meets my eyes.

There isn't anything I can say to that. I reach for his hand and squeeze.

He exhales roughly and clears his throat, swiping at his eye. "So. We bring the baby inside, and there's an envelope with her birth certificate and a note." He lets out a bitter laugh, and when he speaks again, anger laces his words. "She left a fucking *note*, Elodie. Like a coward. I still have it. I wanted to burn it, but Sharon wouldn't let me. Said I might need it one day." His jaw clenches. "My name was listed as the father on the birth certificate. Lauren's name was there as the mother. Rosalie wasn't quite three months old."

"Oh, God," I whisper, the reality of what he must have gone through crashing through me.

He chokes out a laugh. "Yeah. That's about what I said, too."

"But what if she's not—" I begin.

"I had a DNA test," he interrupts. "Not that it would have mattered."

I swallow hard and force the tears away. "And that was it? She never contacted you again?"

"She did. Later that day. But only to make sure I had her. That I—that I was going to keep her." His eyes turn to steel. "She said she would give her up for adoption if I didn't."

I inhale a sharp breath.

"But Elodie, the second I looked at that tiny little girl, all scrunched up in her carrier and eyeing me with all the sass she still gives me today, I was a fucking goner. I hadn't even read the note yet. I didn't need to. I knew. I just *knew*, and in that moment..." He swallows and meets my gaze, a small smile on his lips. "That's when I became a father."

The love in his eyes as he says it, the way his whole body seems to soften at the admission, it simply undoes me. The final thread that had held me together disappears, evaporating into the muggy night. I lean over and kiss him, my heart feeling like it might actually burst with the way I feel about him. "You," I say against his lips.

He pulls me close, not releasing the kiss. "Me, what?"

"You are incredible."

He laughs. "In case you haven't noticed, I'm barely holding it together."

I lean back and study him, pushing his silky hair back from his face, his eyes glimmering with mirth behind his glasses. "Let me help."

His eyes seem to shutter. "I can't ask that of you."

"I'm already helping, Ansel," I remind him, forcing him to look at me. "In case *you* haven't noticed."

He doesn't respond at first. Then he says, "My lawyer is working on things. To keep her away from us. From

Rosalie," he corrects quickly, seeming to realize what he said. "And...it *was* because of her that you and Rosie were followed. I'm not sure how many times it's happened, either."

Fear streaks through me. "And now?"

"Now, I've put a restraining order on her. Or tried to, at least. But I don't know if it'll make a difference. Something tells me..." He sighs. "I have a bad feeling about everything. That's all."

I bite my lip, letting it all sink in.

His eyes dart between mine. "There's one more thing."

I wait.

"Lauren showed up here last night."

"She *what*?" I growl the words, a protective anger rising so quickly in me it's dizzying.

He nods grimly. "That's why I left—I was so angry, and I didn't want you or Rosie to see me like that. I'm sorry I left. But I just—I was furious. I didn't trust myself to go inside."

I grip his hand and squeeze. "Thank you for telling me."

"She threatened to go to the media about us."

I start. "Why? But why would anyone care about us?"

He grins wryly. "I keep telling you we're famous, Elodie."

"I know."

He smiles. "I...don't think you really do. You've not had to see anything since it's the off-season, but..." He trails off and shrugs.

"No one bothered us on that one date, so you're not Travis-Kelce-level famous."

"No," he admits with a chuckle. "I most certainly am not. It's not so much that it's intrusive, per se, but if Lauren says something to the media—"

"Let her," I declare, squaring my shoulders.

Ansel studies me. "I'm not sure you're ready for that."

A flare of indignation courses through me. "What's that supposed to mean?"

"Easy, tiger," he says, rubbing his hands along my thighs. "I only mean that I want you to carefully consider the ramifications of something like this happening. It's not easy, being in the public eye."

I think back to conversations I've had with Kari. The nightmare PR scenarios she's dealt with over the course of her time with the Granite and other companies. "I'm ready."

His eyes flare with surprise.

"Nice Girl Elodie is gone, remember?" I say with a smile. "I can handle it. I can handle *Lauren*."

"Of that, I have no doubt," he says. Then he pulls me to him for a kiss. When we break apart, he says, "One more thing."

I worry my bottom lip, knowing what's coming.

"Tell me. Earlier. When you said—"

My pulse kicks up. I know what he's referring to, but I ask anyway. "That I can't have kids?"

His chin dips slightly in confirmation, then his eyes dart to my neck and chest as I take a huge breath. "It's okay, Elle," he says quietly.

I nod, more to myself than anything. "I know."

He takes my hand in his. "You don't have to tell me if you don't want to."

I clear my throat. "It's fine." It's not fine. It's not even close to fine.

Because I am *terrified*. I don't know what possessed me to blurt it out when I did. I was just...ravenous. And I clearly wasn't thinking. But I gather the reserves of strength that seem, remarkably, to keep going, and clutch it to me. I meet his eyes. His kind, beautiful eyes.

"It's," I start, then stop. *Breathe.* "It's what I said. I can't have kids. There's nothing wrong with me, not anything that doctors can pinpoint, but, um." I break off, swallowing. "My ex and I. He'd wanted kids early, before we got married, so when nothing happened naturally, we both got tested. He was fine. I...wasn't. We never went down IVF. It all—*we*—went downhill pretty fast after that. It just...wasn't meant to be, I guess."

I reach for my drink and take a giant sip, reveling in the cold liquid while I take stock of myself. *I'm still here.* But I'm not the one I need to worry about. It's the man in front of me. What if he thinks I'm just as pathetic as Jeremy did? *What if he rejects me just like my mother?*

I tilt the glass back, finishing the drink off before finally steeling myself to meet his eyes.

And there, looking back at me, is everything I could ever hope for. His caramel brown eyes are filled with understanding, sorrow, acceptance. He puts his hand on the strip of couch between us, palm up. A gesture of comfort.

I press my palm to his, and he threads our fingers together.

Finally, he speaks. "I love you."

I blink. I didn't hear him correctly.

"It's probably not the right time to tell you that," he says. "In fact, it may be the absolute worst time. But I do." He blows out a breath, then gives me a smile.

God, that *smile.* It's bright and beautiful, lighting up his face in a way I have never seen before. My heart cracks wide open yet again, growing so broad and deep that the only thing to fill it—the only person in the world who could possibly fill it—is the man beaming at me. "I love you,

Elodie Cole. And you don't have to say anything back. In fact, please don't. But I—"

I cut him off, palming his cheeks and rising onto my knees as he pulls me onto his lap. Then I kiss the hell out of him. His arms band around me, strong and sure, pulling me as close to him as we can get. I bite back a sob, then a laugh, still kissing him. Utterly unable to get hold of my emotions. Impossible to grab onto any one thing as they swirl and eddy around me. *He loves me.*

He loves me.

He *loves* me.

In seconds, the kiss turns desperate, needy. As if both of us are too full of feeling and need it out. I keen into his mouth, and he hisses in response. "Baby, *fuck.*"

I pull away, yanking his glasses off and tossing them to the side before clawing his shirt. "Skin." I lean back, giving him room to reach behind his neck and yank the shirt off in one smooth motion. I stare as he moves, his tan muscles rippling in the light, before leaning back to kiss him. My hips writhe, grinding on his lap.

He rips his mouth from mine and gasps. But before he can say a word, my hands are already at the waistband of his shorts, God *bless* these mesh shorts and how easy they slide down. And then his hands are moving up my thighs and into my shorts.

He curses, then grinds out, "You aren't wearing anything under here."

"No," I pant, desperate.

In one swift move, he plunges a finger into me, and I gasp. His eyes are bright, watchful, as a second finger joins in.

I move a hand behind his neck to brace myself. "I want—"

"Tell me," he says, his voice raw. "Tell me."

"I want your cock," I breathe out.

His grin is feral. "Good girl," he groans, pulling his fingers out. While I watch, he brings them up to his mouth and sucks them in, slowly, his eyes closing as the taste of me hits his tongue. He moans, then meets my eyes again as he pulls them out, licking them clean.

I whimper. "That's so fucking sexy."

His answering smile is blinding. "God, I love it when you cuss."

I don't answer, just rise and grab his cock. Wordlessly, he moves my shorts to the side, and I lower myself onto him, the feel of him bare just as thrilling and hot as it was earlier today. He groans, tilting his head back and shutting his eyes, finally, *finally* letting himself just feel. It's a small victory, perhaps, but it's so hard-won that I thrill to see it.

He's so sexy like this. Wide open and vulnerable, hiding nothing. Now that he's inside me, thick and long and filling me to the brim, I move slowly, unhurried, luxuriating in the feel of him deep inside me. The soft light flickers against his skin. His throat bobs as he swallows, and the sounds coming out of him, desperate moans and whispers of praise, send my heart racing.

He brings his head back up and opens his eyes, and I lean back down to kiss him. "Ansel," I whisper. I grind against him, and he closes his eyes.

"You feel so good," he murmurs, pushing his hands beneath my shirt and then pulling it off. He angles up, taking a nipple into his mouth through the bralette, soaking the soft cotton and pulling a sound of pleasure out of me.

I rise and down, riding him slowly as he pushes the fabric up and sucks at my nipple again, the sensation a bright, hot thing that brings me closer to the edge. Then he shoves a hand down my shorts, finding my clit and pressing onto it. I hitch a breath, letting my forehead rest on his head as sensations threaten to overwhelm me.

He laughs softly, pulling off my breast and tugging my mouth to his. His tongue thrusts into my mouth, hot and wet, as his free hand wraps around my ass. He holds me in place as his hips rise, pushing him deeper into me.

"Fuck," I let out.

Then he's got both his hands beneath my hips, holding me up as he pushes into me, his strong thighs working over-time as I grip the back of the couch.

"Elodie," he breathes. "Come for me."

"I can't," I say, feeling it so close but knowing it's not going to happen.

"Play with yourself," he says, slowing his thrusts and turning them into swirls.

My cheeks burn, but I do it, sliding my hand down my shorts and pressing onto the bundle of nerves.

His eyes flare. "Fuck, that worked," he murmurs. "I can feel you tighten around me." He keeps moving. "I will always make sure you come, Elodie. Always."

The way he says it, so certain and sure of himself, the future embedded in that promise, sends a wave of desire through me.

He grunts again. "God*damn*, woman." He picks up the pace, and as I press and swirl my fingers around myself, he fucks me. Pushing and thrusting, finding the spot that makes me gasp repeatedly. "There it is," he says triumphantly, still working me. Still fucking me. "Let me hear you, Elodie. Let me hear you come."

I detonate, bearing down on him as I groan, the sound loud enough to drown out any other noise.

He climaxes with me, smacking his hips into mine and

holding through his release. I pull his mouth to mine and kiss him as we both come down. After a moment, he relaxes, pulling me to him as I lay my head on his shoulder, my thighs shaking.

"That is the best sound in the world," he says, running a palm over my curls and kissing my forehead.

"What is?" I murmur against his neck.

"You coming."

Chapter 27
Elodie

I WAKE UP in Ansel's bed, sun streaming through the blinds.

"Good morning, Daddy," a tiny voice whispers on Ansel's side of the bed. "Did you and Elle Belle have a sleepover?"

Well, no hiding this now, I think, rising onto an elbow and smiling at the sweet little girl peering over the bed. Thank goodness I put on one of his T-shirts last night.

Beside me, Ansel's voice is deep and scratchy as he answers his daughter. "Good morning, Rosie Posie. Did you let me sleep late?"

"Yes, but now I'm hungry."

"Me, too," Ansel says. "Maybe I need a Rosie sandwich."

Suddenly, he's grabbing a squealing five-year-old and pulling her into the bed in between us, snorting and smacking his lips while Rosie laughs hysterically.

"Save me, Elle Belle!" Rosie giggles, clinging onto me while Ansel pretends to chomp on her.

"Okay, okay," Ansel finally says, "I guess I can eat regular food. Give me and Elodie a few minutes, okay?"

Rosalie scampers off the bed, leaving the room with an "Okay, Daddy!"

I start to throw the covers off, but Ansel growls and yanks me to him, all warmth and hard body and smelling of sleep and deliciousness. His hand slides up the shirt and cups my breast while he threads our legs together. There's no mistaking the hardness between his...or the wetness between mine. "Where do you think you're going?"

I meet his eyes. They're twinkling and bright. "To get dressed so we can feed Rosie?"

"Not yet." He starts to slide under the covers between my legs, then pops back up, his eyes glimmering. "Let's test my theory."

"What theory is that?"

"The one where I test, yet again, how good you are at staying so quiet that the kid down the hall has no idea you're coming."

I widen my eyes. "Ansel!" I whisper-hiss. But he disappears beneath the covers again. "Don't you—*oh*," I break off as his mouth meets my pussy, my hips bucking up of their own accord.

Of course, I *can* be quiet.

But it's not easy.

We make our way downstairs a short while later, my face flushed and my body humming. Ansel gets the coffee going while I inspect the fridge for breakfast inspiration. After grabbing some ingredients, I turn and find Ansel studying me.

"What?"

"I'd like to tell her," he says, his voice quiet.

"Tell who about what?" I ask. I suspect I know what he means, but I also don't want to hope.

"Tell Rosie about us."

My whole chest warms at the confirmation. "Really?"

"I'm bound to get questions about why we had a sleepover, and if you can spend the night in her bed, and if the three of us can sleep in the same bed, and so on," he says with a grin. "So, if you're okay with it...yeah," he finishes. "I'd like to tell her."

I'm not sure I can smile any wider. "That sounds amazing."

He nods. "Then it's settled."

Over a simple breakfast of eggs, bacon, and toast, Ansel broaches the topic. "So, Rosie Posie."

"Yes, Daddy?" Rosie answers, her mouth full of eggs.

"Mouth." He arches an eyebrow at her, the scar going through it that much more pronounced. When she closes her mouth, he continues, "You like Elodie, right?"

"Mm-hmm," she hums, taking a giant bite of toast and lining the outsides of her cheeks with grape jelly.

"So, what would you say if I told you that I wanted her to be my girlfriend?"

"Like Rapunzel and Flynn Rider?"

Ansel hesitates, so I take over. "Yes, sort of like Rapunzel and Flynn Rider," I answer.

She smiles. "I like that." Then she looks over at me. "Can we go to the thrift store today?"

Now it's my turn to hesitate, because it's Saturday, and normally that's when Ansel and Rosie spend a lot of time together. But Ansel just glances at me, the look on his face wide open even as he gives me the sexiest smile. To Rosie, he says, "You don't want to hang out with me like we always do on Saturdays?"

She shrugs. "I mean, if we have to."

I hold back a snort of laughter.

"But if Elle Belle is living with us now, then won't we all see each other all the time?"

Ansel and I freeze, looking at each other with *now what?* expressions.

"Um," I start.

"We should probably go get Cleocatra," she continues, popping a piece of bacon in her mouth. "I bet she's lonely. And she's *definitely* hungry. Right, Elle Belle?"

"Tell you what," Ansel says. "Let's let Elodie do some things on her own for a bit this morning. I'd like to take you to the park."

She shrugs. "Okay."

Later, as Rosie runs upstairs to get dressed and gather her hair supplies, Ansel pulls me to him in the kitchen.

"Sorry about that." He smiles down at me, then laughs. "I didn't realize we were moving in together."

My cheeks heat. "Yeah...you'll talk to her?"

"Of course. I need to tell her about Lauren, too. Not the bad stuff, exactly, but she needs to know—" He breaks off and sighs. I squeeze him tight, and he tries again. "She needs to know about her, in case things..."

When it's clear he can't finish the sentence, I simply put my head on his chest and hug him. "It's going to be okay."

"Is it?" His voice is thick.

I pull back to look at him. "Yes. You're her father, Ansel. You're the one who's been here the whole time, loving her, taking care of her. *That's* what matters."

Fear, stark and unguarded, lines his face. "I hope you're right. Because if Lauren—if she takes my little girl—"

"That's not going to happen," I insist.

He swallows. "But if it does."

"Ansel. It is not going to happen. In no world does this happen." I sound a lot more certain than I feel, but it doesn't matter. If Ansel needs me to be the strong one, then I will be. It's that simple.

"Okay. Okay," he repeats, looking out the kitchen window. Then he releases a nervous laugh. "I don't suppose you have any ideas on what I should tell Rosie?"

I hold my hands up. "I got nothing, boss."

He winces. "Oh, shit."

"What?"

Gesturing between the two of us, he clarifies, "Us. This. You're her nanny."

"Did that slip your mind?" I smile softly. "I'll keep doing it, Ansel. And if you need someone past August, I'll do that, too."

He shakes his head. "No. No way. The preschool should have a spot. Besides, you have your business to launch. I'll figure something out if I have to, but it should be okay."

Crossing my arms, I press my lips together. "Let me help you, Ansel."

"Nope," he says, pulling me to him and kissing my forehead. "I got this."

Chapter 28
Ansel

I T TOOK ROSIE all of a week to get Elodie moved in with us.

She started out simple, suggesting that Elodie should have some pajamas for sleepovers. Then swimsuits for the pool. Then clothes to change into after the pool. And then the cat.

Frankly, it's impressive, and I can't decide if her ability to make it happen is something I should be terrified of or not. What I *do* know is that, despite me being nervous as hell to explain about Lauren, she took the news pretty well, all things considered. She's known that most kids have two parents, and that we were different because the woman who had her decided to give her to me. Which is a hard enough message to send without making Rosie feel unwanted. I took it farther this time, explaining that I'd heard from the woman who'd given her to me, and that she wanted to know how Rosie was doing. Rosie, of course, wanted to know what I told her, and I responded that I'd been truthful: that Rosie was a monster who ate bugs for breakfast. She seemed to take it in stride, and with each new question she's lobbed at me about it, I've been able to answer.

We haven't seen or heard anything from Lauren, though, and if there's anything to truly be worried about, it's that. It's infuriating. I should be happy. I should be fucking *ecstatic*. Instead, I can't stop the low-grade anxiety that runs through my every waking moment.

It gets worse when Coach texts me for a Sunday afternoon meeting at the Granite headquarters. He won't tell me what it's about, only that I need to be there.

When I walk into the conference room he told me to go to, I'm faced with an entire team of people: not just Coach, but the assistant coach Craig, the president and owner of the team, a woman who looks suspiciously like a lawyer, and Kari and her boss.

"Ansel, have a seat." Coach gestures to the table.

"What's going on?" I don't bother sitting.

"It's not bad," Kari says, ignoring the look of consternation her boss gives her. She inclines her head to the empty chair.

I approach it like I'm coming up on a wounded animal, swiveling it out and easing into the cool black leather. "Is anyone going to start talking?"

"Coach Boden is leaving," Scott Bland, the owner, says.

I frown in confusion and surprise.

"And I'm taking Craig with me," Coach adds. "We're heading to Europe. Team over there made me an offer I can't refuse."

"You telling everyone on the team individually?" I try to joke.

Mr. Bland folds his hands on the table, and I realize that all of them are in suits. Even Kari is polished, her hair pulled back into a sleek ponytail, and she's wearing a deep yellow suit jacket.

"We'd like you to be the interim head coach," the owner says.

I lean back in the chair and bark out a laugh. "Me? That's hilarious. You can't possibly be serious."

"They're serious, Miles," Coach says.

But there's no way. "I've never coached," I tell the table. "Ever. I don't know the first thing about it." My head pounds, uncertainty pumping through me. A glass of water is pushed my way, and I take it, gulping it down.

"I'll get you up to speed," Coach continues. "We'll spend the next week going over everything before I leave."

"You're leaving in a week?" I nearly yelp the words. "How long have you known?"

Kari's boss, Frank, leans forward. "That doesn't matter. What matters is that everyone at this table believes you're the man for the job."

"But—" I start.

"It's just until we find a replacement." Mr. Bland raises his palms as if he's trying to calm me down. "It won't be too long. Maybe a month."

"No way," I protest. "This is ridiculous. *I don't coach.* I have never been a coach. I am the last—"

"We're at a critical point here. Contracts are going out in a couple of days, and we need to keep the team focused while we get someone in place. You're the team captain. You've run practices. You know the drills. You can coach the team in your sleep, even if you don't know it."

I raise an eyebrow at him. Since when does the team president know this much about me? Since now, I suppose.

He keeps going. "Everyone looks up to you."

My head is spinning. And even though I think this is

the dumbest thing they could possibly do, I'm already strategizing. Looking for a way to maximize this opportunity for the team. "Have you decided who's getting renewed? Which tryouts are staying?"

"We thought you might want to have a say in that," Coach offers. "Since Craig and I won't be here."

My eyes nearly bug out. "There's an exhibition game in two weeks. You truly haven't put anyone on *contracts*?"

"It's been...things have been up in the air," Mr. Bland says. "We made sure to pay the boys for the summer intensive you're single-handedly responsible for," he intones, as if it's my fault, "but we've been tied up with other pressing matters."

I fight the rising panic clawing at my chest. "What the hell does that mean?"

"You don't need to know that," he answers.

Judging from his tone, I won't be getting any other explanation. The last thing I want is to be operating in the dark, but at the same time, how much of this shit do I really want to know? Because there's no doubt that the more I know, the more I'll be responsible for. I unclench my fists. "Fine. Are you going to be here for the exhibition game?"

They shake their heads.

Jesus fuck. "What am I missing?" I press. "Why me?"

"Look," Scott says, nodding at the person I presume is a lawyer before returning his focus to me, "you're the highest-paid player in the league."

"Precisely why I should *play*," I remind him.

The lawyer pushes a contract in front of me.

"And you will be," Scott says. "We'll have someone in place before the first game of the season."

"But not the exhibition game," Craig pipes up. "That's likely one you'll be on the sidelines for."

We'll see about that.

"We need you, Miles," Coach says. "You're the only one that makes sense. Look at the contract."

I sigh, but glance down.

And barely manage to keep my jaw from hitting the polished oak table when I see the amount. It's ludicrous. How much are the coaches paid annually if this is what I'm getting for what's likely a month's worth of work?

"I'll be honest with you, Ansel," the owner begins.

I meet his eyes across the table.

"You're the linchpin of this team. We need you. We need you on the pitch, *and* we need you to do this for us."

Well, shit. I take a deep breath and nod, trying to ignore the weight that settles on my shoulders. "Okay," I tell them. "I'll do it."

"Excellent." Scott rises from the table and leaning to shake my hand. He buttons his suit jacket and looks at the table. "I'll leave you all to sort this out, then. See you on the pitch."

I don't have a chance to say anything before he's gone, and the lawyer is setting a pen in front of me.

"I'm Jade," she says, then points at the contract and rises from the table. "I'll give you a few minutes to review."

"My agent needs to look at this," I counter, but she shakes her head.

"Lewis Jones?"

I nod. I took a chance on Lewis when he was straight out of the NFL and starting his agency. He's blown up, so busy with the rest of his clients that he barely has time for me. Lucky for him, I'm easy.

Jade continues, her brow furrowing, "I had him look at it last night. He didn't tip you off?"

I wince. "He texted me, but I was busy." Busy with my

head between Elodie's legs. I'd planned to call him today. In retrospect, I should have called him on the way in.

She shrugs. "Call him now if you want, but I need it signed before you leave." With that, she opens her phone and turns away from me, the dark wooden beads on the end of her braids knocking together as she goes.

Frank slides yet another piece of paper in front of me. "This is the statement we'll release to the media. Have a look at it and make sure you're good with the quote we've written for you."

"Once you're finished with all that," Coach adds, "swing into my office and we'll work out a schedule for the week."

The beginnings of a headache start to form behind my eyes as Kari produces a bag from beneath the table. "What is that?" I ask her.

She, at least, has the decency to look a bit embarrassed. Or at least aware that all of this might be a bit much. "Swag."

"Swag?" I say incredulously. "You're kidding."

"Nope." She pushes it closer. "You'll need coaching gear for the press."

"For the press?" I nearly choke. "I thought you were doing a press release. Surely that's enough."

"It's not," Frank states flatly. "Kari, I'll be in my office. Get that out once he reviews it."

I watch him go. Glancing back at Kari, I say, "He's a prick, isn't he?"

She gives me a wry grin. "Sort of, but look at it this way: at least he's in your corner."

I raise my eyebrows. "That's supposed to be comforting?"

"Believe it or not, yes." She claps my shoulder. "Now, read that quote."

I look at it and shrug. "It's fine." Not like I could come up with anything better, frankly.

She scoops it up with a smile of thanks and leaves, leaving me with the lawyer and my coaches. Or, I guess, former coaches.

What the hell have I just gotten myself into?

Chapter 29
Elodie

"Elle Belle, are you ready?" Rosalie bounces on her toes, looking ridiculously cute in her Atlanta Granite shirt and shorts. Tiny teal and black stars dot her cheeks, and she's clutching Cleocatra to her chest.

"Almost. Is Cleo breathing?" I joke as I check my outfit in the mirror, a little nervous about my choice.

"Cleocatra loves being held," she insists, practically turning her body sideways to look at the cat. "See? She's smiling."

To be honest, I think my cat has simply resigned herself to the force of nature that is Rosalie. "She'd probably like to be put down," I say gently. "Why don't you give her some treats since we'll be gone for a while?"

Rosie cheers and whirls away, Cleo's tail swishing behind her back as they go.

I chuckle and attempt to wrangle the rogue curls into submission, but give up. There's only so much that can be done, and I don't want to be late for the exhibition game.

The stadium is filled with people by the time we get

there, a sea of dark teal and black for the Granite outpacing the red and white for the opposing team. Rosie is almost beside herself, chattering and pointing out the various pieces of merchandise she wants.

"I'll ask Miss Kari," she says, tapping her chin thoughtfully. "I bet she can get it for me."

"I bet she can," I agree, guiding us up to the VIP section where the team's friends and family are. Lucky for us, the suites have both an enclosed section and outside seating, because late August in Atlanta is not for the faint of heart.

Inside the suite, Rosie makes a dash for the fridge to get the juice she's only allowed on game days, then whirls to grab a pre-packaged bag of popcorn before running back to me. "I'm gonna go outside!" she declares.

"Be polite," I remind her, and watch her dash to the door.

"I think she's excited," says a familiar voice, the Australian accent oddly similar to a Southern drawl.

"Sam!" I exclaim, reaching for the woman to give her a hug. "Your brother made the cut?"

She smiles broadly. "He did." Then she nods to where Rosie is situating herself in the front row of the outside section. "Is that Coach Miles' daughter?"

"He *hates* that." I laugh, rolling my eyes. "But yes, that's Rosalie."

Sam scans my outfit, her eyes sparkling. "And what about you? Still just the nanny?" There's no mistaking the suggestion in her voice.

My cheeks burn as I twist my lips. "Not exactly."

Sam cackles. "I *knew* it!"

Allyson appears, and I make the introductions. Kari shows up a few minutes later.

"Miss Ma'am," Kari says, circling her finger at my shirt. "You trying to break hearts today?"

"She doesn't know that Ansel's the one the ladies are here to see, does she?" Allyson jokes.

"Oh, is that how it works here?" Sam says.

"Look at the signs," Allyson says. "I'm not lying."

We grab bottles of water and head to the seats outside, and Allyson starts pointing them out. "See?"

I have to hold back my laughter as I scan the crowd. Sure enough, there are more than a few handmade posters that are Ansel-specific. One proposes marriage, and another begs the opposing team to leave his pretty face intact. A third offers to be the next thing he puts on his thigh. But it's not just Ansel the crowd is here for—plenty of the guys have fans.

"This is really cool," I tell them.

"Not bad for an American crowd," Sam says.

Kari laughs. "Sam, this is *amazing* for an American crowd—trust me."

Soon enough, the announcer brings us all to attention and introduces the New England Free Jacks. The guys run onto the pitch and take their spots on the sidelines. When the Granite is introduced, the crowd loses its mind. But when they run out, I'm shocked to see that Ansel is in gear to actually play, a big number 10 on his back like always, not the coaching getup I saw him leave in.

"Um, what's going on?" Allyson asks.

"Don't look at me," I say with a shrug. Then I grin. "But if he's playing, then that's awesome, because I finally get to see it!"

The announcer seems to be in on the plan, however, because he doesn't break stride in announcing the line-up. Sure enough, Ansel is slated to play fly-half.

Ansel gathers the team around him, and something in my chest squeezes to see him like this: leading. Being looked up to. He's spent the past two weeks utterly focused on getting the team ready for this game, his office utter chaos, strewn in yellow notepad paper sporting half-drawn plays. I want nothing more than for them to win. He deserves it so much.

The game kicks off, and I'm riveted. I've spent the summer learning all I can about the game, watching old videos, and getting Rosie's assistance on things when I can. I could have asked Ansel, sure, but where's the fun in that? It's been far more entertaining to ask Rosie and hear her explanations.

"Go go go!" Sam screams, bringing me out of my haze as she shakes my arm and jumps up and down.

I look, and see Ansel absolutely flying down the pitch, ball cradled against him, his powerful legs moving in a blur as he eats up the yards. But then the other team is on him, and he's tossing the ball back to another guy, who tosses to another, and another. Since it's against the rules to toss the ball forward, the backward tossing moves the ball down the pitch to the try line, but it's slow-going. Ansel gets open again, and the crowd goes wild as the ball makes its way back into his hands. He turns, narrowly missing a tackle by a massive player on the other team, and shoves his arm out to push another player back as he hauls the distance to the try line.

Right as he closes in, two steps away, he's tackled. But it doesn't matter, because Ansel flattens himself out, reaching his arm forward with the ball and getting it right over the line before his body hits the pitch.

"Yes!" I'm yelling and hollering as Rosie's arms fly up, popcorn spilling everywhere.

Ansel pops up and tosses the ball to the ref. Then he turns to the VIP section and points at us before making a heart with his hands and putting it over his heart.

The crowd roars. I don't hesitate to make the same heart over my chest right back, and when I look down at Rosie, she's smiling brightly up at me, her hands in the same position. "Is that something he always does for you, Rosie?"

She shakes her head, beaming. "Nope. That's new. He told me to pay lots of attention because he'd do something new if he scored a try, so that was it!"

I might burst with pride and happiness. *That's my man.* And next to me? The sweetest little girl in the world. I hug her to me.

We continue to watch, and it takes everything in me not to chew my nails to the quick with as stressful as the game is. Ansel plays almost the entire game, and every time the cameras give us a close-up of him on the scoreboard, he looks nothing but stressed.

"You ready for the gala?" Kari asks.

I nod. "I still think it's wild that they have it the same night as the exhibition game."

"Fans love it, but you're right. It's a lot for the players. But tell me you're wearing the gown you showed me."

A swoop of giddy anticipation sweeps through me. "I am," I confirm.

"She looks pretty in it, too," Rosie says.

"Of course she does," Kari agrees, squeezing me to her. Lowering her voice, she asks, "Has he seen you in this, though?"

"No," I confirm.

She waggles her eyes. "Good luck not being late, then."

I shove her playfully and turn my attention back to the game.

"But listen," she says, her voice growing serious. "This gala is a big deal. Lots of press. Red carpet. The whole thing."

I knew where she was going with this. "I'm ready," I promise, then wink at her. "The team's PR person made sure I had my talking points down pat."

"You better," she warns. "Or my boss will have my head."

The game is close, and in the end, the Granite beat the Free Jacks by a mere five points. Kari warned me it could be another hour before Ansel finally got to leave, but time flies, thanks to Rosie running me all around the stadium and saying hello to all the vendors.

"You know, for someone who's only five years old, you sure know a lot of people," I tell her after we've waved to yet another person.

She shrugs. "I like knowing everyone."

I can't help the laugh that escapes, and I pull her up into my arms for a kiss. "I love you, you know that, Rosie bug?"

She wraps around me and squeezes. "I love you, too, Elle Belle."

We make our way back up to the second floor of the stadium, going into the air conditioning and heading for the private area reserved for friends and family. It's emptying out pretty steadily, but Allyson's still there.

"When are you sending me the next round of ideas for review?" Allyson asks by way of greeting.

"Two more days," I answer. "I'm waiting on a travel company to get back to me about some logistics that I know you'll want details of, and then you'll have the final package ready for sign-off."

She squeals. "I'm so excited! Jake is going to lose his mind when I tell him what we're doing."

"I can't believe you're keeping it a secret." They were going to visit the Arctic, for heaven's sake.

"He wanted to be surprised," she says with a wave of her hand. "Not my problem. I'll make sure he's got the right gear, though."

"Daddy!" Rosie's voice clangs through the room as I turn to see Ansel.

He's showered, back in the coach's gear he left the house in this morning: black pants that are tight against his thighs and rear, and a dark teal polo shirt that strains against his muscles. I swear that Kari deliberately got him the tighter-fitting styles, because the previous coach did not look as delectable as this. In fact, no one can possibly look as good as Ansel does.

As he leans down to pick his daughter up, his eyes land on me, darkening immediately.

Allyson laughs. "Ooh, girl. Someone's getting some tonight," she says under her breath before winking at me and shooing me toward him. "See you at the gala."

I make my way to Ansel, who leans in to kiss my cheek. Then he growls, "Where did this come from?"

I glance innocently down at my shirt. "What, this old thing?" I'd taken one of his jerseys and turned it into a crop top, then cut the neck so that it draped off my shoulder. On the back, I'd bedazzled his name and number. I twirl around. "Do you like it?"

A breath saws out of him. "Yes." His voice is low, and his eyes sweep me from head to toe in a promise of everything he intends to do to me later.

Chapter 30
Elodie

We're almost late to the gala, and I put the blame solely on Ansel. The man had me against our bedroom wall in nothing but the jersey the second Sharon retrieved Rosalie. And he kept me there, feasting on me, until I'd come from his mouth and then on his cock. When we got in the shower, it was my turn, backing him onto the in-shower seat and kissing those gorgeous thighs, then licking my way to the proud cock jutting between them. Then he pulled me up and turned me around, practically impaling himself on me as I rode him, my own thighs shaking with the effort.

There are a few cars ahead of us when we pull up to the museum where the gala is being held, and I catch my breath. "Holy crap."

Ansel chuckles, pulling a hand into his and kissing it. "You'll be amazing."

It's far more than I was prepared for. It turns out that this gala isn't just for the Granite. It's also for the city's pro football team, which means the amount of press and fans on either side of the red carpet is absolutely insane. People are ten-deep, lining the street and yelling as we close in. I crane my neck to see the people exiting in front of us and instantly feel underdressed despite the way I'm decked out. I opted for a royal-green silk and chiffon gown that gave Bridgerton vibes and set my ample breasts on full display. At Kari's insistence, and with Ansel's credit card, I also rented a diamond and emerald necklace and earrings, and a diamond tennis bracelet. The entire process made me queasy, but the two of them practically bullied me into submission. Now, looking at the scene before me, I'm incredibly grateful.

We pull into position, and Ansel throws the car into Park. "You look absolutely stunning, Elodie," he says. "I'm the luckiest man here."

I smile softly. "*You're* the one who looks amazing." He was mouth-watering in a form-fitting classic tux that had been perfectly tailored to him. "Though I do kind of wish I could see that tattoo," I tease.

"I can make that happen." He grins wickedly, then leans over to kiss my cheek. "Ready?"

I take a deep breath and nod. "Ready."

He opens his door, and that cues the man on my side to open my door. The man holds his hand out, and I take it, my entire body breaking into a cold sweat. "Good evening, Miss," he says, a bright smile on his face.

"Hi," I gulp.

Cameras flash and voices yell, and I blink, temporarily blinded. I grip the man's hand hard, then let go, horrified. "I'm so sorry," I say, wincing.

Ansel appears on my other side, taking my hand and guiding me close, then tucking my arm into his like I'm his personal rugby ball. He smiles down at me. "You're doing great."

Hot tears appear immediately, and my knees are literally shaking. "I can't do this," I whisper, panicked.

"Look at me," he says, his voice low and calm.

I obey, even though I'm hyper-aware of the cameras still flashing. Capturing everything.

"We will leave right now if you want to. But I know you, and you'll be so mad at yourself if we do."

A strangled laugh leaves me. "You're right."

His mouth quirks up. "Shall we?"

I squeeze my eyes shut, willing the tears away as I nod. When I open them, Ansel is smiling softly at me. "Let's do it."

"That's my brave girl," he says. Then he smiles, all mischief and secrets. "I'll be sure to eat your pussy extra well as your reward."

I choke back a scandalized gasp as he turns me, and we step back onto the red carpet.

"Remember to smile." He grins wolfishly down at me.

We walk slowly, stopping to pose every few feet. Any time I try to pull away so that the photographers can get a shot of Ansel alone, he grips me tight. Finally, we make it up the stairs, where one reporter stands.

"Ansel Miles," she says with a bright smile. "Welcome to the City of Refuge Sports Gala."

"Thank you."

"And who did you bring with you?" she asks, her eyes lighting on me.

Ansel's hand moves to my lower back as he answers. "This is Elodie Cole."

I smile, hoping I don't look as crazed and nervous as I feel. I swear, even my lips are shaking.

"Elodie, so nice to have you. Who are you wearing?"

I give her the name of the designer, and she turns back to Ansel.

"Word is that you're being considered for the permanent coaching position for the Granite, Ansel. Can we expect to see you on the sidelines this season?"

He shakes his head. "Definitely not. I'm grateful for the opportunity to serve my team as interim coach, but I have a lot more to give on the pitch."

The reporter gives a nod and wraps up the interview, and Ansel leads me away.

As we round the corner and begin the short walk to the ballroom, he stops and pulls me to the side, looking down at me with such love and concern that my stomach pitches. "How are you?"

I give him a lopsided smile. "I think I'm okay."

"Really?"

"Really. I'm not shaking anymore." I hold up my hand for his inspection.

He grabs it and presses it to his lips. "One word from you and we leave."

I nod, but he keeps me in place.

"I mean it, Elodie. I love you. None of this matters."

"Well, considering it's a benefit for an organization that helps struggling families, I'd say it matters a great deal."

His eyes soften. "Your heart is amazing, you know that?"

With a shrug, I say, "Any organization that's feeding children is worthy. That's not my heart; that's just humanity."

With another kiss to my cheek, he straightens and leads us in, his hand warm and steady on my back. And thank goodness, because I nearly trip over my own two feet at the glamor we walk into. It's beyond excessive, the attendees dripping in jewels and custom-made clothing, servers darting here and there with trays of champagne and appetizers. The athletes are larger than life, and the people by their side are stunning.

"There's Jake and Carter," Ansel says, nodding toward an area near one of the four bars in the room. "Let's go say hello, and I'll grab you a drink."

"Just one," I murmur as we go. I'm not interested in anything but sobriety when I get in places like this. I think it's all the old pageant training that kicks in, that need to be *on*, to always know what's going on around me and be ready to pivot based on whoever I'm talking to. Probably not the healthiest approach, but there you have it.

We approach the small circle, and Allyson smiles knowingly as she takes me in. "You look beautiful. A little flushed, perhaps?"

I narrow my eyes playfully at her. "Something like that. You must be Jake," I say, turning to her fiancé.

He's a massive man, easily one and a half of Ansel. His long black hair is slicked into a low ponytail, and he looks extremely uncomfortable in his tux. But he gives me a friendly grin as he shakes my hand. "I've heard a lot about you. Wanna tell me where I'm going?"

Allyson whacks his arm playfully. "She'll do no such thing."

Kari appears with Sam, the two of them having declared they'd be each other's dates for the evening, and Lennox shows up with a date as well. After my glass of champagne is empty, Ansel holds his hand out. "Dance with me."

With a smile, I let him lead me to the dance floor, and we wrap our arms around each other, swaying to the music. "Have I told you how stunning you look this evening?" he asks, his expression heated as I meet his eyes.

I smile. "You have. But you can say it again."

His hand is warm and sure on my waist, the other holding mine in a light grip as he moves me across the floor. "It's true. This dress...I'd like to rip it off and sink into you right now."

My cheeks heat. "Mr. Miles, that's quite the mouth you have on you."

"I'd rather it be on you," he growls softly in return.

"You're a great dancer." I follow his lead easily, his steps sure and natural. And he smells utterly delicious, a hint of woodsy cologne this evening on top of his usual masculine scent.

"Changing the subject on me?" he teases.

"I have to, or I'll drag you into a darkened room and let you have your way with me," I counter.

His eyebrows rise, the scar slashing through one of them serving only to make him look like a nineteenth century rake. "And this is a bad thing...why?"

I swat at his chest, and he captures it, pulling it up to press a kiss to my hand. With his eyes trained on mine, his tongue licks at the seam between my first and second fingers, a reminder of his considerable talents. My core heats as my mouth opens in a gasp.

He chuckles. "You're leaving that dress on later."

"Promise?"

"Mm," he hums, his eyes alight. "You're a good dancer yourself, you know."

"Part of my pageant training," I respond. "Mom made sure I knew the basics of all types of dances."

He grunts noncommittally, having learned enough about my relationship with my mom to not be much of a fan. "Was that what you did for the talent portion?"

I scan his face for any hint of teasing, but there's none. "No. I played flute."

"Do you still play?"

I shrug. "I *can*, but it's not good. I donated the instrument to an organization similar to this one after college, actually."

He smiles, his warm brown eyes crinkling. "I love your heart." He pauses. "And I love *you*."

The words are on the tip of my tongue, but I can't make them come out. I rest my head against his chest, and he pulls me tighter. "There's no place I'd rather be," I whisper, hoping it's enough. Loving him is utterly and completely terrifying. But also...perfect.

We leave the dance floor after another song, and the night goes on as we rejoin our friends at a table near the back of the ballroom for the seated dinner. All around us are athletes and their dates, fans who've bought or won tickets to the event, and other people with way too much money.

"It's weird, right?" Kari says, leaning over as the desserts are served.

"Which part?" I joke.

"I get that this is benefiting a charity, but couldn't we just take all the money we spent on clothes and rentals and the event itself and funnel that into the organization? We'd probably double or triple the impact."

I appraise her with a grin. She's gorgeous tonight, resplendent in a ruby-red gown and gold jewelry, half her black bob slicked into finger waves and the other half swinging free to her chin. "Spoken like a woman with a vision."

She shrugs, her eyes sliding to Lennox and his date

before darting away. "I just think these are silly, but I have to attend them."

I stand, and Ansel rises with me. "I'll be back. Powder room."

The restroom is empty when I walk in and take care of things. But when I exit the stall, there in front of me, like the worst nightmare in the history of nightmares, is Lauren.

Shit.

This can't possibly end well.

Chapter 31
Elodie

"What do you want." It's not a question. It's a demand. I keep eye contact with her as I stalk to the sink to wash my hands, and I'm surprised to see they're not shaking.

Given how furious I am at this woman, that's honestly a miracle.

"Seems you're getting awfully cozy with the father of my child," Lauren sneers. It's a terrible look on her, turning a face that should be beautiful into something horrible and ugly. Her dress should be embarrassed to be seen on her.

"Great observation there, genius," I drawl, happy to have found my well of anger brimming and ready to go. "Anything else?" I ask, grabbing a paper towel and drying my hands. For the briefest of moments, I seriously consider balling it up and throwing it at her, too.

She steps forward, putting us about five feet apart. "You need to convince Ansel to do what's right."

"And what's that—pay you to go away, or let you take his little girl away from him?"

Lauren's eyes flash. "She's *my* daughter, you know. Not yours."

A bark of laughter comes out. "Your daughter? Your *daughter*? Bitch, please." I close the distance, getting right up in her face while keeping my hands fisted at my sides. "You lost the right to call her that when you left her on Ansel's doorstep all those years ago. When you told him that if he didn't take her, you were tossing her into the system. When you didn't so much as call to check on her in the years since. So let me be perfectly clear: You. Are. Not. Her. Mother. Not by a fucking long shot."

"And you think you are?" she asks, a hand on her hip.

When I speak, my voice is low, seething. And now? *Now* I'm shaking. Because fuck her. "I'm a hell of a lot better mother than you'll ever be. And if you think for one fucking second that I'm going to let you get your bitch-ass paws on that sweet little girl, you can get fucked. Because she deserves better than you. *He* deserves better than you. The best thing you can do is go back to the sewer you crawled out of."

"Oh, sweetheart," she croons, a vicious smile on her face, "you have no idea who you're messing with."

I look her up and down, years of pageant training roaring back to the surface with a vengeance. "Oh, really? Let's see. You're in an out-of-season gown, your spray tan is so orange it was probably done by an intern, your heels are scuffed, your pedicure is non-existent, your jewelry is fake, your makeup is a decade out of style, and your hair?" I suck my teeth. "Honey." With a *tsk*, I tilt my head. "But please. Do tell me. Who, exactly, am I fucking with?"

She just smiles. "You'll see."

And with that, she turns and walks away, hips swishing

beneath a black glittery gown, a discount sticker on the sole of one of her heels.

The door shuts behind her, and I hiss the anger out in one long exhale. I shake my hands, adrenaline coursing through me, and give myself exactly five seconds to pull myself together. Turning to the mirror, I swipe on some lipstick and give my reflection my best pageant smile. There's no trace of the seething woman I am below the surface. Time to fake it for the crowd and get the heck out of here.

After exiting the bathroom, I force myself to go slow as I walk back to the table, scanning the massive ballroom for any sign of Lauren. But she's gone, likely having fled the moment we finished our little talk.

Ansel stands as I near, his gaze roaming my body appreciatively, then widening as he takes in my expression. "Are you okay?" he asks, voice low as he bends to me.

"We need to leave now," I answer. "I'll explain everything as soon as we're in the car. Right now, we need to pretend like everything is perfectly fine, but it's time to go."

He straightens, eyes narrowing. "Tell me," he bites out.

My own spine stiffens at his tone. "In the *car*."

He jerks his chin down in wordless agreement, then turns to the rest of the table to make our departure known. We leave, his hand once again on the small of my back, and in minutes the valet is running to get our car. Mercifully, I don't see anyone taking photos, and after longer than I'd prefer, Ansel is helping me into the car before shutting the door behind me and walking to his side.

We aren't even ten feet away from the valet before he's looking over at me, ready. "Well?"

I exhale. "Lauren cornered me in the ladies' room."

"She *what?*" The steering wheel leather protests

beneath his clenched hands. He shoots a glance at me before focusing back on the road. "Are you okay? Goddammit, Elodie."

I force myself not to shrink into the seat. "I'm fine."

"Sorry." He catches himself. "I'm not mad at you. I just —I wish you'd told me while we were there. I want to give you a hug. And then find Lauren and shake her," he admits.

I reach over and place a steadying hand on his leg. It works, but only to a point. He reaches down to grab it, squeezing once before pulling it up to kiss my palm. He threads our fingers together before resting our hands on his leg, the other hand still gripping too tightly onto the wheel before him.

"Tell me." It's a gentle request, but tension radiates off him.

I relay the exchange, his jaw dropping with every bit of the conversation I give him. When I'm done, he looks at me longer than he should.

"Holy shit, Elodie," he breathes. "I—I don't know what to say except...thank you."

"You're thanking me?" I repeat, my own mouth agape. "It's a miracle that we didn't come to blows in there."

The corners of his mouth lift. "I'd put my money on you."

I huff a laugh, but the comment releases the rest of my anger. "You're ridiculous."

He kisses my palm again. "Maybe. Maybe not. But I know one thing for sure."

I wait.

With a wink, he says, "I love you."

The words bubble up, *I love you, too*, but my throat tightens again, my body refusing to let them come out. I said it plenty to my ex, and it was never enough. My love wasn't enough. *I* wasn't enough. And even now, in the car with a man who lets the words flow as easily as water, I can't do it.

I blame my argument with Lauren.

That must be it.

We're silent the rest of the way to the house, both of us lost in our own thoughts. When we pull into the driveway, Ansel kills the engine and looks over at me, his expression thoughtful.

"Stay with me."

I grin. "I *always* stay with you."

But he shakes his head. "No. I mean stay. Stay even when the preschool slot opens up in September—"

"Oh my gosh, they finally called you?" I interrupt.

He exhales a laugh. "Not the point, Elodie."

I bite my lip, and his eyes darken in response. He reaches for me, threading his hand into the curls at the nape of my neck and guiding me across the console for a kiss. I melt, happy to fall into the safety of his lips.

When we break away, he studies me in the dim light, his eyes darting over my face. "You don't have to answer now. But the offer stands."

"Look at you, finally learning to ask for what you need," I tease.

He smiles, sweet and bashful. "Not what I need, Elodie. What I *want*."

I pick up on the double meaning and smirk. "And what else do you want, Ansel?"

He opens the door and gets out, tossing a devilish grin as he goes. "Why don't you come inside and let me show you?"

Chapter 32
Ansel

I've got her slammed against the door before she even knows what's happening. God*damn* this woman and her mouth. Her sweet, beautiful, sensuous mouth that she used to tell Lauren off.

It's hot as fuck.

The way she stood up for my daughter? For me?

I sink to my knees and pull the gown up, groaning when I see the flimsy lace fabric barely covering anything between her legs. I press my mouth against her, feeling her wetness and nearly losing my mind in the process. The panties have to go. I rip them with one hard yank of my hands.

Above me, Elodie gasps. "I liked those! I just bought them..." She drifts off with a moan that turns into a curse.

I grin as I run my tongue over her clit just the way she likes it. "Can't help it," I say against her. "Needed to eat this pussy."

Her hands thread through my hair as she lifts a leg over my shoulder and settles against the door, happy to let me have my way with her.

I don't let up, thrusting my tongue into her and following it with my fingers, finding that perfect spot that makes her practically sing with pleasure as I pay attention to her clit, swirling and pressing.

"Fuck, Ansel, fuck, fuck, *fuck*!" On the final curse, she climaxes, shuddering and bucking against my face.

It's fantastic.

But I'm nowhere near done. I pull her through the orgasm, and when she exhales and sags against the door, I rise and scoop her into my arms.

She flails her legs and swats at my chest. "Ansel! Put me down, I'm heavy!"

"Baby, I hip thrust more than you," I promise. "Now quit wiggling and trust me when I say I can handle you. *All* of you."

She blinks slowly, her already-glassy eyes shining with satisfaction. "And what's next?"

"Next, I'm going to bend you over that couch. I'm going to bury myself so deep in you and fuck you so hard that neither one of us will ever recover."

A feline grin crosses her face. "Sounds perfect."

We reach the couch, and I set her down. "Turn around and let me unzip you."

She starts to obey, then shakes her head. "Not yet." She walks around the couch and settles into the center cushion. "You first. You in that tux is almost criminal."

I raise an eyebrow. "You like this getup?"

She licks her lips and looks me up and down. "I do. And I'll like it even better when it's on the floor next to you."

Without breaking eye contact, I toe off the too-tight shoes and pull off my socks. It's not sexy, but damned if she doesn't stop me before I do anything else.

"Next is the jacket. *Only* the jacket."

I shrug it off, letting it fall to the floor.

"Now the cuffs."

"Not the bowtie?"

She shakes her head. "Absolutely not. Cuffs. Undo them and roll them up your arms."

"But—"

"I want those forearms on display, Ansel. Gimme." She makes a *get on with it* motion with her hands.

I laugh. "Who are you, and where did my sweet Elodie go?" But I do as she asks, undoing my cuffs and rolling them up for her inspection. "I feel ridiculous."

She drags her gaze up my chest and finally meets my eyes, ravenous. "But you look incredible."

"Can I take the shirt off now?"

She hums, making a show of thinking about it. "Turn around first. I need to see that thick rugby ass."

I choke out a laugh but do as she commands. "Thick rugby ass? Seriously, who *are* you?"

"A woman who is taking the time to appreciate the fine specimen of a man she's lucky enough to be with, that's who."

After a moment, I turn back around, clocking the adoration on her face even as she blushes. *There she is.* Slowly, I reach up to the bowtie, untying the knot and pulling it out with as much finesse as I can. Then I start on the buttons, undoing them one by one, absolutely riveted by Elodie. She's tense, her body flushed, and her breasts, God fucking help me, they are *heaving* as she watches me.

This might be the hottest thing I have ever experienced in my life.

Actually, it *is*. No contest.

And since I'm just as turned on as she is by this entire thing, I stop when I get to my waist, spreading the shirt wide and letting her get a good look, before pulling the sides back together.

Her mouth clamps shut as her eyes meet mine.

I smile, then pull the shirt back apart. Her eyes drop to my chest, unmoving as I slide one part of the shirt out of my pants, then the other. I unroll the cuffs, delighting in how she licks her lips as I go, and finally let the shirt fall to the floor behind me.

She exhales. "Do you have any idea how hot you are?" She meets my eyes and lifts a weak hand at me. "Your body is *insane*, Ansel. Your chest is...ugh. And your abs? Stupid. But it's those muscles" —she gestures at the ones leading below my pants— "*those* are heaven-sent."

I wink at her, then start taking off the belt. When it's joined the rest of its compatriots on the floor, I unbutton and unzip the pants.

"That's enough," she says, then crooks a finger and beckons me with it.

"Yes, ma'am," I smirk, closing the distance to her as she stands and turns.

"Unzip my dress." She reaches to pull her hair around, but I stop her.

"Let me. Please." These fucking curls. I *dream* of her hair.

I pull them to the side, exposing one creamy shoulder and a sea of russet freckles. My cock twitches as I press a kiss to her skin. She hums as I straighten and begin to unzip the dress, inch by delicious inch, revealing more freckles for me to worship, dotted like paint splatters around her back. I breathe her in, delighting in her scent, fresh and darkly floral.

I reach the end of the zipper, and she shrugs it off,

turning to me in nothing but her heels. When her doe eyes meet mine, I say, "The shoes stay on."

She grins, then sits on the edge of the couch, spreading her legs wide. "Come here," she whispers. When I do, she pushes my pants off, leaving me only in my underwear.

"Black briefs," she says, shaking her head. "Only you could make these look sexy."

I smirk. "Gotta give you what you want, Elle."

She licks her lips. "That is the perfect answer."

Without another word, she pulls them off. My cock springs free, already leaking and aching for her. She pulls me close, one hand gripping my thigh as the other wraps around the base of my cock as her head lowers.

"Fuck." I grit the word out, already seeing stars as she takes me to the back of her throat and out again, swirling her tongue along every part of me.

Her hair falls to the side, and I gather it up, wrapping it around my hand and using it to guide her mouth up and down my shaft. She digs her nails into my leg, and I nearly black out from it all. The bite of pain from her nails against the pleasure of her mouth. I look down, and she's watching me, her eyes never leaving mine as she takes me in over and over.

I'm going to explode.

Pulling her off, I yank her up with a growl. "Bend over. *Now.*"

I give her all of three seconds before I've got her levered over the arm of the couch, raising her hips and shoving a pillow beneath her before spreading her wide. She's flawless, all soft curves gone taut with want, her back arched, golden-brown curls spilling down her back. I notch into place, but pause. Needing just a moment to pull myself together.

She looks over her shoulder. "Ansel. Give me your cock."

My chest heaves as my throat tightens. "Whatever you want, baby."

I slide in, and her head lowers as she lets out a curse. Gripping her hips, I push into her, over and over and over, wanting her to feel every inch of me. Needing it like I need the very breath that's sawing out of my lungs. Desperate never to stop feeling the way her body clenches around mine, the perfection of it. As though we were made only for each other, made to come together like this.

When she tightens around me and lets out a strangled moan, I go harder. Faster. "Yes. Please don't stop—please—Ansel—" She cuts off with a yell, coming so hard that my body immediately tumbles after her. My orgasm hits like a freight train, coursing through me like lightning as I give myself over to it.

Stars. I see stars as I pull out and take the few steps to collapse onto the couch. With a satisfied laugh, Elodie falls into my arms.

Chapter 33
Elodie

My dreams are scattered wisps of things. Crows exploding into a winter sky from a mist-covered field. Jumping into a pool and watching the shimmering sun grow smaller as I sink into an endless blue dark. Walking a red carpet into nothing, cameras flashing like a thousand silver flames, cold and heartless, as I reach for a hand that isn't there.

When I finally wake, warm and safe and tucked into Ansel's body, I take a moment to breathe. To remember last night. The way he took me over the couch, and later in the bed, near feral with need. The confrontation with Lauren at the gala. The way *I love you* refused to come out of my mouth, no matter how many times I tried last night.

But I do. I love him so much. I want a life with him and Rosalie. I want to wake up every morning and know that the man next to me is the one I'll be with for the rest of my life. To live a long, happy life together. To play endless games of Marco Polo in the pool, then collapse into each other's arms at night.

I turn, burrowing deeper into his arms and relishing the

squeeze he gives in return. He opens his eyes, and the love I see in them is breathtaking. And even though the words remain stuck in my throat, I hope he reads the same love on my face as I look at him.

"Good morning." His voice is gravelly and low. Sexy.

"Good morning."

"What time is it?"

With a shrug, I lean up to kiss him, then roll to grab my phone from where it sits on the bedside table. Ansel does the same on his side, and as I wake the screen up, a curse leaves his lips.

"What?" I ask, but I trail off at the notifications. Dozens of them. Texts and alerts from every social media app I have.

Ansel sits up, tension radiating off him as he grabs his glasses and swipes at his phone, stabbing at whatever link is in there. Dread fills my body as I open a text from Kari.

> KARI
>
> Have you seen this? Please tell me it's fake.

I follow the link to the international news site she pasted into the next text, and a gasp leaves my mouth at the headline.

NATIONAL RUGBY LEAGUE STAR'S NANNY MAKES POWER GRAB: "SHE'S NOT YOUR DAUGHTER"

Nausea roils through me as I scan the article. Lauren. Lauren's gone to the press and made me look like an absolute monster.

Beside me, the sound of my own voice wafts from Ansel's phone. *"Stay away from them. You don't deserve them. I'm her mother now."*

Ansel looks over at me. "Is this—"

But I'm already shaking my head, even as guilt and doubt begin to swirl in my belly. "That's not what I said. I didn't say it like that. She edited the recording."

Ansel's phone pings with a text. "This..." he starts, eyes scanning the screen as he moves deftly between apps. His face pales. "This isn't good, Elle."

My body tingles, my heart racing. This can't be happening. None of this can be happening.

He holds up a different post, and it's the two of us on the red carpet. Tears spring to my eyes as I take it in: We're looking at each other, and there's the softest smile on his face. The love and adoration shine through. Beside the photo in bold capital letters is the headline: **NAUGHTY NANNY NABS RUGGER!**

It's endless. Shots of us at the gala overlaid with quotes I never said. Audio that twists my words into things that never came out of my mouth. As far as the world is concerned, I'm a money-grabbing home wrecker who's deliberately keeping Lauren away from her daughter.

"I think I might be sick," I mutter, letting the phone slide out of my hands as I stumble to the bathroom.

Ansel doesn't answer, his attention focused on the phone he's bringing up to his ear. "Lewis. I guess all those years of being your easiest client just went out the door."

I try to pull myself together in the bathroom, splashing water on my face and staring hard at my reflection. This will blow over. It *has* to.

Then I turn and retch into the toilet.

When I pick my phone back up from where I dropped it on the nightstand, a new text waits for me.

MOTHER

I don't know what you've gotten yourself
into this time, Elodie, but you need to fix it.
I have pageant press all over me. You know
how hard I've worked to finally get to
where I am. I can't have something like this
getting in the way.

A wrecked laugh escapes me. Of *course* my mother would reach out. Of *course* she would worry only about how this makes her look to the pageant world, and not about the toll this might be taking on her daughter.

I don't bother answering.

An hour later, Kari appears at the front door, waving her phone like it's her personal weapon. The scowl on her face drops as soon as she sees me. "Oh, babe."

That's all it takes. I start sobbing as she steps over the threshold, lunging into her arms and squeezing her tight. "I didn't say any of those things," I manage to say between gasps of air.

"That's good," she says, shutting the door behind her with her foot and running a hand down my back. "But we have to figure this out."

"I don't know what to do," I whimper. This is my nightmare. My absolute *nightmare*. And because it's Kari, I admit the rest. "My mother texted."

She stills, then leans back to meet my eyes.

"Seems she's worried how this will look as she's rising through the pageant ranks. God forbid anything stop her from becoming the head of the organization." I want to be pissed. I want my voice to be razor sharp. But instead, the words come out in a choked sob. A series of whimpers revealing the soft underbelly that only Kari knows.

"Come here," Kari says, pulling me into her arms. "I'm so sorry, Elodie. We'll figure this out."

"I don't think so," I whisper. That text tells me everything I need to know about her. "I think I need to have a long talk with her when this blows over."

Kari winces. "That...might take a while."

My stomach drops. "Is it that bad?"

She fidgets, and instead of answering, she asks, "Where's Rosalie?"

"Next door. Ansel called and asked Sharon if she minded keeping her a few more hours."

"I need you to fix it!" Ansel's voice rises from where he paces in the kitchen behind us. "That's what I pay you for." A pause. "Then find me someone who can." The unmistakable sound of a phone clattering to the counter. "Fuck! Fuck, fuck, fuck, *fuck!*"

My eyes go wide as they meet Kari's.

But hers only narrow as she squares her shoulders. "Time for me to do my job."

Then it hits me like a physical blow to the chest. She's not here for me. She was *never* coming over for me. She's here for Ansel. For the Granite.

"Oh," I whisper.

Her expression is full of sorrow as she steps forward to pull me into another crushing hug. "I'm so sorry, Elodie."

A knock at the door has her pulling away and tucking my hair behind my ears. "That's going to be Lewis," she says, her voice turning businesslike. "I've got to handle this."

This being the mess that I've made.

"Are you going to be okay?"

I swallow and shrug. "Do I have a choice?" I mumble as she turns to open the door.

A giant hulk of a Black man stands there, and he is

easily the biggest human I've ever laid eyes on. He's immaculately dressed in dark jeans and a cream knit short-sleeved sweater, with gleaming retro Air Jordans that I'd wager he spent a pretty penny on. His fade and beard are sharp, not a line out of place, and the diamond studs in his ears are probably two carats each. "Kari Edwards," he says, his voice a soothing rumble against my frazzled nerves. "Should have figured I'd see you here."

Kari gestures for him to come in, her smile bright but polite. "You know you'll find me where the scandal is. Have you met Elodie Cole?"

Lewis turns his attention to me and extends a hand. It's warm and calloused, and my eyes snag on the Super Bowl championship ring he wears. "Nice to meet you, though I wish it were under better circumstances."

I try to smile back, but it's forced. Then I realize with horror that I'm still in my pajamas. "I...should go get dressed."

"Lewis." Even Ansel's voice is different as he comes up behind me. "Come on into the kitchen. I've got some of that matcha shit you love."

"Always knowing the way to my heart," Lewis jokes.

Ansel barely looks at me as he steps to the side and waves Lewis toward the kitchen. Kari follows, throwing me a wince as she goes.

All I can do is watch them file off, ready to tackle a problem I created.

"I've got a list of talking points," Kari says, her voice fading as they move into the kitchen.

"And I've already lined up some calls to your sponsors," Lewis says. "I don't think they'll be too worried about this, but we can't be too careful."

I swallow, fighting back a fresh round of frustrated tears.

The thing is, this *isn't* my fault. Not really. Sure, I lit into Lauren—because she deserved it. But she's the one who baited me. Who took my words and spliced them into the hateful vitriol making its way across the internet. And now I'm the one taking the fall.

But it's worse than that. Because why is Lauren even doing this, if not to get back at Ansel? If she uses this as the way to somehow force Ansel to share custody, or worse?

What have I done?

I head upstairs and take a long shower, dressing in my comfiest clothes and wondering if I need to start packing up.

No.

He loves me.

But am I enough?

Chapter 34
Ansel

The past few days have been an absolute blur. The Granite's owner called shortly after the news broke and reamed me six ways to Sunday, but once calmed down enough to listen to my side of things, he seemed to be okay. Not that it was the last time he called or anything. I spent the weekend holed up with Lewis and Kari, strategizing on talking points, reaching out to my personal sponsors and team sponsors, and generally trying to keep my shit together. Which was nearly impossible when my lawyer reported on what she was doing on the legal side.

Spoiler alert: There's pretty much nothing she can do. Which is utter and complete bullshit. And I was quick to tell her that, but she swore that she and her team were doing everything they could.

Rosie managed to remain relatively oblivious to the whole thing, which has been the only silver lining to all of this.

And Elodie...

Fuck. Elodie.

It's ninety-five degrees, and she's curled up on the screened-in patio couch wearing sweatpants and a hoodie, eyes glued to her phone. Beside her, Rosie chatters about one thing or another while she puts her favorite puzzle together on the coffee table.

I pour them both some lemonade, cutting the juice with water and dropping freshly sliced jalapeños in it for Elodie just the way I know she likes.

Rosie's eyes sparkle when she sees the glasses in my hands. "Lemonade!" She jumps up and takes it from me, doing a little happy dance as she sips it through a curly straw. The curly straws are mandatory, as I've been informed they make everything taste better.

Elodie's eyes are the opposite, dull and sad, as I ease down beside her and hand hers over. "Thanks."

"You really shouldn't pay so much attention to all that." I tip my chin to her phone. "We both know that none of it is true, and it's not good for you."

She shakes her head, a lone tear tracing down her cheek. "I'm so sorry. I never should have gone to that gala."

I've lost count of how many times she's apologized. "We couldn't have seen this coming, Elodie."

"It's my worst nightmare. Everyone knows who I am. My mother won't stop texting with updates on how bad this is for her pageant presidency bid and keeps demanding that I make it all stop, as if I have control over anything. Complete strangers are DM'ing me and telling me I don't deserve to live," she says, her voice low. "I thought that maybe it'd die down, you know? But it's only gotten worse. The freaking *British* tabloids have caught on, Ansel! They're gleeful that the 'Yank ruggers' finally have some drama. Do you know how bad this is? What they're calling me?" Her voice is shrill, and I watch as she works to rein herself back in.

"I'm aware," I tell her. "Well aware. I have agents asking if they need to find a new team for their player. Marketing called this morning to tell me sales are either going to take a hit because of this, or they'll explode, and they're not sure which yet. The owner called me again. We've talked more in the past three days than I ever wanted to talk to the man. Lewis is earning every cent he makes off me. And Kari's blowing up my phone. The press are hounding me for a quote, but Kari's holding us off until this afternoon's press conference."

She whips her head toward me. "Press conference?"

I keep going. "My parents have called. The players have called, half of them to see if I'm okay and the other half to see if we're practicing this week." I huff out a dry laugh. "So. Yes. I'm aware."

Her face is pale. "And...Lauren? Have you heard anything from her?"

I shake my head. "That's the worst of it. Through everything, I can't figure out what she gets out of stirring all this up. She can't really want custody."

Because I will crumble if she takes my little girl.

Every reasonable part of me knows that it's impossible, that no judge in their right mind would grant her custody after she literally abandoned her child to my care, but reasonable packed its bags about two days ago. Reasonable is long gone, and in its place is nothing but dread, cold fury, and a thirst for vengeance.

"She's..." Elodie cuts herself off with a meaningful look at Rosie, who's humming to herself while she works on the puzzle nearby. "It doesn't matter. What matters is that Rosie stays here."

"That's *all* that matters," I say vehemently.

Elodie studies me quietly, her eyes puffy and smudged with purple from lack of sleep, while my mind whirls with everything I need to do.

"You're good to watch her?" I ask, indicating my daughter.

"It's my job, Ansel," she reminds me wryly. "I'm definitely good to watch her."

I still check one last time before I leave for the Granite's facilities.

I'M TRYING to pull my shit together in the coach's office for the millionth time when Mark, the head of finance, stops by. "Certainly one way to make a splash, Coach." He grins as he speaks.

"Don't call me Coach," I shoot back, thankful for the immediate friendliness he offers.

Mark smiles back. "Being interim coach not a big enough spotlight for you, man? I thought that check I cut you was plenty."

"No one wants this over with more than me," I tell him. "What's going on? I know you're not just here to shoot the breeze."

He shrugs. "Honestly? Wanted to check on you. See how you were doing. How's your daughter?"

The question is an emotional tackle, and it feels like Mark just took me down a yard from the try line. I force away the tightness in my throat and answer, "Good. Doesn't really know what's going on, which is good."

With a nod, he taps his ring on the doorframe. "You've got a lot of people in your corner, Coach. See you later."

He disappears down the hall, and I stare after him, not quite sure what to make of the visit, but grateful nonetheless.

Kari and her boss, Frank, appear right before the press conference. Frank leads the way, shark-like as ever in a fitted three-piece suit. His bald head gleams beneath the fluorescent lights as he takes one look at me and barks, "Are you ready?"

I stiffen. I really don't like this man. It's obvious that Kari is the real brains and workhorse of the operation, but Frank operates as though he's going to get all the glory. So, screw him.

"I am. No thanks to you."

He stares at me, expressionless. Behind him, Kari's eyes go wide with shock.

But Frank doesn't seem fazed. "I've been busy ensuring our team sponsors don't bail on us thanks to your inability to keep your dick in your pants. The *nanny*, Ansel? Really?"

Kari inhales sharply.

"Watch your fucking mouth," I bite out, rising from the desk and closing the distance between me and the smarmy asshole.

Frank rolls his eyes. "Whatever, bucko. My job is to protect the organization, not you. If you can't handle it, then you shouldn't have said yes to the job. All you are is one more athlete falling prey to pussy. Twice, if I'm not mistaken."

I square my stance and am seconds from punching him when Kari clears her throat.

I glare at Frank. "You're a fucking asshole, you know that?"

He shrugs and picks a piece of invisible lint off his jacket. "Yeah, well, I'm a fucking asshole who's seen just about everything and covered most of it up. So, if you're ready to do what you've been told, then we can get this over with."

Chest heaving, I look past him to where Kari stands, iPad clutched against her chest. "Shall we?"

She nods stiffly, her eyes darting at both of us before she pivots and leads us to the press room down the hall. She slows as we approach, turning and opening her mouth to say something. Frank brushes me without even so much as looking at Kari, and her mouth clamps shut as tiny dots of red appear on her cheeks.

"Would you believe it if I told you that was pretty mild?" Kari says.

"Would *you* believe it if I told you I was prepared to beat him to a bloody pulp?" I counter, shaking my head and blowing air out of my mouth, needing to re-focus on the task at hand.

The room is a pretty standard conference room, with rows of chairs for the press set up to face a long, thin table set up on a raised dais. In the center of the table sit about twenty microphones, all turned on and ready to capture everything I say. All the camera operators stand about halfway back from the dais, and the quality of those cameras depends on the news outlets covering the story. Sometimes, the "camera" is simply someone aiming an iPhone.

There are two entrances into the room: through the rows of double doors at the back of the room, or through the single door that's hidden behind a well-placed column. That's where we stand now as Frank calls the room to order.

I take another deep breath and exhale, using these final moments to center myself and brace for the worst.

"You'll do great," Kari murmurs.

"Tell that to my sweaty palms," I say back, my voice low.

She chuckles. "Being nervous means you care," she assures me. "Just picture all of them naked."

I snort a soft laugh. "Most of them are fat and hairy, Kari. I'll do no such thing." With that, I step into the room.

Cameras immediately start flashing, reporters calling out questions. Frank turns to me, a gleaming smile on his face as he gestures to the center chair. I take a seat as he slithers off.

I've been in the room plenty of times, but never like this. Never as the coach—interim or otherwise. Never as the one the meeting has been called for. And as the cameras keep flashing, the questions still coming, all I can do is remind myself why I'm here.

I hold my hands up, and the room eventually quiets. "I was told to prepare a statement for this. And I did. But I'm going to speak from the heart instead."

Hidden behind the pillar, Frank throws his arms up. I'm willing to bet that if I turned and looked at him, I'd see steam coming out of his ears.

I swallow. "How many of you are parents?"

A few hands raise, and after a moment, a few more.

With a wry smile, I nod at them. "Being a parent is tough. I'm willing to bet that most of you had time to adjust to the idea—say, eight or nine months. But I didn't. I became a parent the day that my daughter's birth mother decided she'd had enough and left her on my front porch."

Murmurs and more camera flashes. "Is that true?" someone shouts.

"You really think I'd make that up?" I ask, then I reconsider. "Don't answer that."

The reporters laugh.

I continue. "Yes, it's true. I didn't know she was pregnant. She kept it from me and then decided she didn't want to be a mom. She left my almost three-month-old daughter on the porch with a note and a birth certificate." I let that sink in, then forge ahead. "Here's the thing. What's happening right now between my daughter's birth mother and me is private. It's not your business. It's no one's business but ours."

"But what about the nanny?" someone yells.

"What *about* the nanny?" I ask.

"The audio—"

"Is completely doctored," I finish.

"I've got an expert who says that's the nanny's voice."

Anger starts to simmer. "I don't give a damn what your 'expert' says," I growl.

Kari appears beside me. "What Coach Miles—"

"*Interim* Coach," I correct.

"What Interim Coach Miles is trying to say," Kari says, eyeing me with no small amount of exasperation, "is that while the words you hear on the file are, in fact, Elodie Cole's, they weren't said in that order, and she contends that many of the words never came out of her mouth. This is a clear use of AI in a smear campaign designed to put Coach Miles on the defensive. Miss Cole and interim Coach Miles are the victims here. Not Lauren Williamson."

Frank is practically dancing a jig in my periphery, and based on Kari's smooth delivery, I'm beginning to suspect that she's seen way more things in this rugby club than I want to know.

I stand. "We're done."

Reporters immediately begin to lob more questions at me, but I ignore them as I make my way down the dais.

Frank blocks my way, his arms crossed.

I don't break stride, aiming straight for him.

And when he doesn't move, I shoulder-check him so hard he hits the wall behind him.

I don't bother saying a word.

Chapter 35
Elodie

nsel's side of the bed is cold when I wake up at seven.

I sit up and focus my bleary eyes, realizing that not only is his side cold, it's also not even been slept in. Which means it's the third night—no, fourth—he's slept somewhere else. He was on the couch once, surrounded by rugby playbooks, but every other morning, I've found him on the floor of Rosie's room, his head on a stuffed unicorn and his massive body partially covered by a rainbow comforter.

This morning, though, he's not in Rosie's room when I poke my head in. Rosie herself still sleeps, her arms thrown wide, the covers askew, surrounded by more dolls and stuffed animals than should be possible. I gaze at her, allowing myself the peace that comes with watching her little chest rise and fall.

She's the reason this matters. I will do whatever it takes to protect this little girl, from now until the end of time. I love Ansel, without question. Wholly and without reservation. But my love for Rosalie is something entirely different, both tender and fierce, and so, so precious. Together, she and Ansel have become the complete center of my world, and I wouldn't have it any other way.

Facing everything that Lauren has thrown at us is simply something that has to be done. A gauntlet to run. A mountain to climb. And I'll do it. No matter the pain, I'll do it.

Turning and leaving the door open a crack, I make my way downstairs. When I don't find Ansel immediately on the couch or in the kitchen, I figure he's probably in the office. I start some coffee and unlock my phone to see what new things the press and social media have to say.

The first thing I see is a short clip of the press release I didn't watch. In the clip, Ansel scowls at the audience as you hear someone ask, *"What about the nanny?"* And Ansel's immediate answer is to dismissively growl, *"What about the nanny?"*

Um, ouch.

A new article focuses on my time at Fore Gone, which is new. Seems my old buddy Dan decided he wasn't on my side after all, not to mention my old boss, hungry for any spotlight she can get. According to them, I was a 'terrible worker' with a 'poor attitude' and neither seems surprised at my new, gold-digging ways.

Spending days reading lies about yourself is nothing I'd recommend to anyone. But what it has done, remarkably, is honed me. It's sharpened my focus and made what's important to me very, very clear. It's made *who* is important to me clear. It's crystalized a few other things, too.

I take a deep breath and pull my phone out, then press call on a contact I've not spoken to in two years.

"Look who finally decides I'm worth talking to." My mother's voice, sugared and vicious as always, comes through the speaker. "You have a lot of explaining to do."

"Hello to you, too, Mother," I answer. "And how like you to jump right into insults and inferences without so much as a how are you."

She sighs, and I hear the clatter of her many bracelets knocking against each other as she waves my comment off. "I raised you better than this, Elodie."

"You raised me like a tyrant," I interrupt. "You only showed affection when I was winning, and the second I put on weight and stopped winning those ridiculous pageants, you made my life hell."

"You were *fat*, Elodie."

I laugh. "I was a perfectly normal girl, Mother. You weaponized your love."

"Because you needed discipline!" she shoots back. "I won't apologize. The only thing I'm sorry for is not being stricter. For God's sake, look at you now," she *tsks*. "Fatter than ever, embroiled in a scandal with a rugby player and trying to insert yourself between a mother and her child, of all things. Just because you can't have your own children doesn't mean you steal someone else's. You should have begged Jeremy to keep you, babies or no babies. Maybe then, none of this would be happening."

"That's not what happened," I say, managing to keep my voice even.

"Oh, so every single news article is lying?"

"Yes!"

"Please." The way she dismisses me cuts like a knife.

I shouldn't have called. I thought I could confront her and walk away without injury. But it's impossible to maintain the shield I'd constructed. Not when every word out of her mouth seems tailor-made to strike true.

Tears streak down my face as I stand in the center of the kitchen, one arm wrapped around my waist as I press the phone to my ear. She's still talking, but I stopped hearing it.

"We're done." My voice is flat, dull.

"Excuse me?"

"Until you can be nice to me, we're done," I repeat.

"Absolutely not," she says. "You owe me. You need to talk to the pageant commission and tell them—"

A harsh laugh escapes. "You honestly think I'm going to help you? Go to hell, Mother."

And with that, I end the call. Before I can overthink it, I block her number.

Beside me, the coffee maker beeps merrily, announcing that coffee is ready. I stare numbly at the phone in my hand, then set it on the counter and push it away.

"Well, that could have gone better," I mumble to myself. I have a feeling that I need to spend some quality time digging through the trauma my mother inflicted. Time on my own and with a therapist. But right now, I'm going to tuck Mother into a tight little box with a **Do Not Open** sign on it and take care of the people I love.

With two mugs of coffee in hand, I make my way to the office. Sure enough, Ansel is there, and he looks up as I enter.

His thick hair is mussed from sleep and his beard needs trimming. Behind his glasses, dark smudges have taken up residence beneath his warm brown eyes, eyes that have dimmed with every passing day since the gala. On the desk in front of him are a pile of papers strewn from one side to the other, along with sticky notes, pens, and highlighters.

"I brought you coffee," I offer, raising the steaming cup and stepping into the office.

He leans back in the chair and scrubs at his face. To the side of the desk is an old couch, lumpy and stained, and the last remnant of Ansel's college days. A pillow is at one end, an Atlanta Granite blanket bunched at the other.

"I wish you'd come sleep in the bed," I say quietly, handing him the coffee.

He takes it and brings it to his mouth. The steam fogs his glasses as he takes a fortifying sip. "Thank you." His voice is scratchy.

I tilt my head toward the couch. "Come sit. Take a break."

He clenches his jaw and shakes his head. "I'm behind. I need to review—"

"You need to take a break." My voice is soft, insistent.

His gaze seems to finally focus on me then. "I don't get to take a break. I have videos to review and practice schedules to confirm. I have emails from sports press around the world that Frank has decided I'll be responding to instead of Kari. I have an eighteen-year-old kid joining the team, against my wishes but hey, I'm just the *interim* coach when my decision isn't one they want to hear. I have to figure out who's going to be his mentor in a ridiculous attempt to keep him from falling prey to every rugger hugger out there, because thanks to all this," he gestures at his phone, "the entire fucking world seems to think the Granite's fly-half is open for business!" he snaps.

My spine straightens at his tone. "I've already had one person yell at me this morning. I don't need you doing it, too. It's not nice."

He blows out a breath. "Yeah, well, neither is this."

"Let me help you." An idea takes hold as the words

form. "We can do this together. I've done nothing these past few days except read lie after lie. We can have another press conference. I can explain—"

"That's not a good idea, Elle."

But I press forward. "Just think about it. We can start a counter-campaign. If Frank won't let Kari do it, then I bet your agent knows the right people."

"*No*, Elodie."

His tone stops me immediately. I meet his eyes. "Did— did something else happen?"

Emotions fly across his face, too fast for me to track. Anger, sadness, desperation, fury, determination. And when he finally speaks, his voice is cold and distant. "I got notice of a custody hearing."

My stomach turns to ice. "No."

His laugh is harsh. "You think I'd lie about something like this?"

I shake my head. "That's not what I meant. Why didn't you tell me?"

"And when would I have told you? During your doom scrolling yesterday afternoon, or before your session of doom scrolling last night?"

I ignore the hateful jab. "You got it yesterday? You've carried this by yourself for a full day and didn't tell me?"

He shrugs. "It doesn't matter. There's nothing you can do about it."

That's not the point. That's entirely *beside* the point. "Did you tell anyone else?"

"Other than my lawyer? I called my parents."

"But you didn't tell me?"

"What do you want me to say, Elodie?" His voice is clipped, harsh. "No. I didn't tell you."

"But I could have helped!"

"How?" he demands. "How could you have helped?"

"I could have—I don't know, but—"

"Exactly," he says, cutting me off. "You don't know. You couldn't have helped."

"Because I love you, Ansel!" Oh. Holy crap. The words came out. They came out! I can't help the smile that forms as I say the words again. "Because I love you. Because we're a team. Because everything we're doing here is supposed to be *with each other*."

He blinks at me, shaking his head. "You say that *now*? Seriously?"

"Probably not the best timing," I admit. "Guess we're the same that way."

"Elodie." My name is an exhale as he drags his hand through his hair.

My stomach twists. *This is what happens when you tell people you love them. They reject you.* I shove the thought away, focused on Ansel. I've just told my mother to go to hell. I can face this. "We can do this. We can get through this together as a team."

He's not having it. "Unbelievable. How could you possibly know anything about being on a team? Nothing in your life has been calibrated for that. I'm not saying that's exactly your fault—pageants are decidedly a one-person thing—but, Elodie. There's no team here. None."

I swallow down the tears. "You know that's not true. You know I'm trying."

"Do I?" He leans forward in his chair. "Here's what I know. I have spent the past five years busting my ass to be the best father I can be. I have read more books on parenting than is probably healthy. I have accepted every damn sponsorship that comes my way and shoved it into a college savings account because I am *terrified* that I'll get hurt and lose everything and won't be able to provide for my little girl. I have let one nanny after another take care of my daughter because I haven't had a choice. And then I finally think I'm going to catch a break this summer, but no. Of course not. And you waltz in."

My whole body trembles as slick, oily dread courses through me. He can't mean this. The coldness in his eyes— that's just fear. It's not about me.

He keeps going. "I had it all under control. Barely, and it sure as fuck wasn't perfect, but we were making it. And then you come in and upend everything. You let both of us fall for you, just in time for Lauren to come in and use you as a weapon. For her to take aim and threaten everything that is good and precious in my entire fucking world. You can't possibly understand what it feels like to face down the threat of losing your daughter. You can't possibly know what it's like for your entire heart to exist outside of your body and run around in pigtails. You cannot begin to feel the absolute *terror* I have at the thought of that snake taking my daughter. So, no. No, you can't help. No, we aren't a team. And no, we won't get through this together."

Every word is a blow. Each sentence a punch that he isn't pulling. And as I stand before him, his voice growing increasingly harsh as he lashes out from behind his desk, all I can think about is the last thing that Jeremy said to me.

I can't love someone who can't give me a child.

And here I am, finally able to tell a different man that I love him, having already loved his daughter the moment I laid eyes on her, only to have him rip her away from me, too.

You should have begged Jeremy to keep you, babies or no babies.

Just because you can't have your own children doesn't mean you steal someone else's.

I won't apologize.

I try to stand straight. I try to square my shoulders. And I really, *really* try not to cry. But I fail on all three counts, and the despair and loathing I feel for myself is stratospheric. I simply nod, tears streaming down my face. I grit my teeth together and meet his eyes one last time. "Okay. I understand."

Chapter 36
Ansel

Fuck.

Chapter 37
Elodie

Kari's eyes widen when she opens the door. "Elodie? What's going on?"

"It's over," I manage to get out between hiccuping sobs. "Me and Ansel. I told him I loved him, and it's over. And I told my mother to go to hell."

"You *what?*" She looks me over, taking me in. The massive bag hanging off one shoulder, the cat carrier in the other hand, the tear-streaked face that I didn't bother washing, the pajamas I'm still in because I didn't bother changing.

Once I ran upstairs, I threw everything I could into a bag and got out of there quickly. I didn't want to face Rosie. I was already in a bad headspace, and seeing her would have absolutely destroyed me.

I take a deep breath and try to focus my thoughts. "I told him I loved him, and he doesn't want anything to do with me," I sob. "It's all my fault. All of this—everything that's happened—is all my fault, Kari!"

Her face falls. "Oh, no, sweetheart. No. Come in, come in."

I step over the threshold, and she takes the carrier out of my hands to let Cleocatra out. The cat yowled the entire drive over, and I truly wasn't sure if she was angry about the car ride or that I'd lured her away from a still-sleeping Rosalie's bed. Kari unlatches the door, and Cleo's calico head pops out, her pink nose sniffing the air.

Kari looks up from where she kneels in front of the carrier. "Coffee?"

It's only then that I realize what time it is. "You're about to go to work, aren't you?" My shoulders sag, and the massive overnight bag slides off my shoulder and thuds to the wooden floor beside me.

She stands and takes my hand. "I *was*. But now I'm not. I just need to call Frank."

I wince, the tears coming back in force. "Everything is all my fault," I wail.

She pulls me into her arms, shushing me and rubbing my back. "Nothing is your fault," she soothes.

Her kindness only makes me cry harder. "It is," I promise her, sniffing and failing miserably at keeping the tears from falling. I can't see a way out. That beautiful clarity I'd somehow woken up with is gone. It disappeared into ash the second Ansel told me we weren't a team. "It definitely is."

Kari releases me from the hug and studies me, her hands on my shoulders. "Hey. It's going to be okay. You're going to tell me everything that happened, and we'll fix it. Because that's what we do. Okay?"

I sniff. "Okay."

She gets me settled onto her couch and presses a cup of coffee into my hands, then grabs her phone. "Let me call Frank, and I'll be back."

She leaves the room, her voice growing distant as she speaks. "Frank? Hey. Listen..."

She's back a few minutes later, sinking onto the couch and tucking her feet beneath her. "Start at the beginning. What's going on?"

A fresh wave of tears begins as the magnitude of what I've done starts to hit me. "I have to move. I told my mother to go to hell. Ansel's got a custody hearing. If he loses—no. He can't lose. But I'm never going to see her again. He'll never let me see her. She'll forget about me, and so will he, and it'll be like I was never there," I sob, unable to breathe. "Oh, God." This is worse than the other day. So much worse.

"Let's start with the mother from hell," Kari suggests softly. "Did she call you?"

"No," I hiccup. "I called her because I woke up and had all this clarity. I finally understood something vital."

"Which was?" she prompts.

"That my mother is a horrible, selfish monster and I needed to tell her that."

"Okay, maybe not the best timing in the world, babe, but sometimes that's just what needs to happen."

I give her a watery smile. "You've always told me I need to tell her off."

"I have," she agrees. "So you had that call."

Nodding, I continue, "And then I took Ansel some coffee, and I was finally able to tell him I loved him. But the timing was bad on that, too." My lip trembles and I bite down on it.

It takes a while, but eventually I'm able to tell Kari the full story. When I finish, she studies me for a long minute. Then she stands and holds up her phone. "This calls for day drinking. With friends. Now, go take a shower and get dressed. I'll handle the rest."

I let out a stuttered breath. "I don't think so."

She snorts. "I don't care. This is happening. Come on. Up you go." She waves me away, shooing me to the bathroom.

"I can't."

"You can."

"Kari—"

She purses her lips. "Move it, woman. Go. Go go go. We're fixing this."

My heart squeezes, and more tears emerge. "It won't help."

She tilts her head, and when she speaks, her voice is soft again. "Well, it sure won't hurt. So go."

Defeated, I sigh and make my way to her shower. I take my time, washing my thick hair and using a body scrub before shrugging and using her razor on my armpits and legs. None of it helps, exactly, but the soothing routine of self-care lulls me into a sense of false calm. Like everything will be okay if I just stay numb.

And numb is what I need. Numb is necessary. I don't want the clear-headedness I woke up with. Look where that got me: blurting out *I love you* to yet another person who doesn't want it. My body finally let the words out, only it was at the exact wrong time. Because it was too late. Way, way too late.

I pull on my favorite pair of Costco lounge pants and a loose crop top over a lacy black bralette and make my way out of the steamy bathroom. Kari bustles around the kitchen, but I don't bother her as I beeline for the couch and pull a blanket over me. I grab my phone, forcing myself not to open any of the social media apps or my email. Instead, I open my reading app and attempt to get lost in the historical fiction I usually love to read.

I must fall asleep, because the next thing I know, I hear voices coming from the kitchen. After a few moments, I recognize the husky laugh of Allyson and the Australian lilt of Sam. The temptation to throw the blanket over my head and pretend to keep sleeping is strong, but I make myself get up and fold the blanket instead.

Padding into the room, I find all three women chattering away, all smiles and happiness, and it hits me then. How empty I feel. I can't fathom feeling as light as they seem, as unburdened. It's no surprise that tears once again spring to my eyes.

Allyson chooses that exact moment to turn and gives me a big smile. "Elodie!" Then she scowls. "Nope. We're not crying."

And that, of course, makes me cry.

All three women surround me as I boo-hoo and generally make a mess of myself, but eventually Sam pulls away.

"All right, enough of that," she scolds playfully. "We were called over for day drinking, and that's exactly what we're going to do."

"But first—did you hear back from that whale-watching company?"

"Allyson!" Kari exclaims.

"What?" Allyson asks. "No better way to get her mind off things than to talk about me."

I can't help the laugh that comes out even as I grab a paper towel to blow my nose. "Yes, Allyson, I did."

She wiggles her eyebrows and rubs her hands together. "Ooh, is it gonna work out?"

I nod. "It is."

Allyson whirls to the counter. "Okay, *now* it's time to drink. Are we starting with straight tequila shots?"

"*No*," all three of us respond.

I don't know how much time passes, but I do know that we impart some serious damage to Kari's liquor collection and put a hurting on Jake's DoorDash account. No one remembered who ordered what, but once the delivery driver deposited Taco Bell, at least five different kinds of chips from the convenience store, and an entire cheesecake from the Cheesecake Factory on Kari's front porch, it didn't matter.

I tell them everything. The way I loved Rosalie from the second I met her, the way Ansel and I slowly fell for each other. How Ansel steadily pulled me out of my "nice girl" shell and told me he loved me, and how I loved him, too, but couldn't get the words out. And this morning, when he ended it.

In exchange, Allyson spilled all the tea about the team, giving us the gossip on everything from which players the old coach had it out for to which ones were being scouted for moving to Europe. Sam told us how she'd left Melbourne not just to accompany her brother—who honestly doesn't need his older sister to look after him—but to break free from the monotony that had become her life. Kari simply watched me from across the room, quietly making sure I was okay.

I wasn't. I'm not.

I don't know when I will be.

Kari clears her throat and raises her glass of wine. "A toast," she declares.

We raise our drinks, Allyson and I drinking expensive and delicious tequila, and Sam joining Kari in the wine department.

"Here's to us. Strong women taking chances, leaping into the unknown, and making ourselves brand new all over again."

"Here, here," Sam says, and we toast.

My phone pings as we drink. I pick it up from its spot on the coffee table and open it, half expecting it to be a text from Ansel, and half knowing he's not sending me squat.

UNKNOWN

Told you not to fuck with me.

I stare at the text as another comes in, then another.

How's it feel to be a pariah? To be used and discarded just like I was?

Hope you enjoyed the free ride. Because it's over.

A wave of hot, bright anger washes over me, and I growl. "That fucking *bitch*."

"Whoa," Kari breathes.

Allyson and Sam gape at me.

"Did you just curse?" Kari continues.

I keep staring at the texts, rage building inside me. Absolutely nothing she's done has been out of love for her daughter. Nothing. And the fact that she sent this tells me she's still got someone watching the house. Which is frightening and disgusting in equal measure.

"I hate her," I seethe. "I hate her fucking guts."

Kari nods appreciatively. "Okay. I like where this is going. This is better than crying."

"Amen," Allyson agrees. "But who do we hate?"

I hold the phone up for them to read. "Lauren."

They're quiet as they read the texts, then they explode into righteous cries of indignation and fury.

"What the *fuck?*" Kari demands.

"She really just sent that," Sam says.

Without a word, Allyson stands and walks to the hallway, then returns with her laptop.

I narrow my alcohol-blurred eyes at her. "What are you doing?"

"Y'all know what my job is, right?"

"Glamorous Black Goddess?" I guess.

She laughs. "Close. I run a private investigation company."

"Wait. You *what?*" Sam's eyes are round.

"You never told us that!" Kari accuses.

Allyson flashes a predatory smile. "You never asked."

Chapter 38
Ansel

There is absolutely nothing worse than seeing your daughter cry.

Actually, I take that back.

It's bad to see your daughter cry. But it is gut-wrenching to know that you're the reason she's crying.

"Does she not love us anymore?" Rosie's tear-filled eyes look up at me as I tuck her into bed.

I managed to distract Rosie from the fact that both Elodie *and* Cleocatra weren't around all day, but now that it's nighttime, all bets are off.

"Of course she still loves you," I tell her softly. That's not the problem.

"Us, Daddy. Does she still love *us*?"

I grimace. How is she so damn perceptive? It's both annoying and wonderful. But right now it's mainly annoying. Still, I know the answer to the question. "Yes, sweetheart. She still loves us."

"Then why isn't she here?" Rosie clutches Violet to her chest, the lookalike doll still sporting braids from Elodie's handiwork last week.

"I…. That's hard to answer," I admit.

Rosie pats my hand even as she sniffs her tears away. "It's okay. Take your time and find your words."

I huff a laugh. "That's *my* saying."

But she simply waits. And I'm filled with so much love for her that I might burst. "Okay," I relent. "I think I messed up."

"You never mess up, Daddy."

"Oh, I mess up plenty," I say wryly, bopping her nose with my finger. "I just keep it hidden from you."

She sits up, adjusting the blanket around her and Violet. "You always tell me that everything is fixatle."

"Fixa*ble*," I correct.

"Fixable," she repeats, then looks at me expectantly.

Sighing, I meet her big hazel eyes. Eyes that remind me so much of Elodie it makes my heart hurt.

Does she *really* love me? After all this, I don't see how she can. Lauren has done everything she can to come after me, and Elodie was a victim of circumstance. She's been dragged through the mud and had more vicious things said about her than I can count.

But how can I ask her to stand beside me as I fight all this? Especially after what I said to her. It doesn't matter that I didn't mean it, that I was scared and lashing out at the one person who's been beside me through all of this. How can she forgive me? What right do I have to ask her forgiveness?

"I said some really mean things to her. Things I didn't mean."

"Were you hungry when you said them? That's when I say things I don't mean," Rosie says, nodding sagely.

"Maybe," I admit. "But I think more than anything, I was scared."

Rosie's little brow furrows. "Why?"

"I'm still figuring all that out," I say, evading the truth. She really is only five, and there's only so much I can sort out to tell her.

"Sounds like you need to say sorry, Daddy."

My shoulders fall. "You're right. I do."

She purses her lips. "Tomorrow."

"Tomorrow...what?"

"Tomorrow we go get her, and you apologize. And then we ask her to stay with us forever." She gives a firm, decisive jerk of her chin before snuggling back under the covers.

I lean down and press a kiss to her forehead. "You're right."

"Good night, Daddy."

"Good night, Rosalie. Sweet dreams."

"Sleep tight."

"I love you."

"Love you, too." She delivers it with a wide, cracking yawn.

Downstairs, I text the only person I can think of who might know where Elodie is.

> Is she with you?

KARI
> Sorry I'm not talking to meanies right now

> Please.

KARI
> Why should I tell you if she's next to me, plastered out of her mind and holding a slice of cheesecake with her hand?

> So she's with you?

KARI

Why would I tell you that she's been here
all day?

I'm coming by in the morning.

KARI

I don't know why you would because why
would I tell you she probably needs to
sleep it off till at least ten?

Thank you.

KARI

I don't know what you're talking about.

Chapter 39
Elodie

I wake up to a glass of water and some ibuprofen on the coffee table in front of me. Beside them is a note from Kari explaining that she's gone to work and that we'll tackle things when she gets home later. Curled up at the end of the couch is Cleocatra, blinking her green eyes at me in what I can only assume is silent judgment for how drunk I got yesterday.

I shower and have some coffee, then hear a knock at the door. My breath catches when I look through the peephole and see Ansel and Rosalie.

With my heart beating wildly, I open the door, only to gape at what they each hold. Rosie holds three different bouquets in her little arms: a dozen red roses, a dozen tulips of different colors, and then a mix of flowers. Clutched in Ansel's hand are three giant vellum balloons: SpongeBob SquarePants, Bluey, and a massive rainbow balloon with the words *My condolences* on it.

"Hi," Ansel croaks.

"We brought you flowers and balloons because girls deserve a lot of flowers when boys mess up. And Daddy told me he messed up big-time." Rosie offers this last tidbit with no small amount of pride.

The relief I feel at seeing Rosie is unmatched. I kneel before her, so grateful to see her sweet face that tears spring to my eyes. "They're very pretty."

Rosie hands them over, then launches herself into my free arm. "I missed you, Elle Belle," she whispers.

I squeeze her tight. "I missed you, too, Rosie bug."

Finally, Rosie lets go and leans back. "Is Cleocatra here?"

I stand and gesture inside, sniffing back my tears. "Oh, yes. She's somewhere in there."

Rosie dashes inside without so much as a backward glance, making Ansel and me chuckle.

"Well," I mutter, watching her disappear around the corner, "at least she's got her priorities straight."

Ansel looks terrible. Much worse than yesterday, with sallow-looking skin and hair in disarray. His beautiful caramel eyes have lost their sparkle, and they gaze back at me with trepidation.

"Do you want to come in?" I ask. "I mean, I know Rosie just took off in there, but I can go get her if—"

"I want to," he says softly. "If you'll have me."

I take a deep breath. Despite the flowers and balloons, I'm still not sure what this conversation is really going to entail. "Okay."

He follows me in, still holding the mylar balloons as they clunk against each other while we make our way to the living room. "Is Kari here?"

I shake my head as I get a good look at the balloons. *"My condolences?"*

He shrugs and gives me a shy smile. "Rosie insisted on

three balloons, and since there wasn't one that said *I'm sorry*, she decided that this one would work."

"Of course she did." I can't help but be amused.

"I tried convincing her that *Happy Birthday* might be better, but." He shrugs again. "Obviously, they're for you. So are the flowers." He gestures at the bunches in her hand. "Want me to take them and put them in water?"

"Um, no. Just hang on, and I'll go do that."

I leave him there, shifting on his feet as I go to the kitchen and find a pitcher to fill and put the bouquets in.

Ansel is winding the balloons together and trying to get them to stay put in a corner of the living room when I return. He's sweating.

My mouth quirks up as a spark of hope flares to life inside me. "Do *you* need water, too?"

He hesitates, then gestures awkwardly at the couch. "No, thanks. Can we sit?"

We sit.

"I'm sorry," he blurts. "I'm so fucking sorry, Elodie."

I stare, unable to believe it.

"Hang on. I need—" He blinks rapidly, swaying a bit.

Jumping up, I say, "I think you *do* need water. Hold on."

I'm back in moments, handing him a glass of water that he gulps down like a man on fire. When was the last time he ate? Once I'm sure he's okay, I sit back down in front of him.

He works his jaw, seeming to wrestle with himself before finally settling on a path forward. "This morning, I woke up at the butt-crack of dawn to tackle coach business. I emailed all the agents at once and then I emailed all the reporters at once. I'm through. I've had enough of being distracted, because all it's done is made things worse. I don't know that any of it could have stopped the looming custody battle, but I'm tackling one thing at a time. This morning was rugby business. Now, my actual life gets attention." He pauses. "*You* are my actual life, Elodie. You and Rosie.

"You are nothing I expected," he continues. "When we talked that first day, I had no idea—I couldn't possibly fathom—that we'd end up like this." He rakes his fingers through his hair. "Elodie, meeting you has been one of my life's greatest joys. You are exactly what I needed. You push me, you challenge me, you make me a better man. You make me a better father. And I can't imagine my life without you."

Oh. *Oh.* "Ansel," I breathe.

He pulls my hands into his, his expression hopeful. "I was out of line yesterday. *Way* out of line. I've been under a lot of pressure, but that doesn't excuse the way I behaved. Getting that custody summons was...fuck, that's the scariest thing that's ever happened to me."

I bite my lip. "I just wanted to help."

"I know." He squeezes my hands, then brings them up to kiss them. "I'm still learning to accept help. Same as you," he teases gently, raising a scarred eyebrow.

Can he really mean this? "I don't know if we should...do whatever it is we're doing. Your words yesterday—"

"Were utter and complete crap," he admits. "Hurtful, and untrue."

I study him. "Maybe, but the fact is..." I stop, look away. Swallowing, I meet his gaze again. "I love that little girl so much it's terrifying. But I'm not her mother, Ansel. I'll never be her mother. And if Lauren—"

"Fuck Lauren," he growls, making me flinch at the harsh tone. Gentler, he says, "You've acted more like her mother in the past months than her own ever did. Rosie's never had a mother, Elodie. And I'm not apologizing in some misguided attempt to get you to watch my kid. I'm here because I love you. I love you so much that it takes my breath away. I love you for *you*. Your laughter. Your heart. I love you for the way your eyes crinkle when you laugh. For the love on your face when you look at my daughter. I love your freckles—seriously, I can't get enough of those." He quirks a smile. "And I love that you grade Rosie's cannonballs more harshly than I do. I love that you're building your business and not hesitating for one second about it. I love how you're learning the rules of rugby, even though you keep calling me a half-fly instead of a fly-half."

"That *might* be on purpose," I mumble with a grin, my eyes filled with unshed tears.

"I know." He smiles, the color back on his face. "I love you, Elodie. So wholly and completely that it nearly paralyzes me. But you make me brave. You make me want to take the risk. And I don't know if you'll ever forgive me for what I said, or if you can ever fathom being by my side again. Loving me. Loving Rosalie. Being a team with us. But God, I hope you do."

My heart swells as he speaks, my entire body heating with unbridled joy and hope. He loves me. He *still* loves me. After everything. "This is the only team I ever want to be a part of," I say, leaning forward to cradle his face. "I love you, too, Ansel. I'm sorry it took me so long to say it. And I'm sorry I let Lauren bait me in the bathroom—"

He cuts me off with a kiss, a ragged breath leaving him. "Fuck, I missed this," he breathes. "I missed you."

"It was only twenty-four hours," I protest softly, giggling as he keeps kissing me even as we talk.

"Twenty-four hours is too much," he says.

I giggle, meeting those caramel irises and seeing them filled with light once more. "I love you."

"Damn, that sounds good." He grins and traces a finger

along my bare shoulder, sending goosebumps down my body. "Say it again."

With a smile, I happily obey. "I love you, Ansel Miles."

"Does this mean you're coming back home now?"

We both turn to see Rosie in the doorway, Cleocatra held precariously in her arms and sporting what can only be described as a look of resigned indignation.

We look back at each other. Ansel asks, "What do you say, Elle Belle? Are we worth the try?"

My smile is bright and sure. "Absolutely."

Chapter 40
Ansel
One week later

I lug the last bag into the spare bedroom and heave a breath, looking at Elodie. "Your shoes are oppressive." We unloaded the storage unit the other day, and today marked the moving of all her things over from the guesthouse.

She laughs. "I thought you were a big bad rugby player. You can't handle a little old bag of shoes?"

I give her a flat stare. "That bag could be used for weight training for the forwards, Elodie. *That's* how insane it is."

She shrugs, unapologetic. "Well, you seemed to be perfectly fine with my shoes when I wore the strappy ones while you fucked me from behind the other night."

My eyes nearly bug out of my head. "Elodie Cole. Did you just say a cuss word when I wasn't buried deep inside you?"

Her eyes twinkle as a blush stains her cheeks. "Maybe."

I step around the bag, my arousal evident through the gray sweatpants I'm wearing. "Get over here."

She giggles and backs away. "We still have more bags to bring up from the truck!"

I shake my head and keep stalking toward her. "They can wait."

She tries again. "Rosie is downstairs!"

"I can be quick," I say, making grabby hands as I close in.

"The bed's not made!" She gasps as I snag her around the waist and pull her to me, her back to my front.

"It's the guest bedroom, and it's a *good* thing it's not made." I lick her neck and slip my thumbs into the waistband of her yoga shorts. "Tell me something," I say against her ear as I push the fabric down.

"Yes?" It comes out hoarse.

"Do you ever wear panties with these?"

"N-no," she stutters, her breath catching as I slide my finger along her slit. She's soaked.

I push my sweatpants and boxers down. "Good." I bend her over the bed and glide my hand down her back before notching myself at her entrance. "Don't ever start."

She wiggles her hips, and the sight of her is almost enough to make me come right now. I slide into her on a grunt. The feel of her, velvety hot and tight, is the sweetest sensation. *Home.*

She gasps, then moans as I thrust again. "Fast and hard, Ansel."

"Yes, ma'am." I grip her hips and slam into her, watching my cock disappear into her over and over. I will give this woman whatever she wants. Today, tomorrow, a decade from now.

I GET a call from my lawyer later that night, as Elodie and I watch Rosie work on yet another puzzle. Frowning at the phone, I pull it up to my ear. "Jennifer?"

"Is Elodie there?" Jennifer asks. "Put me on speakerphone."

"Hang on," I instruct, and Elodie and I walk to the kitchen so that Rosie doesn't hear. "Okay, go."

"Elodie, are you familiar with a woman named Allyson Fields?"

I scrunch my brow and mouth, *"Jake's fiancée?"*

She nods and answers, "Yes, I am."

"Mm. And do you, by chance, know what she does for a living?"

"I do," she says, drawing out the words.

"I don't," I state.

"Interesting," Jennifer answers. "Because Allyson is a private investigator. One of the South's finest, in fact. Her company, and her reputation in particular, is top-notch. My clients can't afford her."

"She's my friend," Elodie says.

Jennifer continues, "Imagine my surprise when I got a call from her, followed by a zip file filled with all sorts of information on Rosalie's birth mother."

My eyebrows are practically on the ceiling with how high I'm raising them. "What? How? What's it say?"

Meanwhile, Elodie's grinning like a fool. Her smile makes me start to shake. Could something good actually be happening with this?

"Turns out that Lauren Williamson is actually Laura Williams, who's wanted in Nevada for embezzlement. And in California for the same thing. And South Carolina. There's also a, and this is a legal term, *shit-ton* of speeding tickets attributed to her various monikers." Jennifer pauses. "It's safe to say that the custody hearing is a no-go, Ansel. You can stop worrying."

"Holy shit," I breathe in disbelief. Goosebumps fly across my body. This can't be real. But it is. I think. "Seriously?"

"Seriously." Jennifer's smile comes through the speaker. "This is my favorite part of the job."

I laugh. "Until I pay that bill."

She chuckles. "That's nice, too. Congratulations, Ansel. And Elodie, tell your friend thank you."

"I will."

Jennifer signs off, and I pick Elodie up and whirl her around the kitchen, my grip on her tight. She laughs, her relief just as palpable as mine. I let her down only to pull her back for a kiss, smiling the entire time.

"I knew Allyson was impressive. I had no *clue* she was a next-level spy master," I mutter. "But—how? What made her look into it?"

"Oh." Elodie waves a hand nonchalantly. "It was after Lauren texted me the night we got smashed."

"She *what*?"

"It doesn't matter." Elodie presses a hand to my chest. "She's getting what she deserves." Then she winks. "But I will never forget the look on Allyson's face when she opened that laptop. Just remind me never to get on Allyson's bad side, okay?"

I have to sit down. My knees are literally weak. "It's over. It's really over."

"Well, that part's over." Elodie holds up her phone for me to see the text that's just come in for both of us.

KARI

Y'all know Allyson tipped me off and as your PR rep I must demand a PRESS CONFERENCE.

I shake my head. "Tell that woman to give me at least a full day of relief first."

With a knowing grin, Elodie sends the message, and Kari's response comes through moments later.

KARI

I knew you'd say that. You have a press conference to introduce the new coach next week anyway.

Immediately below the text is a link to someone's rugby coaching bio. "Let me see that." Elodie hands over her phone, and I click the link, reading the bio. "Huh. Seems like we've got ourselves a good one."

"Yeah?"

"Yeah. Colin Thicke is one of the winningest rugby coaches in the collegiate circuit. I remember him from my own college days." If memory serves, he's no-nonsense, gets shit done, and has a squeaky-clean reputation. Whether and how that translates to professional rugby, I don't yet know. What I *do* know? That I can't wait to hand the reins back over to an actual coach. Another text from Kari swings in filled only with question marks, and I snort. "She's impatient."

"You've met her, right?" Elodie jokes.

I pluck my own phone off the kitchen counter and type a response.

Chill out, Kari. Of course I'll do your damn press conference. Any chance you can get me poster-size glossies of Lauren's arrest photos?

KARI

Don't threaten me with a good time.

Chapter 41
Elodie

Ansel's eyes darken as he comes into the bedroom after getting Rosie set up with yet another viewing of *Brave.* "What is that?"

I twirl in the short sundress, letting it flare up and around to give Ansel a show. It's September, but that doesn't mean squat in Atlanta. Unless you count 'no longer sweltering' as a temperature. With a smirk, I meet his eyes. "This old thing?"

Cursing darkly, he walks across the plush rug and drops to his knees before me. His deep brown eyes meet mine as he says, "Yes, this old thing. You and these damn short dresses are going to be my undoing." His hands skim up the back of my calves, then move farther up the back of my thighs before encountering the cheeky underwear I'm wearing.

He growls. "And I'm going to die a very, very happy man." Then he ducks under the dress.

"Ansel." I laugh, but it turns to a deep, guttural moan as he slips the panties down and presses his hot mouth to the apex of my thighs.

"You taste so good, Elodie." The words are barely intelligible as he begins to worship me, tongue and teeth and lips, and I give myself over to him. The man has been nothing but insatiable since I moved in permanently after we made up. Sex with a kid in the house, it turns out, doesn't happen any less than when she *isn't* in the house; it's just more creative.

Ansel licks my center, focusing in on that glorious bundle of nerves as his hands hold me steady against him. I tremble, and he bears down. Ecstasy comes hot and fast, and I'm panting through the orgasm in minutes. It's barely ended before I'm gasping, "More. I need more."

He lifts the dress off his head and grins up at me, pure male satisfaction on his face. "Then take off this pretty sundress and let me have you."

I pull it off and unclasp my bra as he stands and removes his clothes, then we tumble onto the bed. I spread my legs, eager and wanting, as he positions himself between them. But instead of pushing inside me like I need him to do, he drops his head to mine for a kiss. The taste of my arousal is on his tongue, and it sends me soaring. I grind my hips against him, silently begging. "Want you," I murmur. "Now."

He gives a low laugh as he thrusts up, slow and hard, his cock sliding through my wetness and skimming along my clit. "You want this, sweetheart?"

I reach up and take his glasses off, setting them to the side before taking his face in my hands. His beard is soft on my skin. "I want *you*."

He groans, taking my mouth with his and drifting a hand to my breast before lazily circling my nipple. His tongue licks inside my mouth as he pinches the stiff peak.

The pain it brings is exquisite, and perfect, and I raise my hips again.

"Please," I whisper against his lips.

But he doesn't do it, kissing my jaw and neck while his hand travels the length of my body. On a frustrated groan, I roll us, putting him on his back as I straddle him. I press my palms against the tight, muscular planes of his chest, feasting on the sight of him.

He grins mischievously. "Wondered how long it'd take you."

"You should know that I take what I want now."

His smile turns sincere. "And I love watching you do it. You are a wonder, Elodie."

The praise turns me to goo inside. *This man*, I think. *I love this man so much.* I take his length into my hands as I hold his stare, then lower myself onto him, memorizing the way his eyes glaze at the sensation.

"Elle," he whispers. "Fuck."

I swirl my hips slowly, letting my body get used to him before leaning down for a kiss. His arms encircle me as my hair curtains around us, blocking the world out. He fills every inch of me, thick and hot. I lay my brow on his, the bond stretching between us an almost physical thing. As if a length of velvet ribbon stretched between us and into us, knotting us into a tangle so unbreakable that no one could ever shake it. "I love you," I tell him. Then I say it again. "I love you."

"I love you, too." He cradles my cheek, never looking away as he gently thrusts into me. When we kiss, it's with intention. With need. Desire. Love.

Finally, I rise, taking the full brunt of him inside me as I straighten. He feels so good, so deep within me that I whimper.

"Ride me, baby," he urges softly, his palms coming to rest on either side of my bottom. "I'm yours."

"And I'm yours," I whisper. I begin to move, letting my body take over. We work as one, his hands helping me move up and down, his body chasing my own, every movement designed for pleasure. Emotion soars through me, and tears prick my eyes. The sex is beautiful, tender and soft.

He moves us again, repositioning our bodies in confident, swift motions that have him cradled between my legs as he settles me onto the mattress beneath him. "Let me," he murmurs, driving slowly into me.

I gasp, and he captures my mouth, swallowing the sound. Our eyes meet as he pulls almost all the way out, then pushes back in. He does it again, and my body opens even more as I take him deeper. "Ansel," I moan, the pleasure almost too much to bear.

"Yes?" His grin is sexy, confident.

I dig my nails into his ass, and he takes me again, going deep. Our eyes never leave the others' as we let our bodies speak. *I love you. I want you always. You're perfect. This is perfect. I love you.* Emotion is stark on his face, mirroring my own.

He pulls almost to the edge and thrusts in, slow and sure, again and again, until I'm a quivering mess. "Please," I repeat. The pace is luxuriously slow, and nearly unbearable. "More. *More.*"

He pulls my leg up and over his shoulder, and thrusts.

"God, *yes*," I hiss.

Again, he pushes. "How's this?" He pushes again, his voice low and sensual. "You want my cock like this?"

I arch my neck, and he leans down to lick it, thrusting again as his teeth scrape along my jaw. "Yes," I breathe.

"I'm going to take you like this forever, Elodie." He

slams into me, and I moan at the pleasure of it. "Fuck, this pussy." Another deep thrust as he grunts, "You're so tight around me."

I squeeze him in answer, and he curses, starting to lose the rhythm.

It's exactly what I want. I want him undone. Feral. As wild with love as I am. I grip his jaw, and his eyes meet mine again. "Fuck me, Ansel. I want to feel you so deep inside me I scream."

It's all he needs. He snaps, letting go of all control as he pounds into me. It's everything. *He* is everything. Because even as our bodies lose control, his eyes stay on mine. He moves a hand to my breast, squeezing, then pinching my nipple. I hiss, and he does it again. "Come."

The one-word command is all I need to let go, shattering into a million pieces as I bite down on his shoulder. He grunts at the sensation, and I feel him release inside me. He keeps going, swirling and moving, drawing the orgasm out as much as he can. When we come to a stop, he raises his head and kisses me. "You're incredible," he says.

I grin and tangle our legs together, unwilling to let him go. "Only with you."

"Untrue." He nuzzles my neck, his hand stroking down my body before he lifts onto an elbow and looks at me. "Promise me something."

"Anything."

He brushes a curl from my face. "Promise me that no matter what comes our way, we'll do it together. No more facing things alone. We're a team."

My heart swells. "A team."

His eyes crinkle as he beams. "Always."

"Always."

Epilogue: Elodie

"We're late," I chide Ansel as we walk up the driveway.

"We wouldn't have been if someone hadn't decided to twirl around in a sundress," he retorts, a grin plastered on his face. "I apologize for nothing."

Rosalie walks between us, her little hands yanking us forward. "Come *on*. You said that Tia was gonna be here!"

Ansel laughs. "She is. Go on if you want—Coach said to head straight through the side fence. Be *careful*!" he yells at her retreating back.

I wink at him. "I mean, you *did* say she could go on."

"Didn't think she'd take off at rocket speed," he mutters.

"This, coming from the guy who sprints down the pitch like a madman?" I tease.

He takes my hand and pulls me to him, leaning down to plant a kiss on me before we get to the gate. "Behave," he admonishes.

"Me? I'm not the one who needs to behave."

He opens the gate and sketches a bow to wave me in. "One can never tell when you, Kari, and Allyson are all in one place."

I giggle as I spy those very same women across the expansive lawn. I find Rosalie, who's already grabbed the little girl who must be Tia, and then blow a kiss at Ansel. "Guess I'll go get into some trouble, then."

Lennox approaches with a couple of bottles of water in one hand and a non-alcoholic beer in the other. He gives me a sweet smile before turning and offering Ansel his choice of beverage.

Across the yard, Kari and Allyson envelop me in hugs before turning to walk me to the picnic table filled with all manner of drinks. "Where's Sam?" I ask.

"On her way," Kari answers.

"Still can't believe she's going to be the team's new phys-ical therapist." The other one left with the old coach, and the timing was too perfect.

"Now all we have to do is get Frank fired, and Kari can head up the PR division," Allyson declares.

Kari lets out a derisive snort. "That will never happen. He's in tight with the president."

"Who's not great," Allyson says pointedly. "But he'll do."

I chuckle, then look around at the house. "So, this is the new coach's place?" It's big, sprawling to fill the massive yard with two stories and what's probably a furnished attic.

Allyson raises an eyebrow. "You wanna know what I found out about him?"

Kari laughs. "Tell me you didn't investigate him."

"Tell me you think I *didn't*," she counters, flipping her braids behind her shoulder. "Gotta make sure my Granite guys are covered."

I roll my eyes. "You're a menace—and I love you for it."

"Have you met him yet?" Kari asks. "He's over there. Your man's talking to him."

I follow her direction. Sure enough, Ansel is on one side of him, and Lennox is on the other. He's tall, easily the same height as the players, with broad shoulders and a trim waist. "He was definitely a rugby player," I muse, taking in the muscled legs that flex as he shifts in place. He seems at ease with himself, calm and cool, even though every person here is absolutely taking his measure.

"His stats are good," Allyson says, as though she's reading my mind. "Took a number of colleges to the championships and won. Is definitely responsible for the steady increase in rugby programs at the collegiate level. Big on community outreach. Single. Never married. No kids. No criminal record. Dude's even got a curated social media presence."

"Yeah, and he's got a big dick, too."

We whirl to see Sam, who came up behind us while we stared at the coach. She's a little pale, her ice-blue eyes blinking as she plays with the charm on her necklace.

"*What?*" Kari hisses.

"I didn't know. I swear. He was just a good-looking guy in a bar." Her voice is panicked as she meets each of our eyes in turn.

"So you—" I start.

"And he...," Kari finishes.

Sam nods slowly.

"Oh, shit," Allyson says.

Sam swallows audibly. "Yeah. Oh, shit."

Acknowledgments

Thank you to my family. Your continuous, unwavering support is the very definition of love and forms the foundation of all my stories.

Thank you to the Brat Pack. Being a part of your crew is the best part of this publishing journey. And thank you to Katie, my editor, for never letting me get away with simply skimming the surface of the story. Excavation is your specialty.

When I started this book, I had no intention for it to feel as personal as it became. While my own story isn't remotely like that of Rosalie's, my own childhood was fraught with drama that included an accusation of kidnapping, an incredibly cruel stepmother, and the revelation of a father I didn't know I had when I was sixteen. I most definitely have gotten my own happily ever after, but it's taken decades.

Thank you to The Neighbourhood, Mansionair, Zola Blood, Bob Moses, and Hozier for your sexy as hell music. This book—and its spicy scenes in particular—rests on your collective backs.

And finally: thank you to rugby thighs. All hail those beefy, yummy legs.

Also by Valerie Pepper

GUIDED TO LOVE

~Small town romcom with men in uniform~

The Mechanic's Guide to Getting the Boss's Daughter (series prequel novella)

The Widow's Guide to Second Chances (Book 1)

The Barista's Guide to The Perfect Steam (Book 2)

The Grump's Guide to Chaos (Book 3)

LUCKY IN LOVE

~Beach town romcom shenanigans~

Dining for Love (Book 1)

Dashing for Love (Book 2)

Late to Love (Book 3)

Hate to Love (Book 4)

ATLANTA GRANITE

~Rugby romance~

Worth the Try (Book 1)

The No Try Zone (Book 2)

SACRED RIVER

~Small town...with witches!~

Love Potion No. 69 (Novella, Book 1)

Karaoke Chemistry (Book 2)

About the Author

 Valerie Pepper writes steamy small town and sports romance hot enough to fry an egg on. Naturally, she's an incurable optimist and a firm believer in happily ever afters, even if it takes more than one try. She's fascinated with the idea of a capsule wardrobe, but loves clothes and shoes far too much to make a real go of it. She's living out her own second-chance romance in Birmingham, Alabama, with her family (and maybe too many shoes).

Get a free short story at www.authorvaleriepepper.com and follow her @authorvaleriepepper on most social media.

9 798988 857082